WATTERS • LEYH • SOTUYO • LAIHO

LUMBERJANES ™

JACKALOPE SPRINGS ETERNAL

BOOM! BOX ™

BOOM! BOX™

LUMBERJANES Volume Twelve, July 2019. Published by BOOM! Box, a division of Boom Entertainment, Inc. Lumberjanes is ™ & © 2019 Shannon Watters, Grace Ellis, Noelle Stevenson & Brooklyn Allen. Originally published in single magazine form as LUMBERJANES No. 45-48. ™ & © 2017-2018 Shannon Watters, Grace Ellis, Noelle Stevenson & Brooklyn Allen. All rights reserved. BOOM! Box™ and the BOOM! Box logo are trademarks of Boom Entertainment, Inc., registered in various countries and categories. All characters, events, and institutions depicted herein are fictional. Any similarity between any of the names, characters, persons, events, and/or institutions in this publication to actual names, characters, and persons, whether living or dead, events, and/or institutions is unintended and purely coincidental. BOOM! Box does not read or accept unsolicited submissions of ideas, stories, or artwork.

For information regarding the CPSIA on this printed material, call: (203) 595-3636 and provide reference #RICH – 844879.

BOOM! Studios, 5670 Wilshire Boulevard, Suite 400, Los Angeles, CA 90036-5679. Printed in USA. First Printing.

ISBN: 978-1-68415-380-0, eISBN: 978-1-64144-363-0

THIS LUMBERJANES FIELD MANUAL BELONGS TO:

NAME:_____

TROOP:_____

DATE INVESTED:_____

FIELD MANUAL TABLE OF CONTENTS

LUMBERJANES
FIELD MANUAL

For the Intermediate Program

Tenth Edition • December 1984

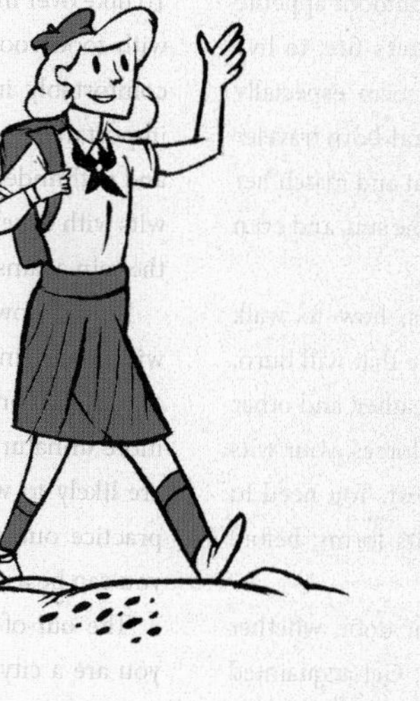

Prepared for the

Miss Qiunzella Thiskwin
Penniquiqul Thistle Crumpet's

CAMP FOR [redacted] HARDCORE LADY-TYPES

"Friendship to the Max!"

A MESSAGE FROM THE LUMBERJANES HIGH COUNCIL

miss
Quinzella
Thiskwin
Penniquiqul Thistle Crumpet's
Camp for
HARDCORE LADY TYPES
FRIENDSHIP to the MAX!

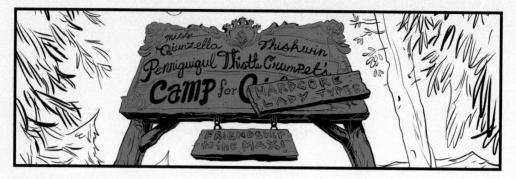

There is something about being a child in the summertime that has a grandiosity in and of itself. We of the High Council hope that these languid and lazy days spent with friends will be some that you can cherish as you grow older, just as we still hold dear the hours we spent playing hopscotch and other games in the hot July sun, although our summer memories vary greatly, from High Councillor to High Councillor. In a strange way, these weeks of summer can feel like both the longest days and fastest hours of one's youth: both never-ending, and a precious commodity to be savored before they run out.

We know that when you are in the midst of them, summer days can also sometimes seem unimportant, overly similar from one to another, or even common...but they aren't. Yes, summer will come back every year, but the things that make up the Junes, Julys, and Augusts of your childhood—the games of tag, the fireflies, and the flavors of ice pop that stained your tongue—are unique to you, and you alone.

Whether you spend your summers at camp, surrounded by new friends and experiences, or at home engulfed in the places and people you know best, we hope that you will not only make the most of these days, but find the things that make them *your* days. Make the most of air so hot it seems to curl as it rises up from the earth, of rain storms so powerful they soak you down to your bones, and of early mornings with nowhere you need to be, but full of the promise of places you want to be. Make the most of time with friends, and of inventing new games to play, stories to tell, and rules to follow simply for the fun of walking backwards, or speaking only Pig Latin, or sending secret messages back and forth across camp or town. Remember the good you felt each day, and strive to do good as well, so that the memories you forge now as a young person will be ones that you can revisit in your older years and look back on both fondly and proudly. Make this season one of well-spent youth, to the best of your ability.

THE LUMBERJANES PLEDGE

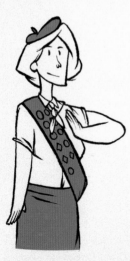

I solemnly swear to do my best
Every day, and in all that I do,
To be brave and strong,
To be truthful and compassionate,
To be interesting and interested,
To pay attention and question
The world around me,
To think of others first,
To always help and protect my friends,
[redacted]
And to make the world a better place
For Lumberjane scouts
And for everyone else.

THEN THERE'S A LINE ABOUT GOD, OR WHATEVER

LUMBERJANES ™
JACKALOPE SPRINGS ETERNAL

Written by
Shannon Watters
& Kat Leyh

Illustrated by
Ayme Sotuyo

Colors by
Maarta Laiho

Letters by
Aubrey Aiese

Cover by
Kat Leyh

Designer
Marie Krupina

Associate Editor
Sophie Philips-Roberts

Series Editor
Dafna Pleban

Collection Editor
Jeanine Schaefer

*Special thanks to **Kelsey Pate** for giving the Lumberjanes their name.*

Created by **Shannon Watters, Grace Ellis, Noelle Stevenson & Brooklyn Allen**

LUMBERJANES FIELD MANUAL

CHAPTER
FORTY-FIVE

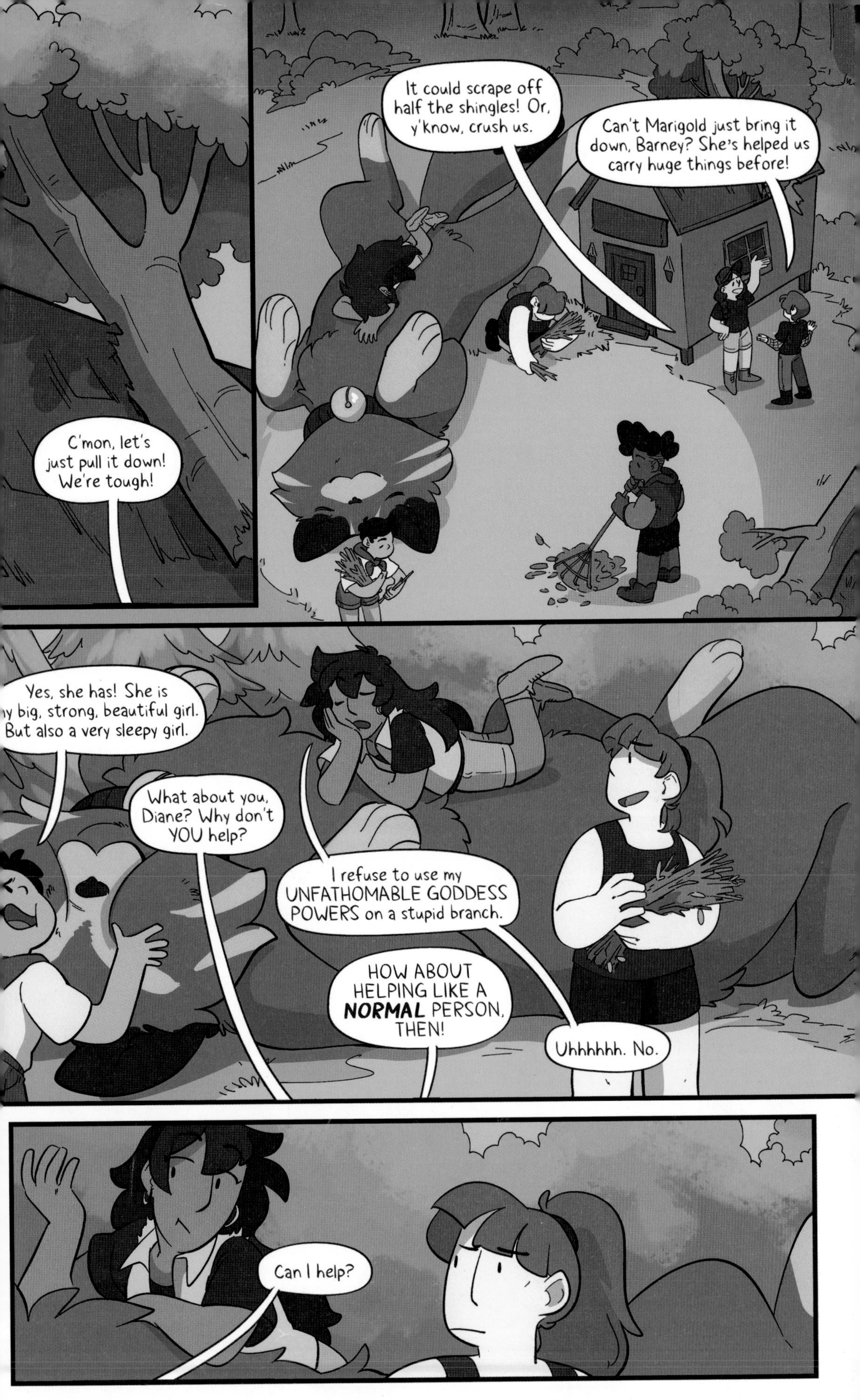
It could scrape off half the shingles! Or, y'know, crush us.
Can't Marigold just bring it down, Barney? She's helped us carry huge things before!
C'mon, let's just pull it down! We're tough!
Yes, she has! She is my big, strong, beautiful girl. But also a very sleepy girl.
What about you, Diane? Why don't YOU help?
I refuse to use my UNFATHOMABLE GODDESS POWERS on a stupid branch.
HOW ABOUT HELPING LIKE A **NORMAL** PERSON, THEN!
Uhhhhhh. No.
Can I help?

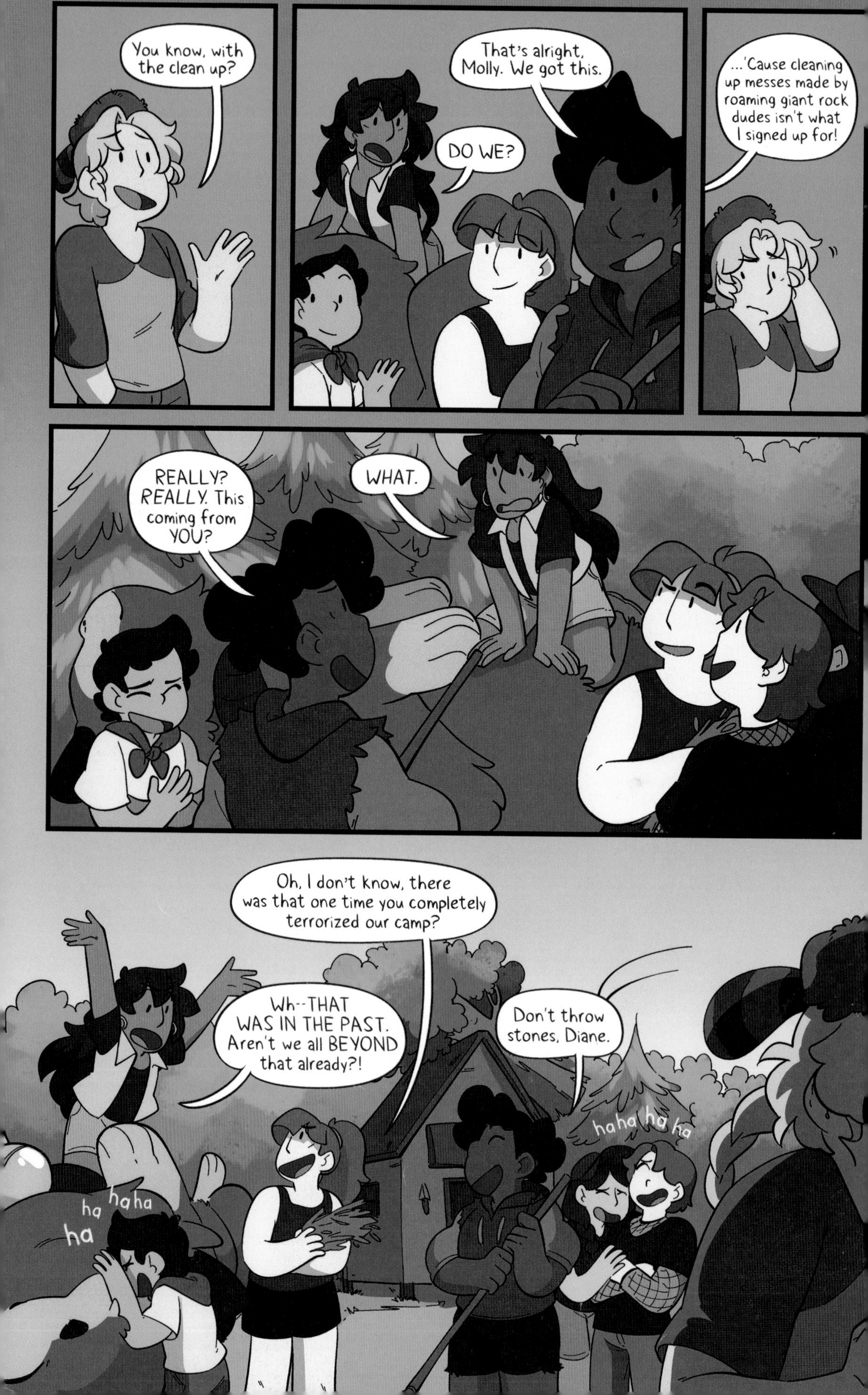
You know, with the clean up?
That's alright, Molly. We got this.
DO WE?
...'Cause cleaning up messes made by roaming giant rock dudes isn't what I signed up for!
REALLY? REALLY. This coming from YOU?
WHAT.
Oh, I don't know, there was that one time you completely terrorized our camp?
Wh--THAT WAS IN THE PAST. Aren't we all BEYOND that already?!
Don't throw stones, Diane.
ha ha ha ha
ha haha ha

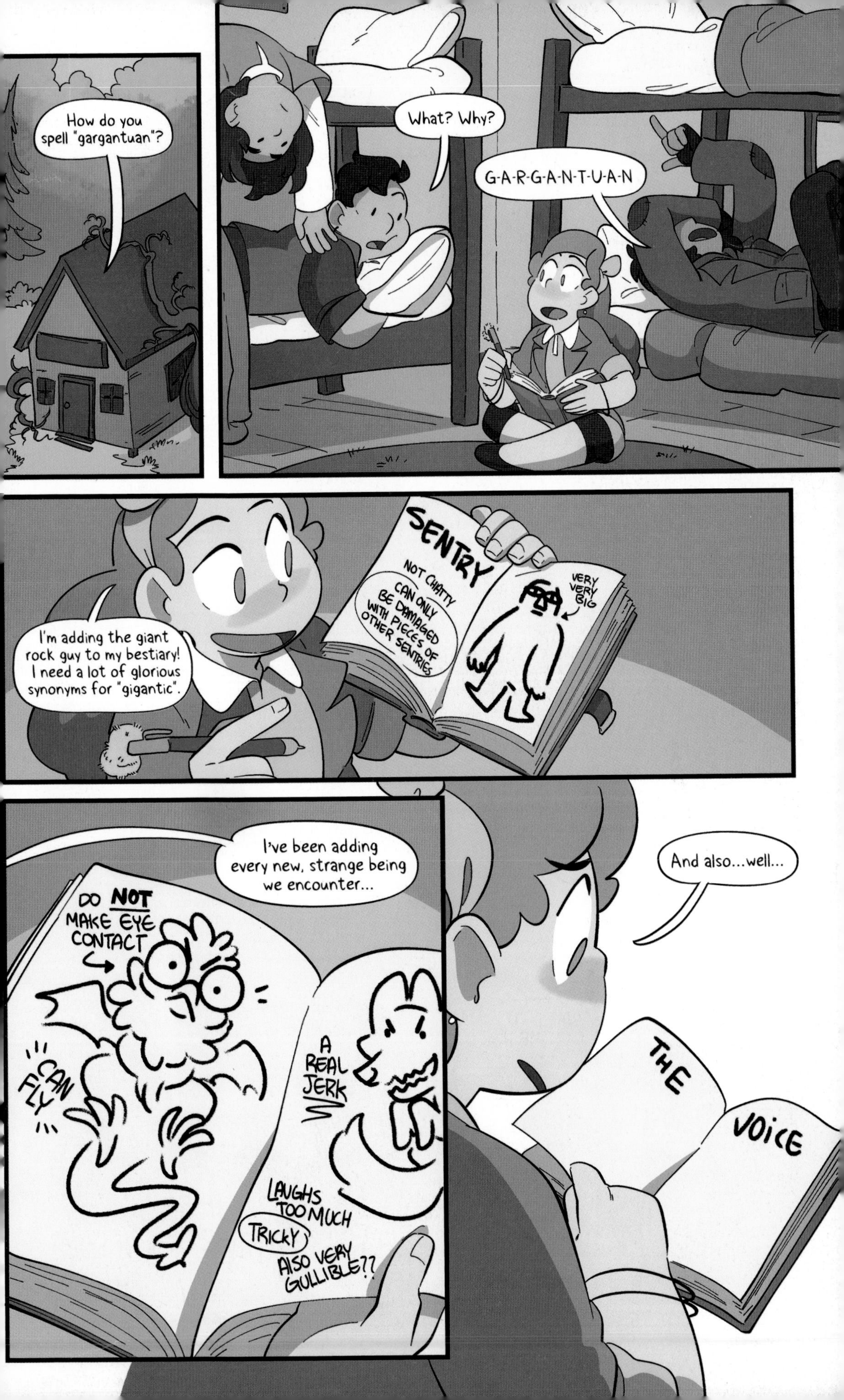
How do you spell "gargantuan"?
What? Why?
G-A-R-G-A-N-T-U-A-N
SENTRY
NOT CHATTY
CAN ONLY BE DAMAGED WITH PIECES OF OTHER SENTRIES
VERY VERY BIG
I'm adding the giant rock guy to my bestiary! I need a lot of glorious synonyms for "gigantic".
I've been adding every new, strange being we encounter...
DO NOT MAKE EYE CONTACT
CAN FLY
A REAL JERK
LAUGHS TOO MUCH
TRICKY
ALSO VERY GULLIBLE??
And also...well...
THE
VOICE

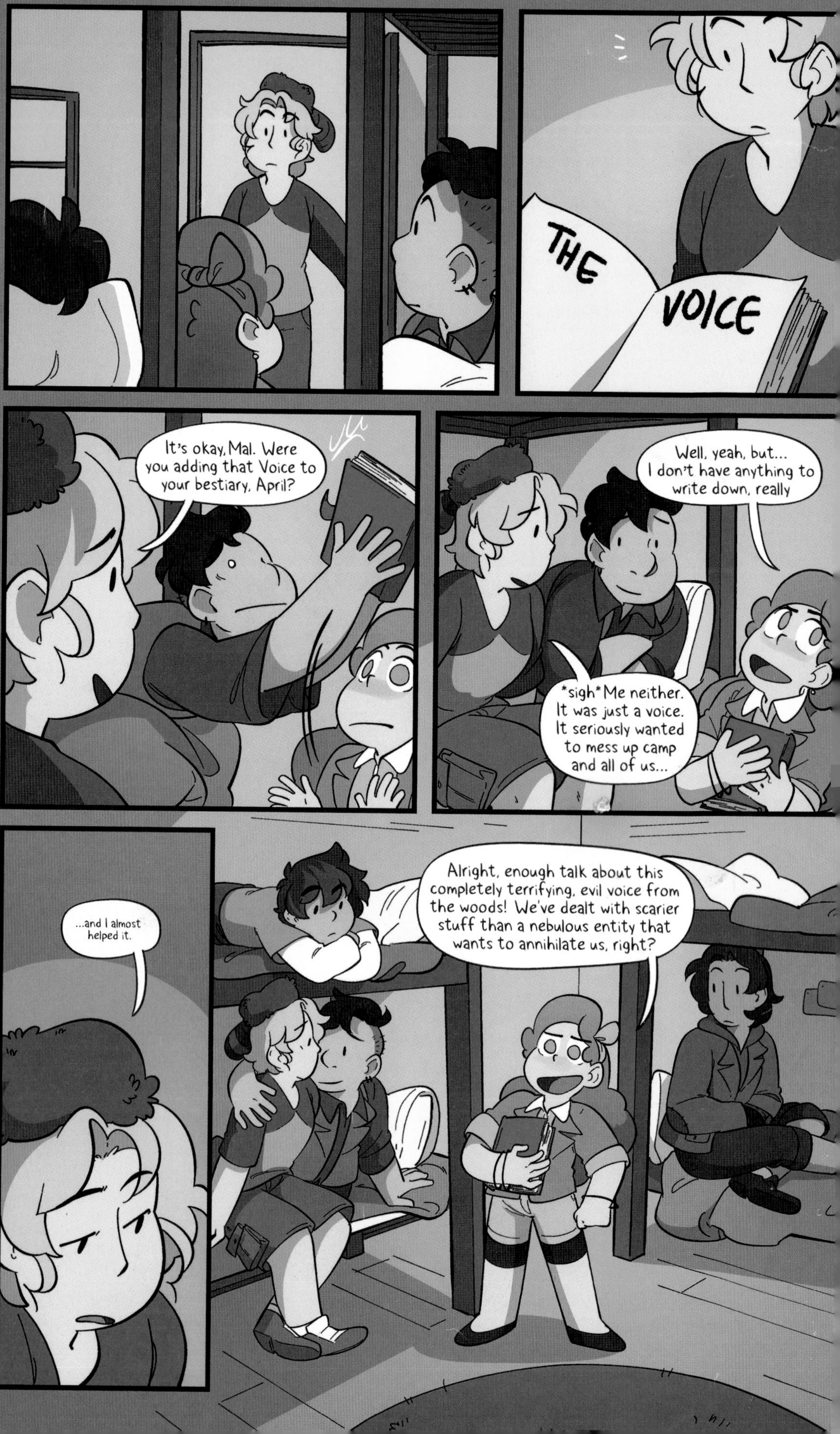
THE VOICE
It's okay, Mal. Were you adding that Voice to your bestiary, April?
Well, yeah, but... I don't have anything to write down, really
sigh Me neither. It was just a voice. It seriously wanted to mess up camp and all of us...
...and I almost helped it.
Alright, enough talk about this completely terrifying, evil voice from the woods! We've dealt with scarier stuff than a nebulous entity that wants to annihilate us, right?

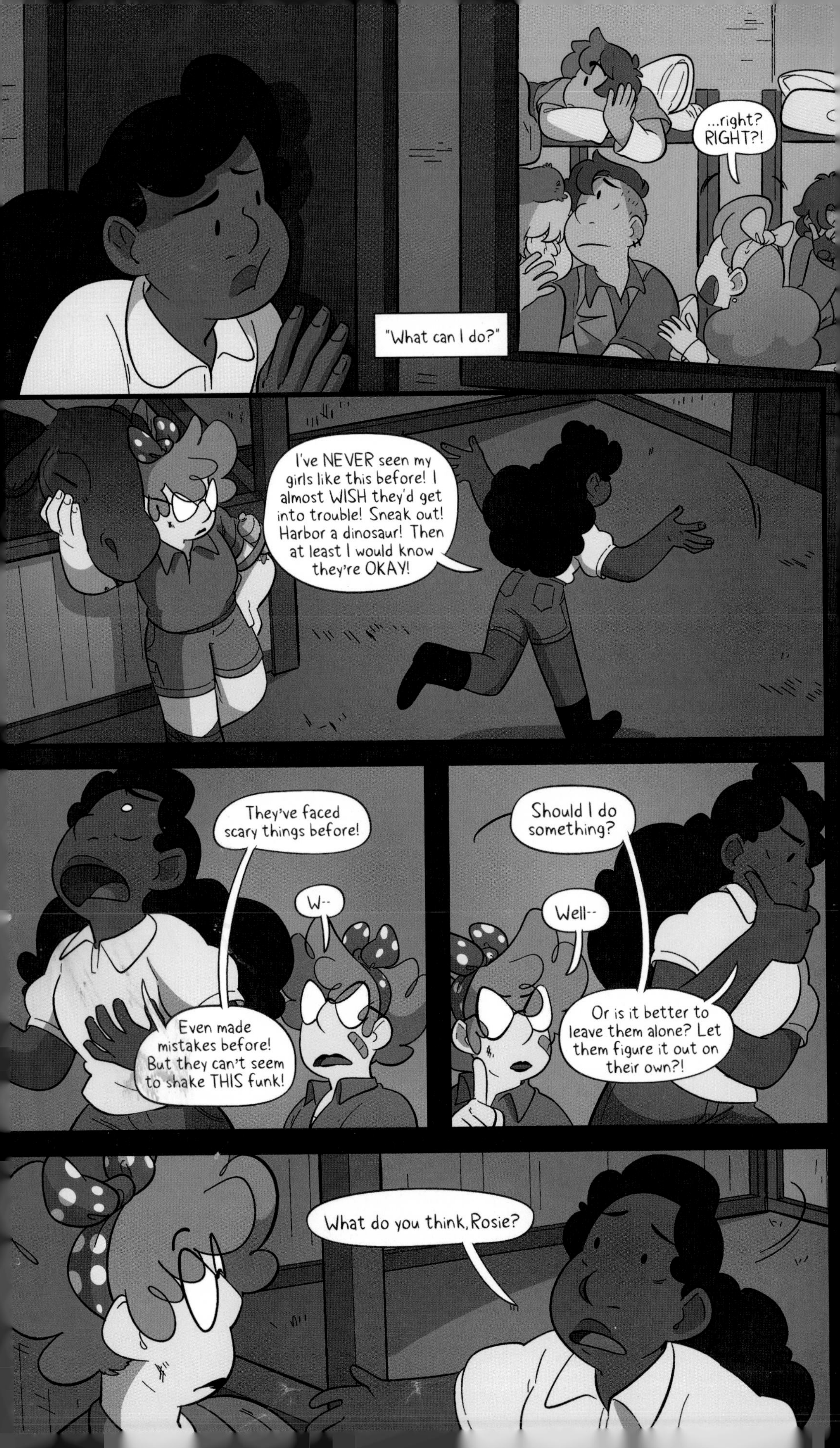

...right?
RIGHT?!
"What can I do?"
I've NEVER seen my girls like this before! I almost WISH they'd get into trouble! Sneak out! Harbor a dinosaur! Then at least I would know they're OKAY!
They've faced scary things before!
W--
Even made mistakes before! But they can't seem to shake THIS funk!
Should I do something?
Well--
Or is it better to leave them alone? Let them figure it out on their own?!
What do you think, Rosie?

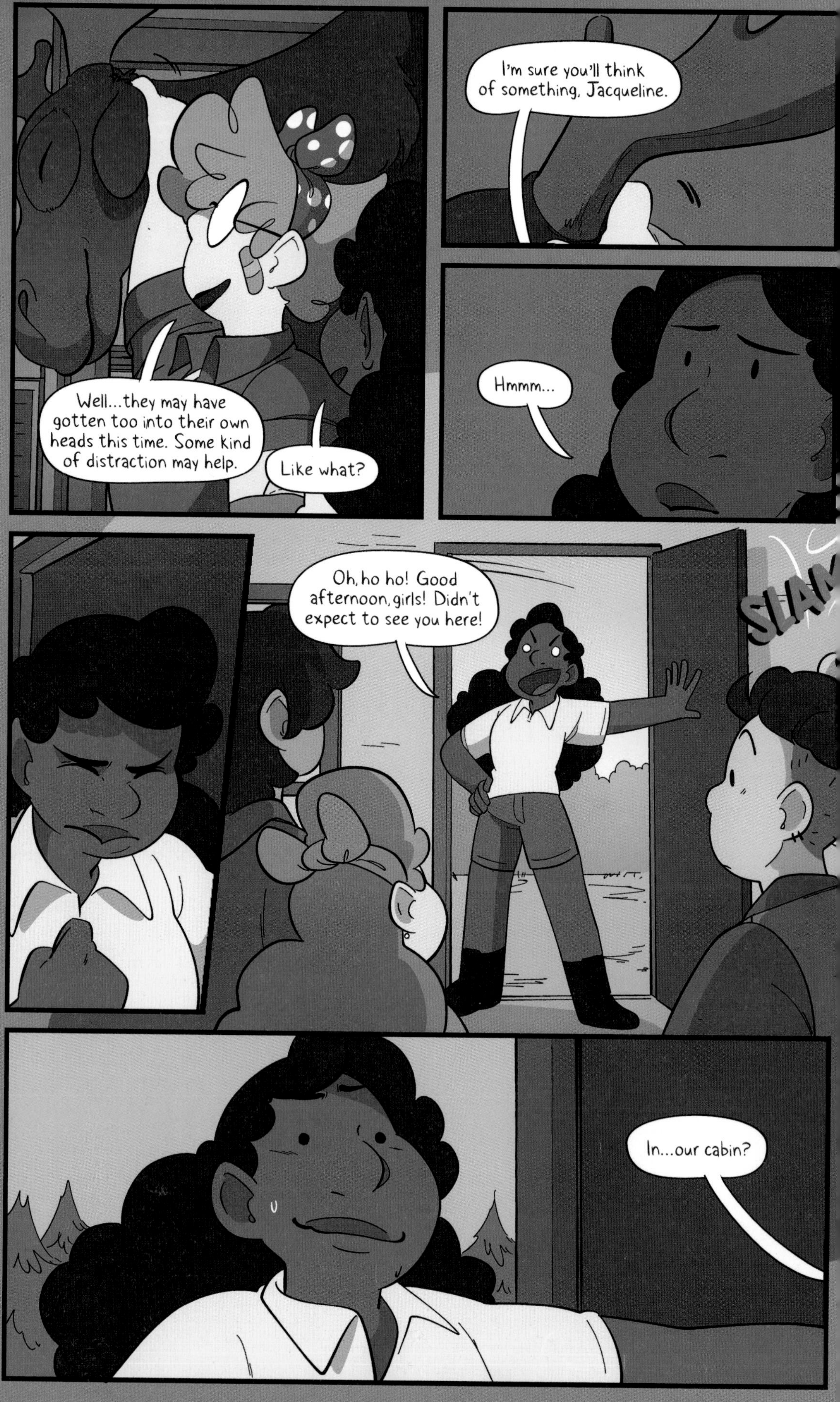

Well...they may have gotten too into their own heads this time. Some kind of distraction may help.
Like what?
I'm sure you'll think of something, Jacqueline.
Hmmm...
Oh, ho ho! Good afternoon, girls! Didn't expect to see you here!
In...our cabin?

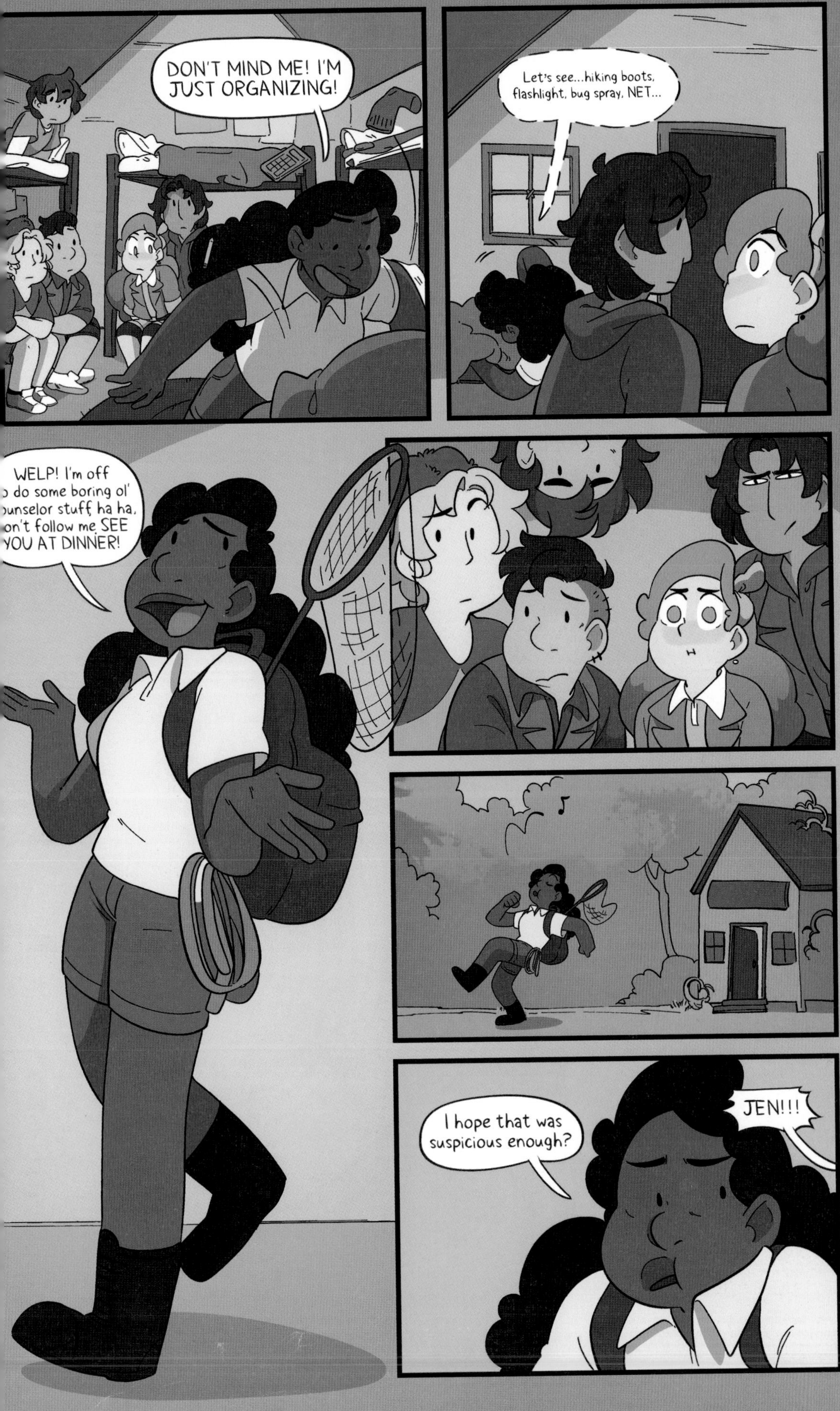
DON'T MIND ME! I'M JUST ORGANIZING!
Let's see...hiking boots, flashlight, bug spray, NET...
WELP! I'm off
o do some boring ol'
ounselor stuff ha ha,
on't follow me SEE
YOU AT DINNER!
I hope that was suspicious enough?
JEN!!!

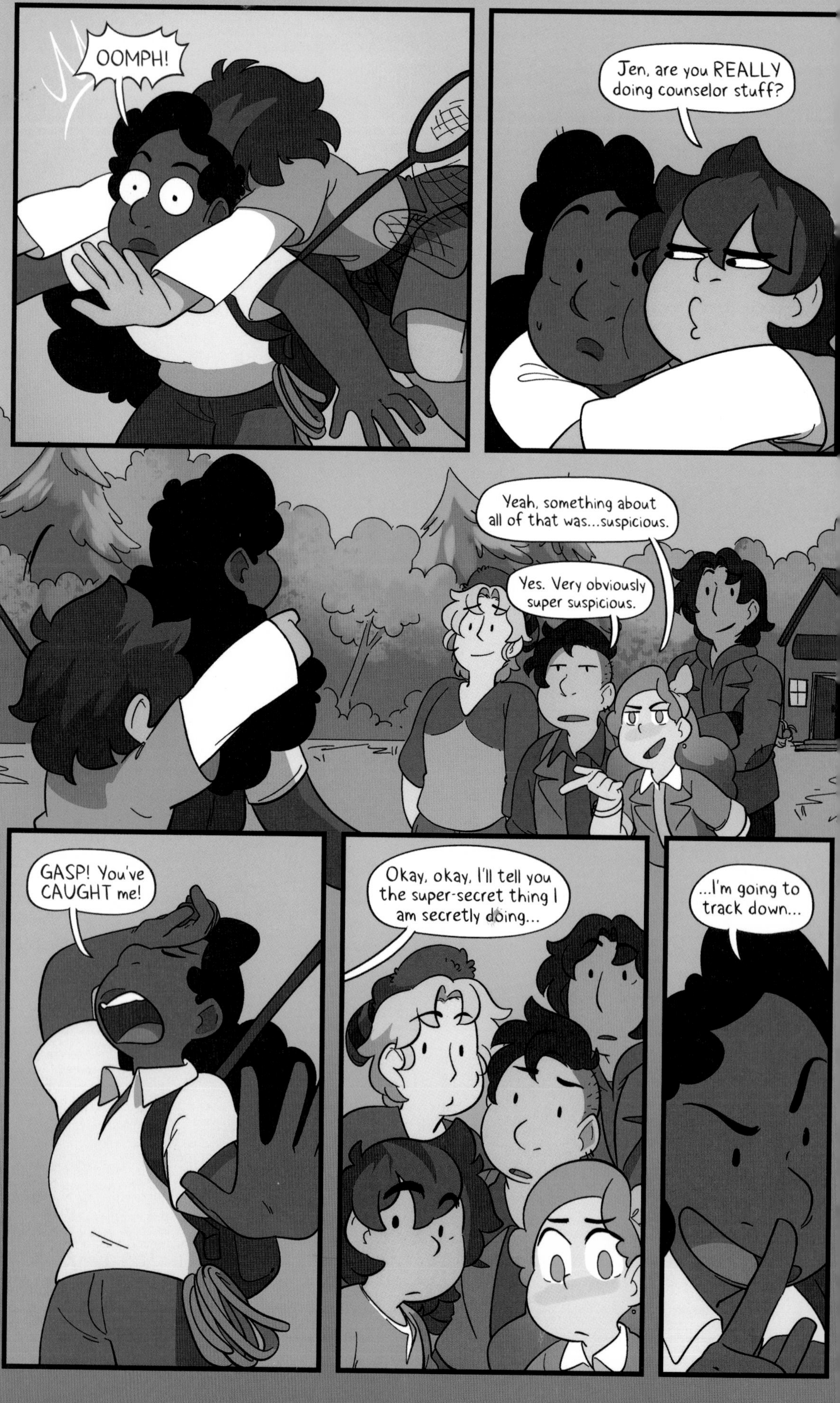

OOMPH!
Jen, are you REALLY doing counselor stuff?
Yeah, something about all of that was...suspicious.
Yes. Very obviously super suspicious.
GASP! You've CAUGHT me!
Okay, okay, I'll tell you the super-secret thing I am secretly doing...
...I'm going to track down...

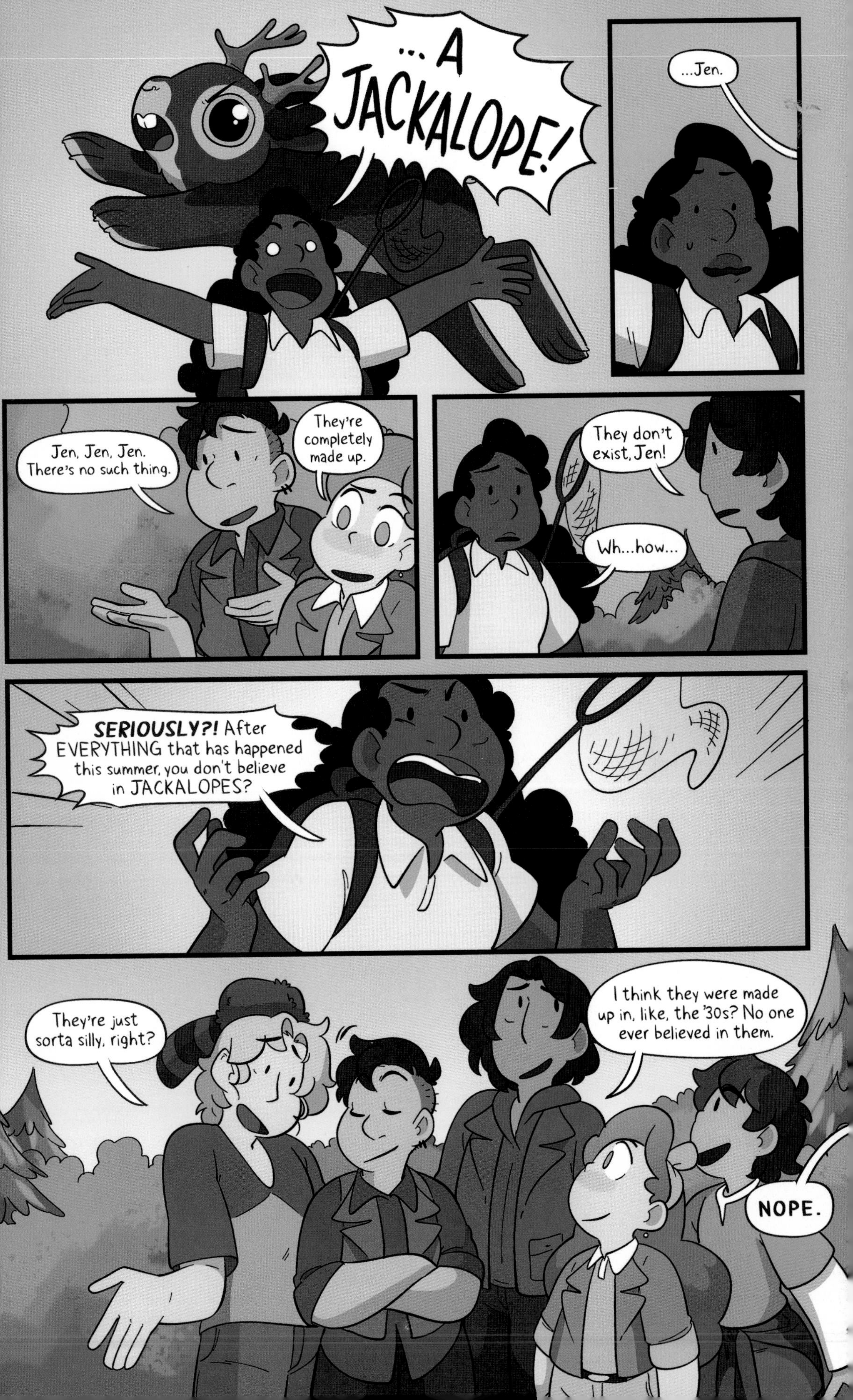
...A JACKALOPE!
...Jen.
Jen, Jen, Jen. There's no such thing.
They're completely made up.
They don't exist, Jen!
Wh...how...
SERIOUSLY?! After EVERYTHING that has happened this summer, you don't believe in JACKALOPES?
They're just sorta silly, right?
I think they were made up in, like, the '30s? No one ever believed in them.
NOPE.

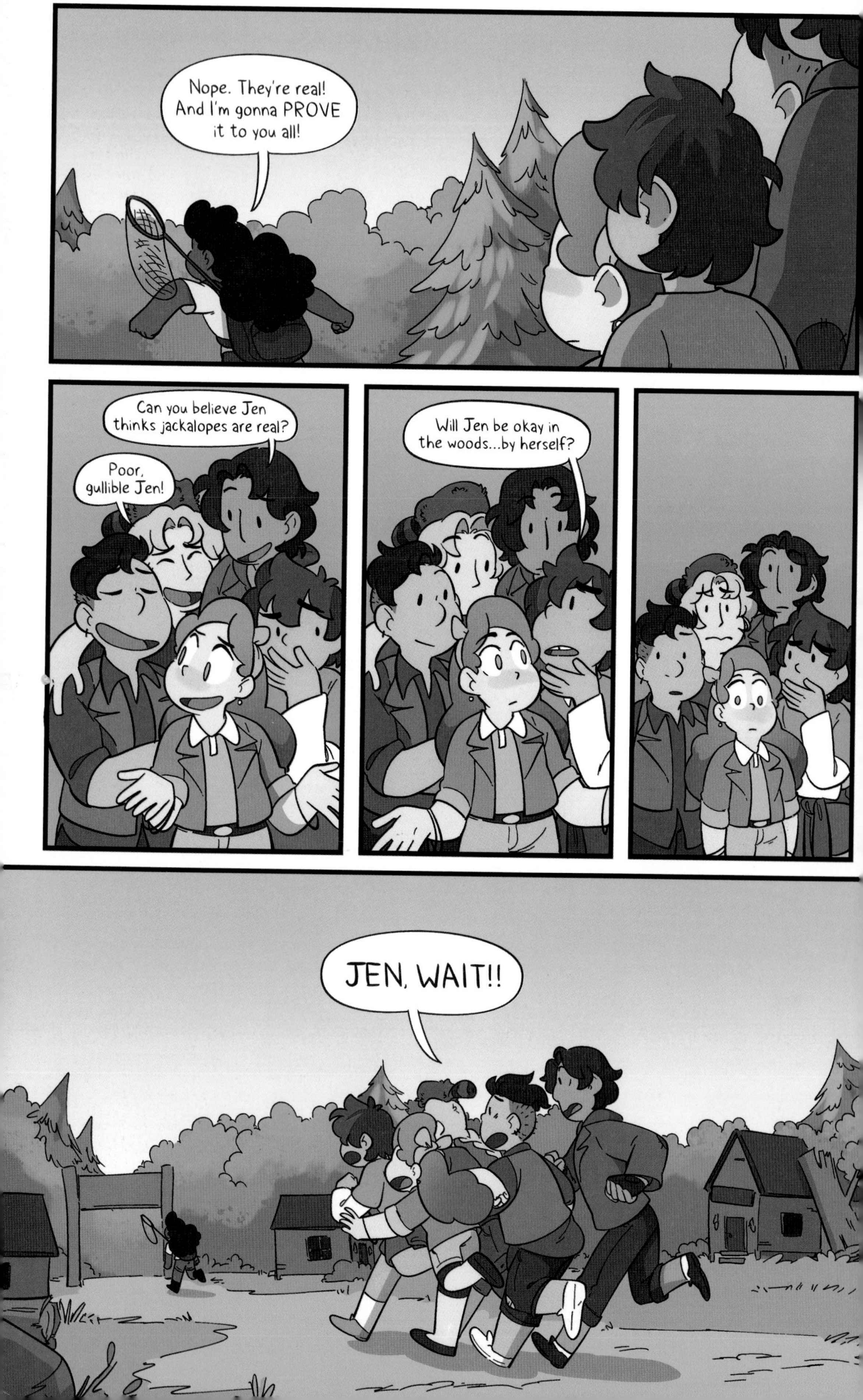
Nope. They're real! And I'm gonna PROVE it to you all!
Can you believe Jen thinks jackalopes are real?
Poor, gullible Jen!
Will Jen be okay in the woods...by herself?
JEN, WAIT!!

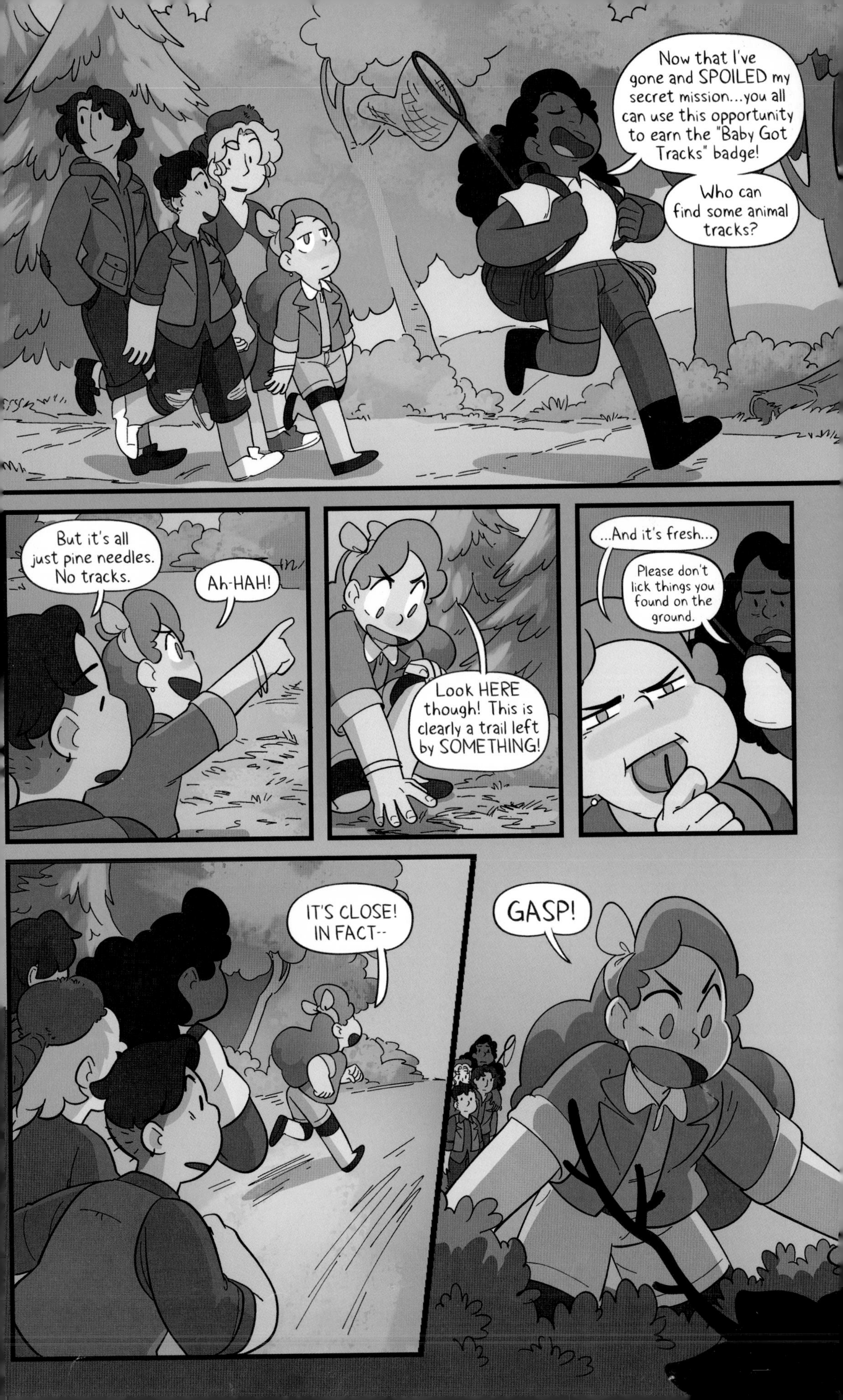
Now that I've gone and SPOILED my secret mission...you all can use this opportunity to earn the "Baby Got Tracks" badge!
Who can find some animal tracks?
But it's all just pine needles. No tracks.
Ah-HAH!
Look HERE though! This is clearly a trail left by SOMETHING!
...And it's fresh...
Please don't lick things you found on the ground.
IT'S CLOSE! IN FACT--
GASP!

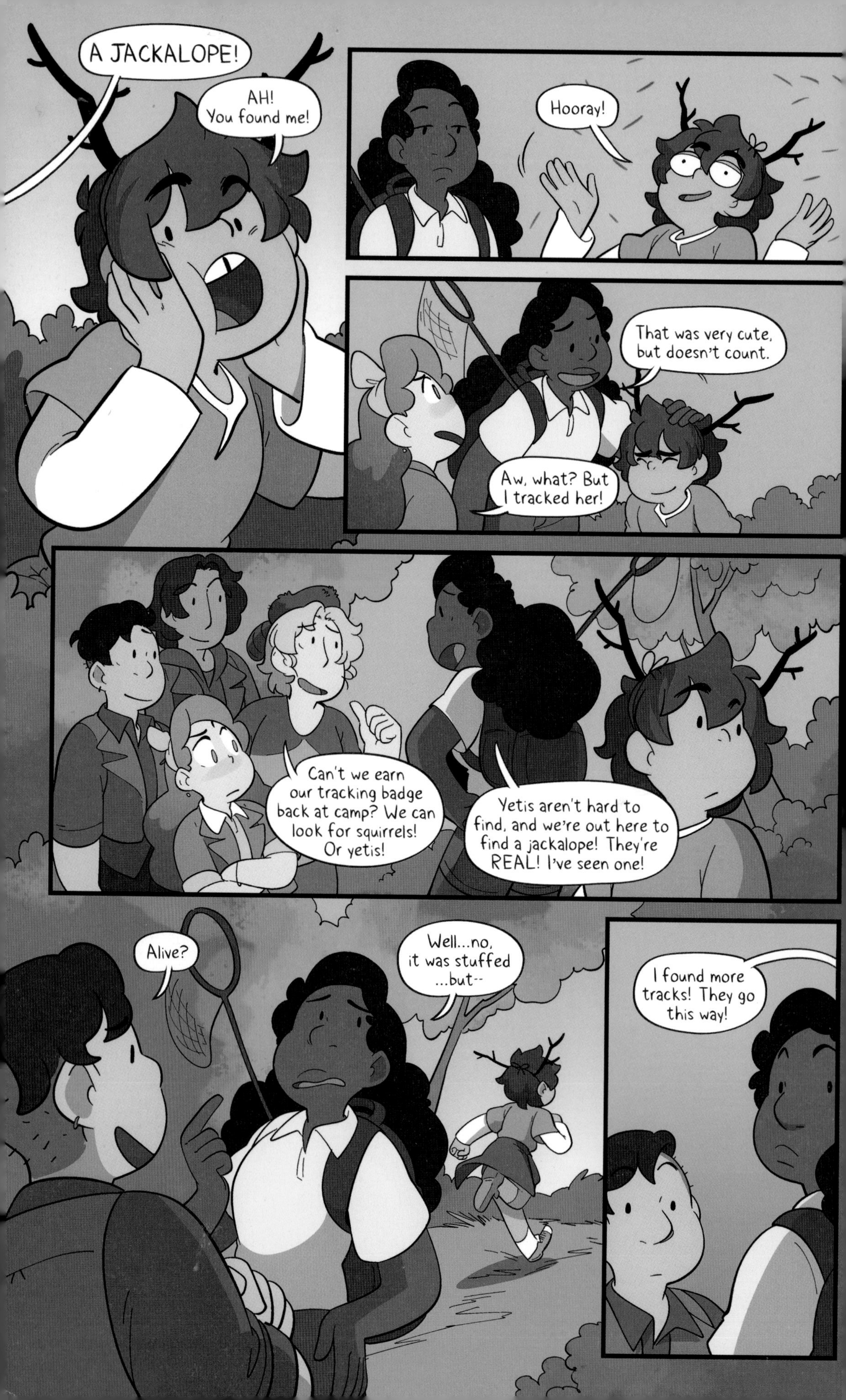
A JACKALOPE!
AH! You found me!
Hooray!
That was very cute, but doesn't count.
Aw, what? But I tracked her!
Can't we earn our tracking badge back at camp? We can look for squirrels! Or yetis!
Yetis aren't hard to find, and we're out here to find a jackalope! They're REAL! I've seen one!
Alive?
Well...no, it was stuffed ...but--
I found more tracks! They go this way!

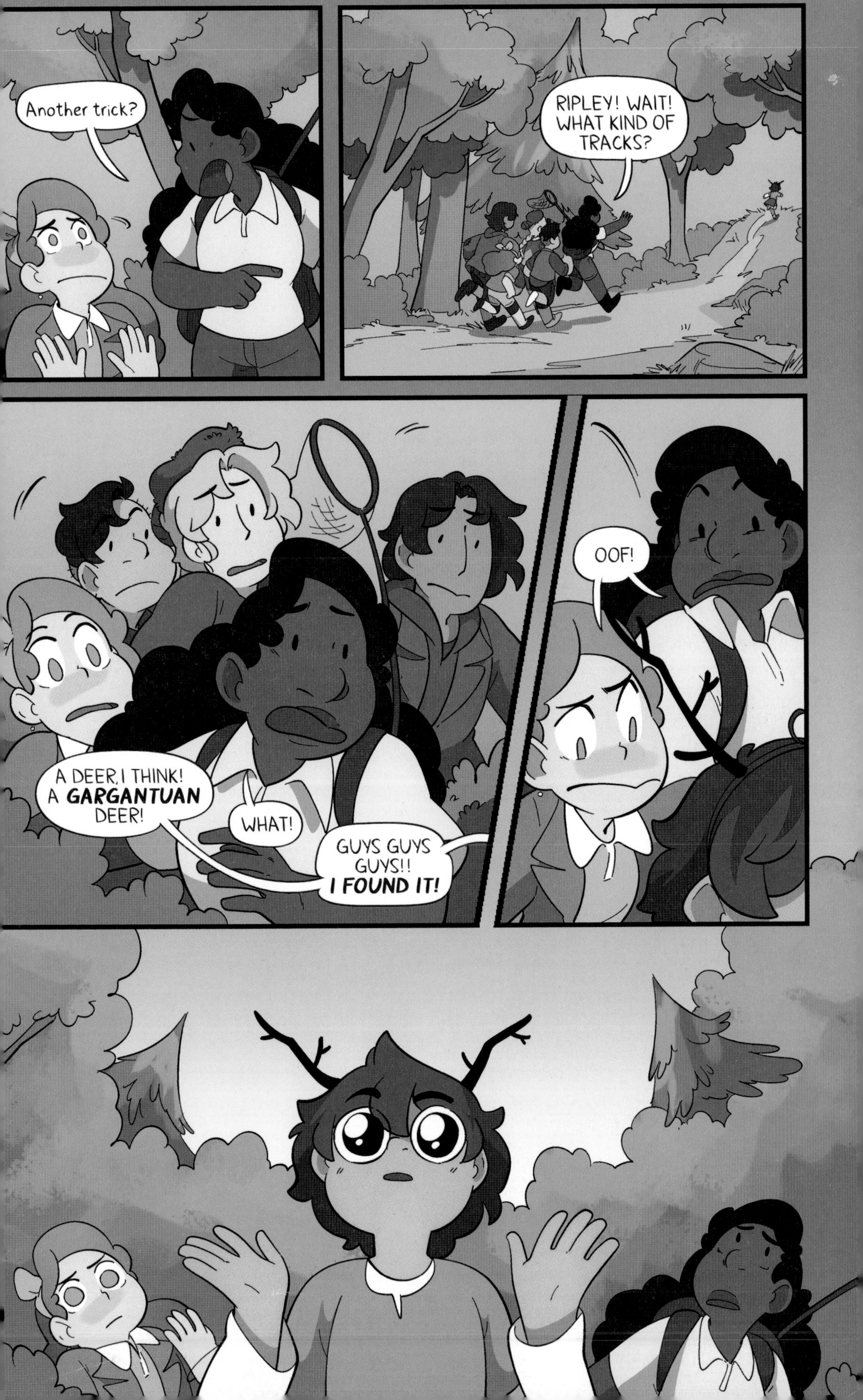

Another trick?
RIPLEY! WAIT! WHAT KIND OF TRACKS?
A DEER, I THINK! A **GARGANTUAN** DEER!
WHAT!
GUYS GUYS GUYS!! **I FOUND IT!**
OOF!

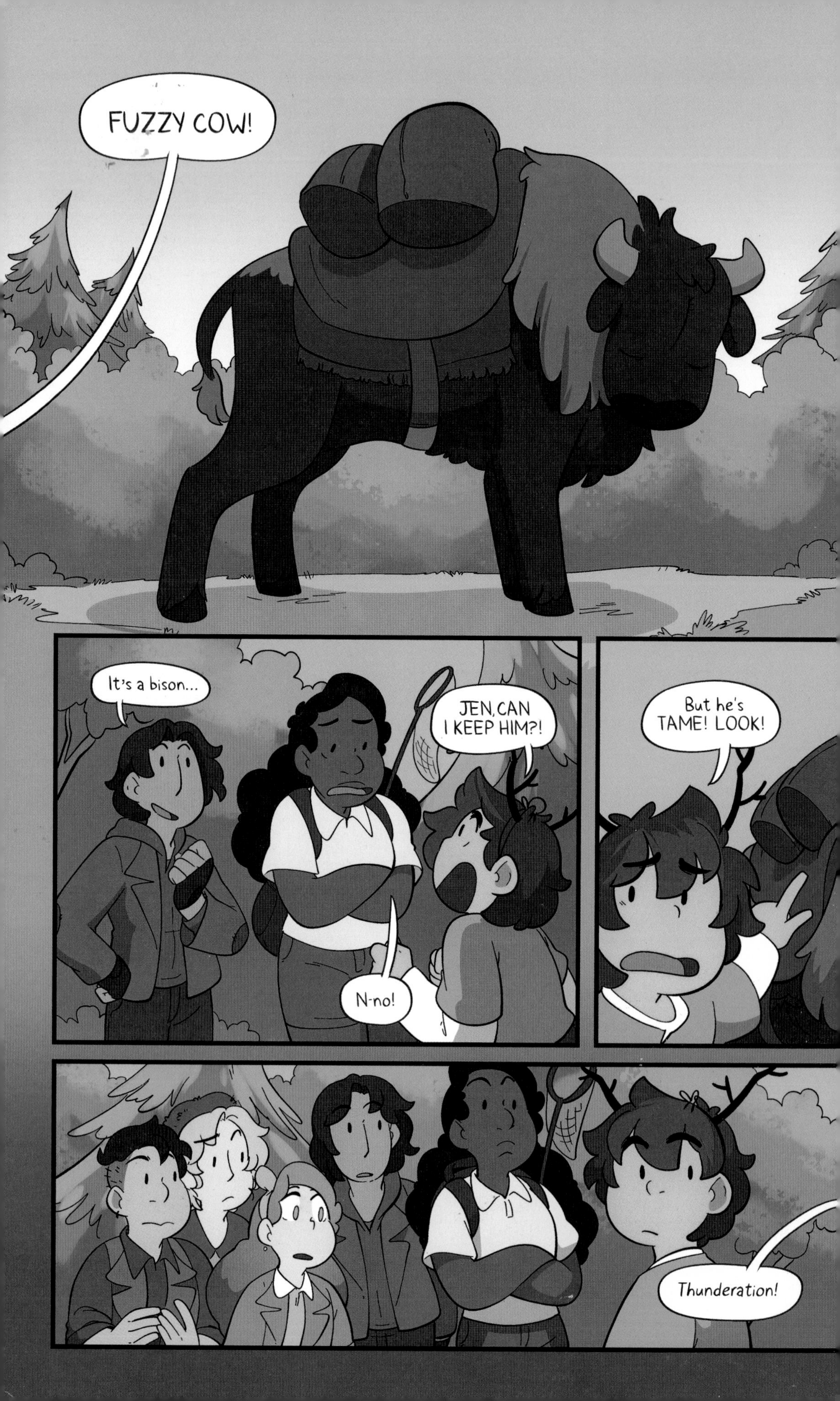
FUZZY COW!
It's a bison...
JEN, CAN I KEEP HIM?!
N-no!
But he's TAME! LOOK!
Thunderation!

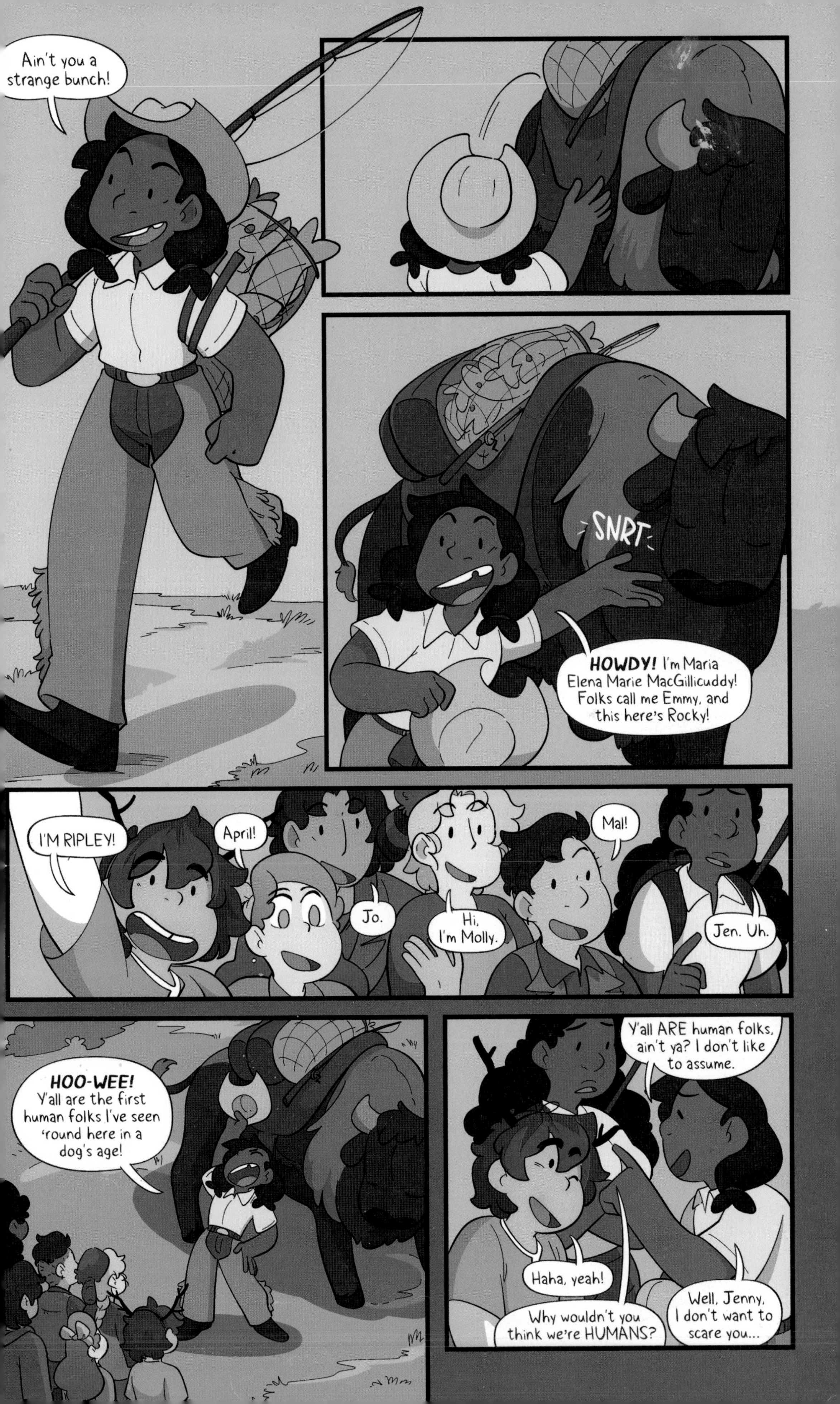
Ain't you a strange bunch!
SNRT
HOWDY! I'm Maria Elena Marie MacGillicuddy! Folks call me Emmy, and this here's Rocky!
I'M RIPLEY!
April!
Jo.
Hi, I'm Molly.
Mal!
Jen. Uh.
HOO-WEE! Y'all are the first human folks I've seen 'round here in a dog's age!
Y'all ARE human folks, ain't ya? I don't like to assume.
Haha, yeah!
Why wouldn't you think we're HUMANS?
Well, Jenny, I don't want to scare you...

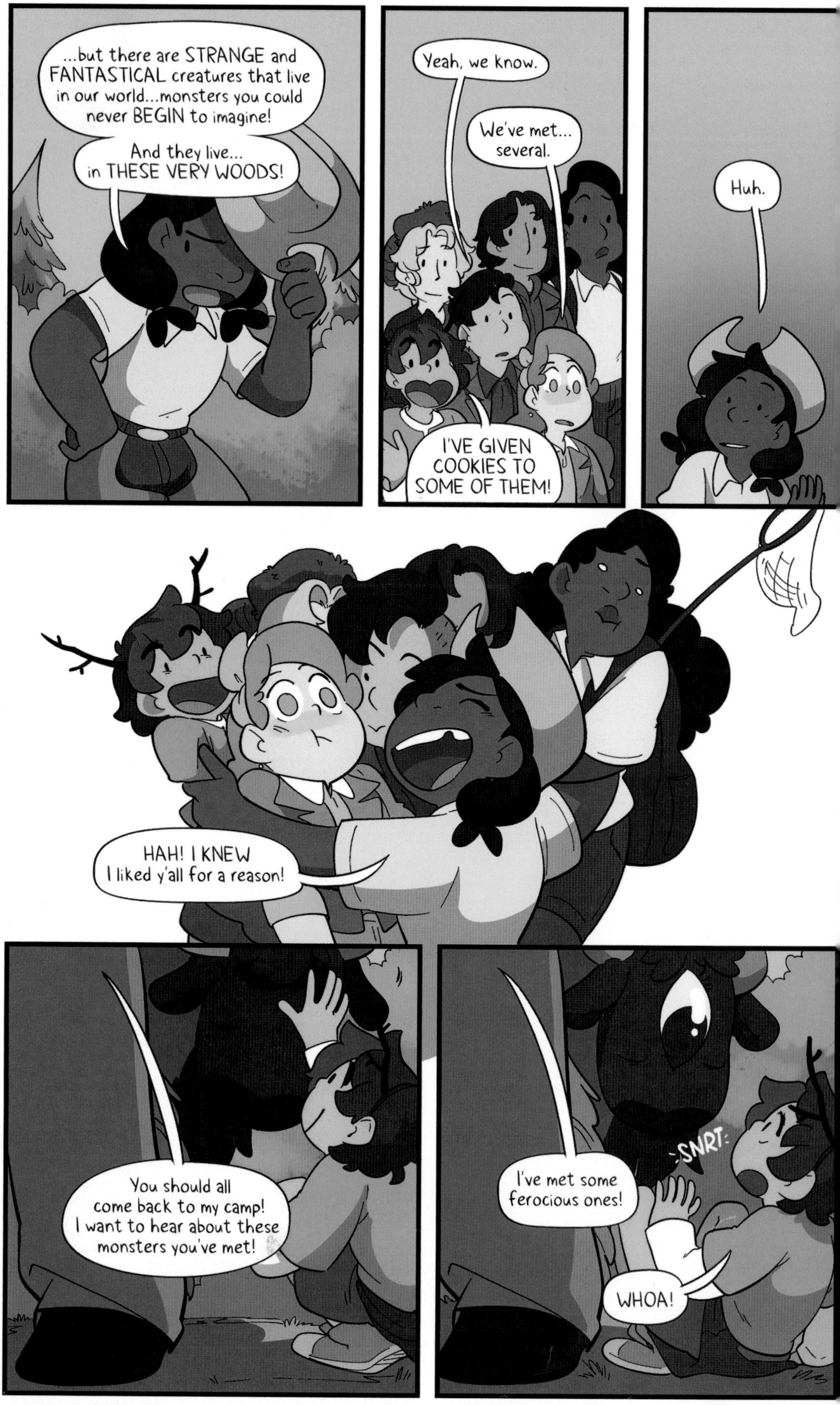
...but there are STRANGE and FANTASTICAL creatures that live in our world...monsters you could never BEGIN to imagine!
And they live... in THESE VERY WOODS!
Yeah, we know.
We've met... several.
I'VE GIVEN COOKIES TO SOME OF THEM!
Huh.
HAH! I KNEW I liked y'all for a reason!
You should all come back to my camp! I want to hear about these monsters you've met!
I've met some ferocious ones!
SNRT
WHOA!

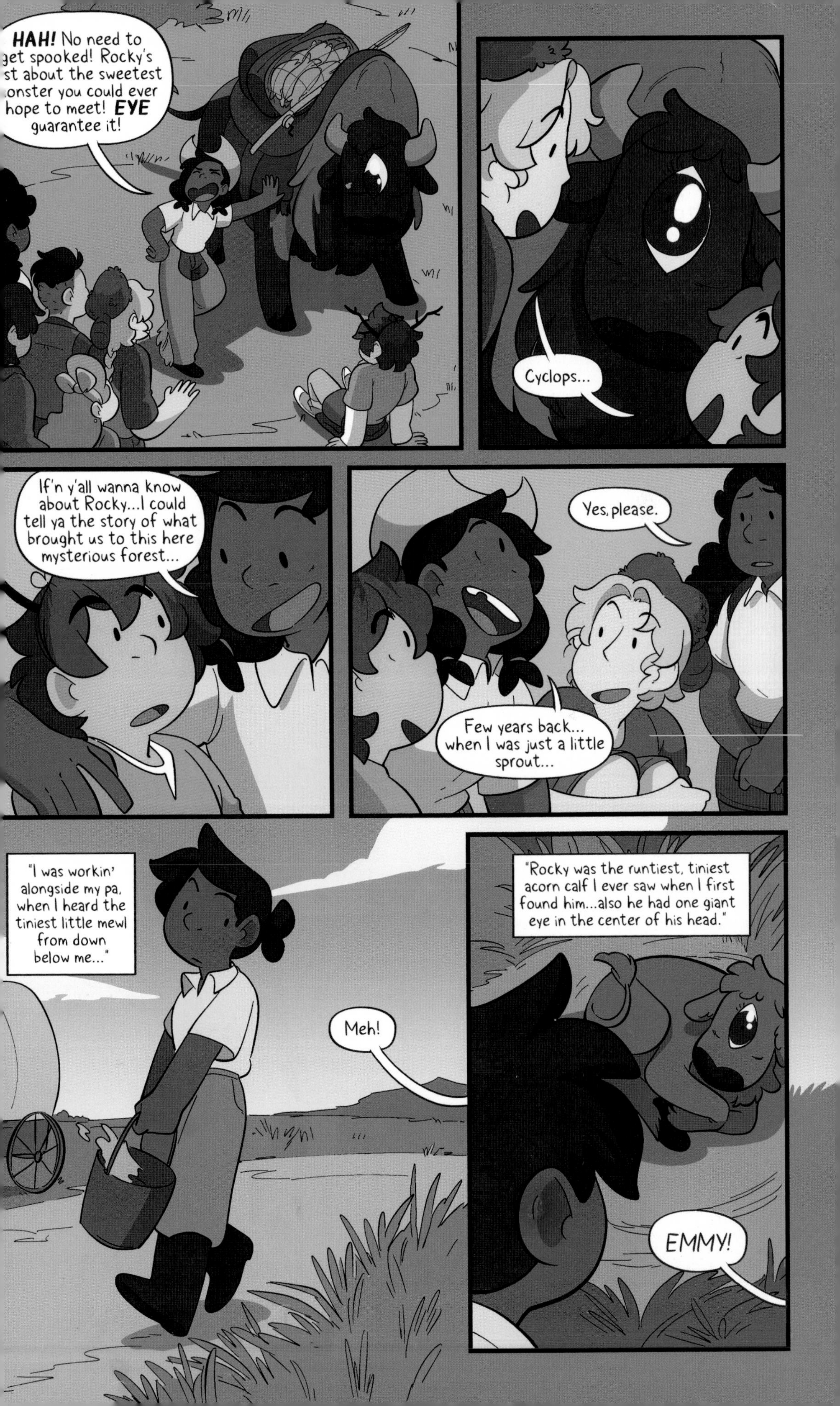

HAH! No need to get spooked! Rocky's st about the sweetest onster you could ever hope to meet! EYE guarantee it!
Cyclops...
If'n y'all wanna know about Rocky...I could tell ya the story of what brought us to this here mysterious forest...
Yes, please.
Few years back... when I was just a little sprout...
"I was workin' alongside my pa, when I heard the tiniest little mewl from down below me..."
Meh!
"Rocky was the runtiest, tiniest acorn calf I ever saw when I first found him...also he had one giant eye in the center of his head."
EMMY!

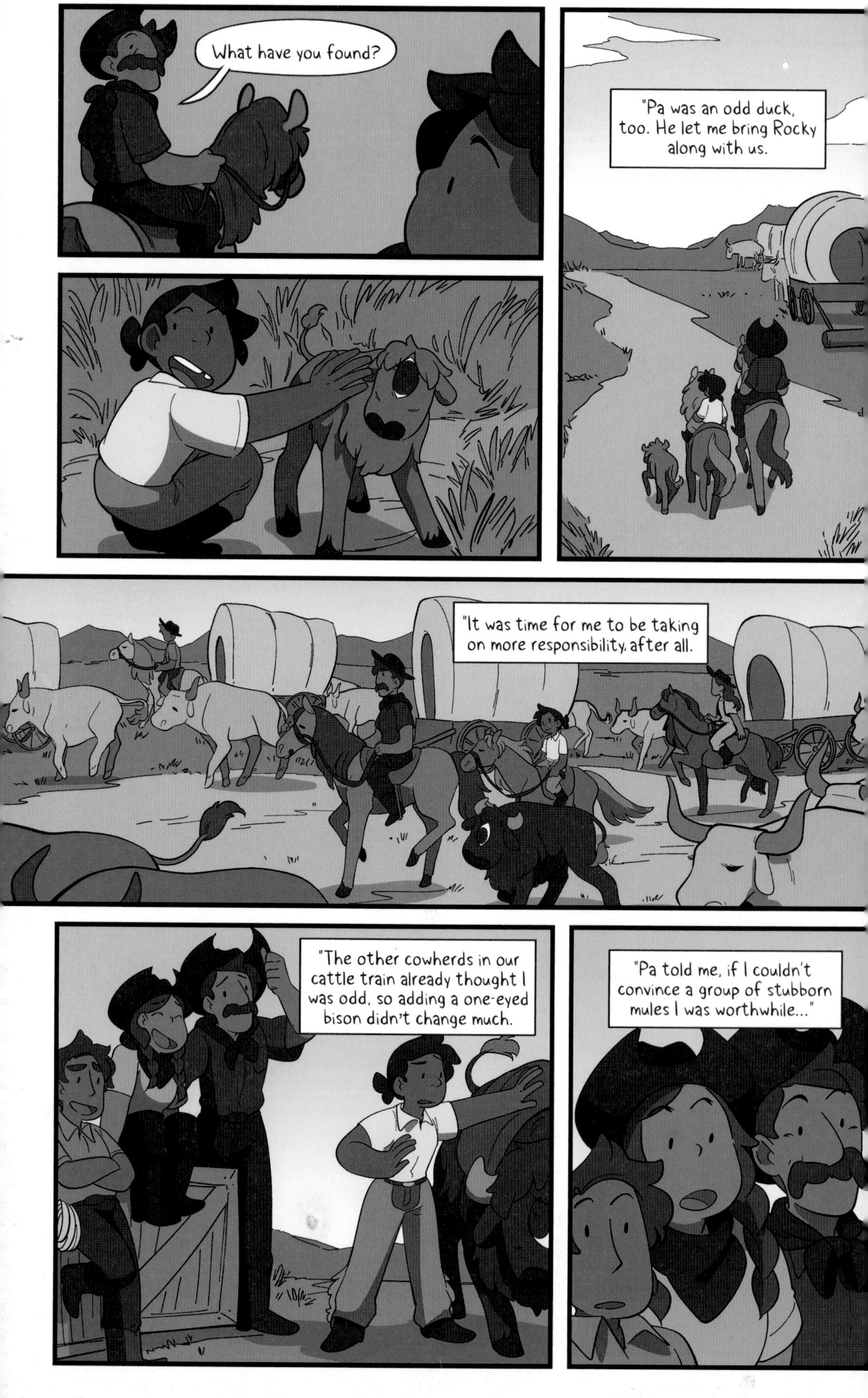
What have you found?
"Pa was an odd duck, too. He let me bring Rocky along with us.
"It was time for me to be taking on more responsibility, after all.
"The other cowherds in our cattle train already thought I was odd, so adding a one-eyed bison didn't change much.
"Pa told me, if I couldn't convince a group of stubborn mules I was worthwhile..."

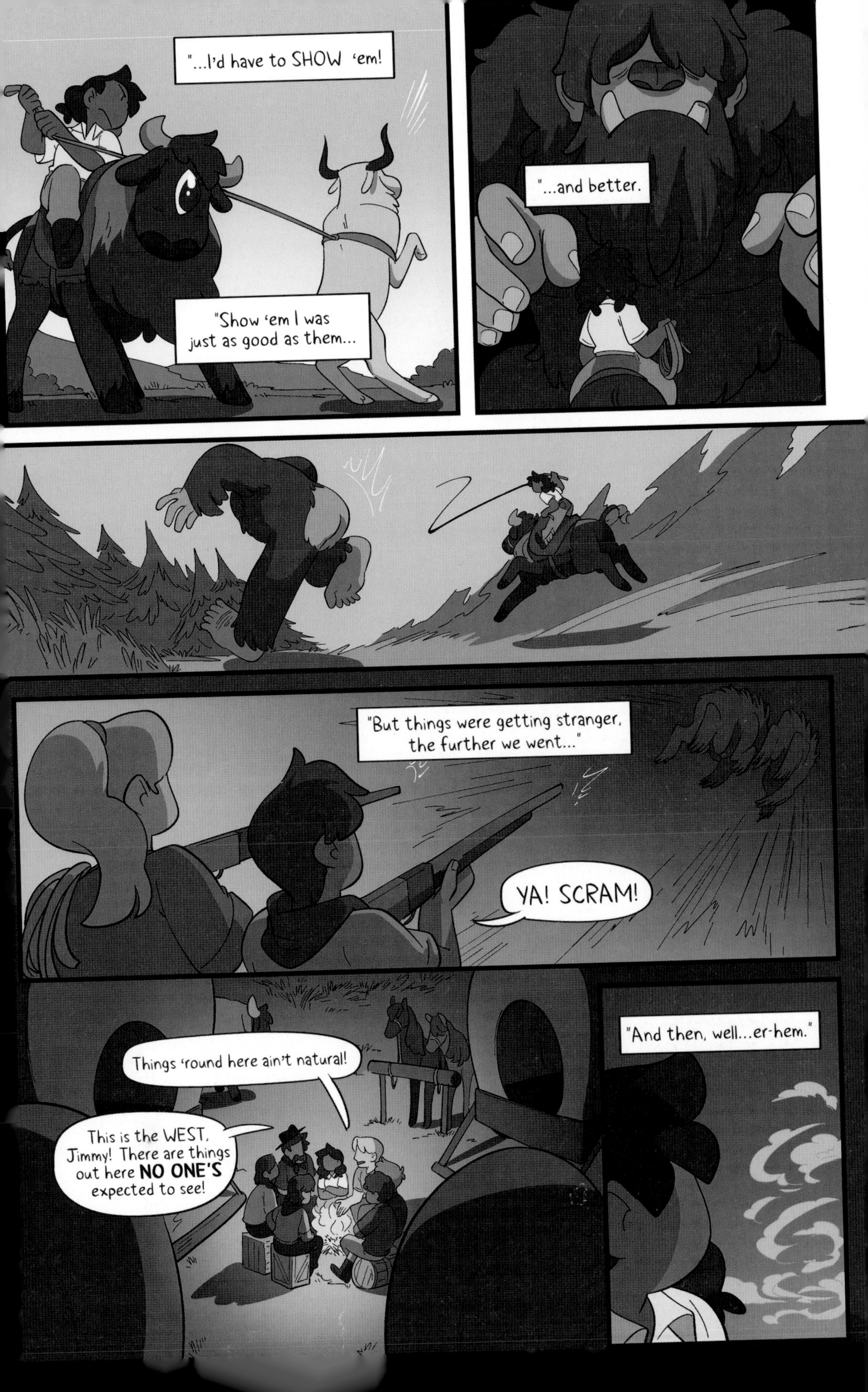
"...I'd have to SHOW 'em!
"Show 'em I was just as good as them...
"...and better.
"But things were getting stranger, the further we went..."
YA! SCRAM!
Things 'round here ain't natural!
This is the WEST, Jimmy! There are things out here **NO ONE'S** expected to see!
"And then, well...er-hem."

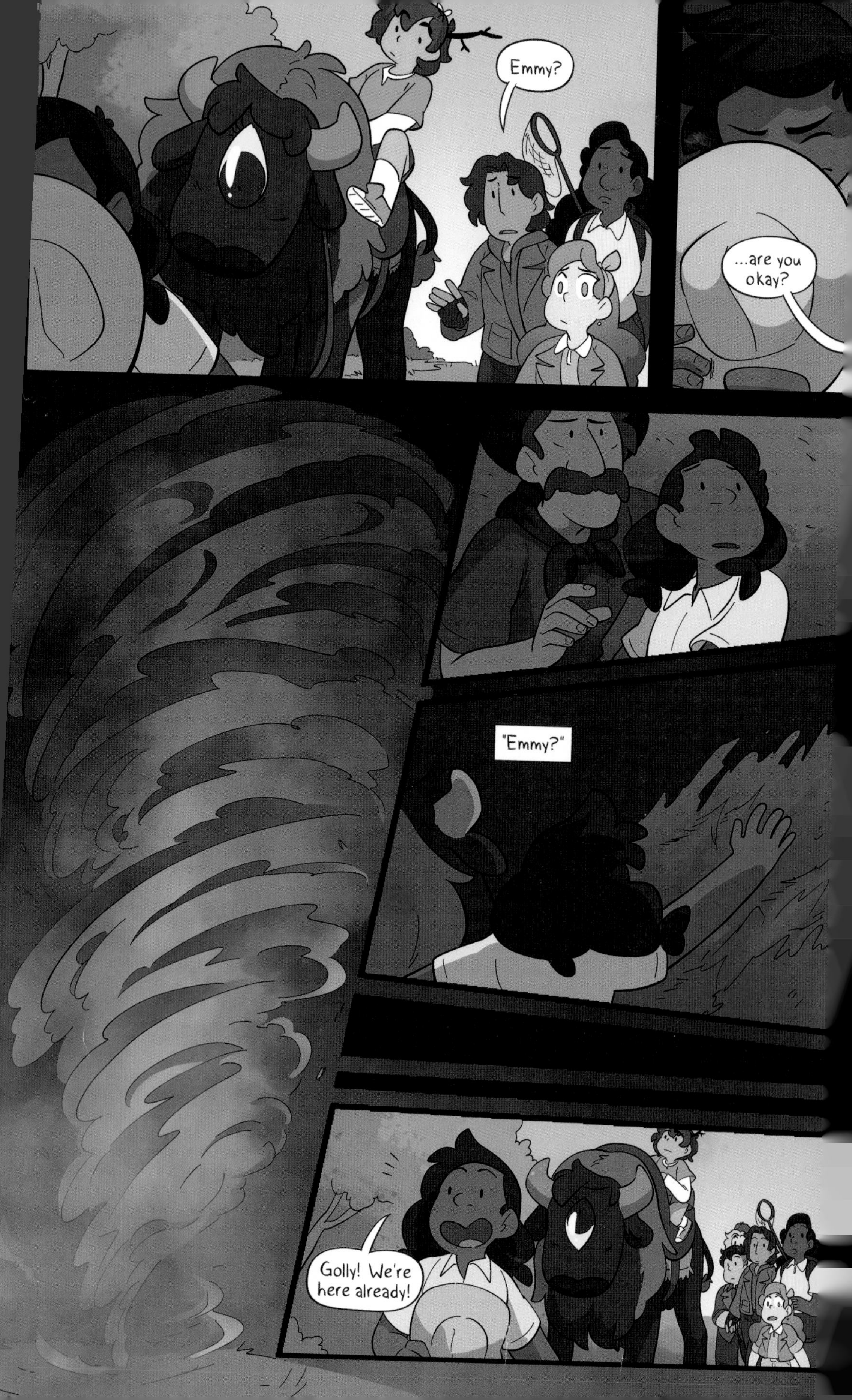
Emmy?
...are you okay?
"Emmy?"
Golly! We're here already!

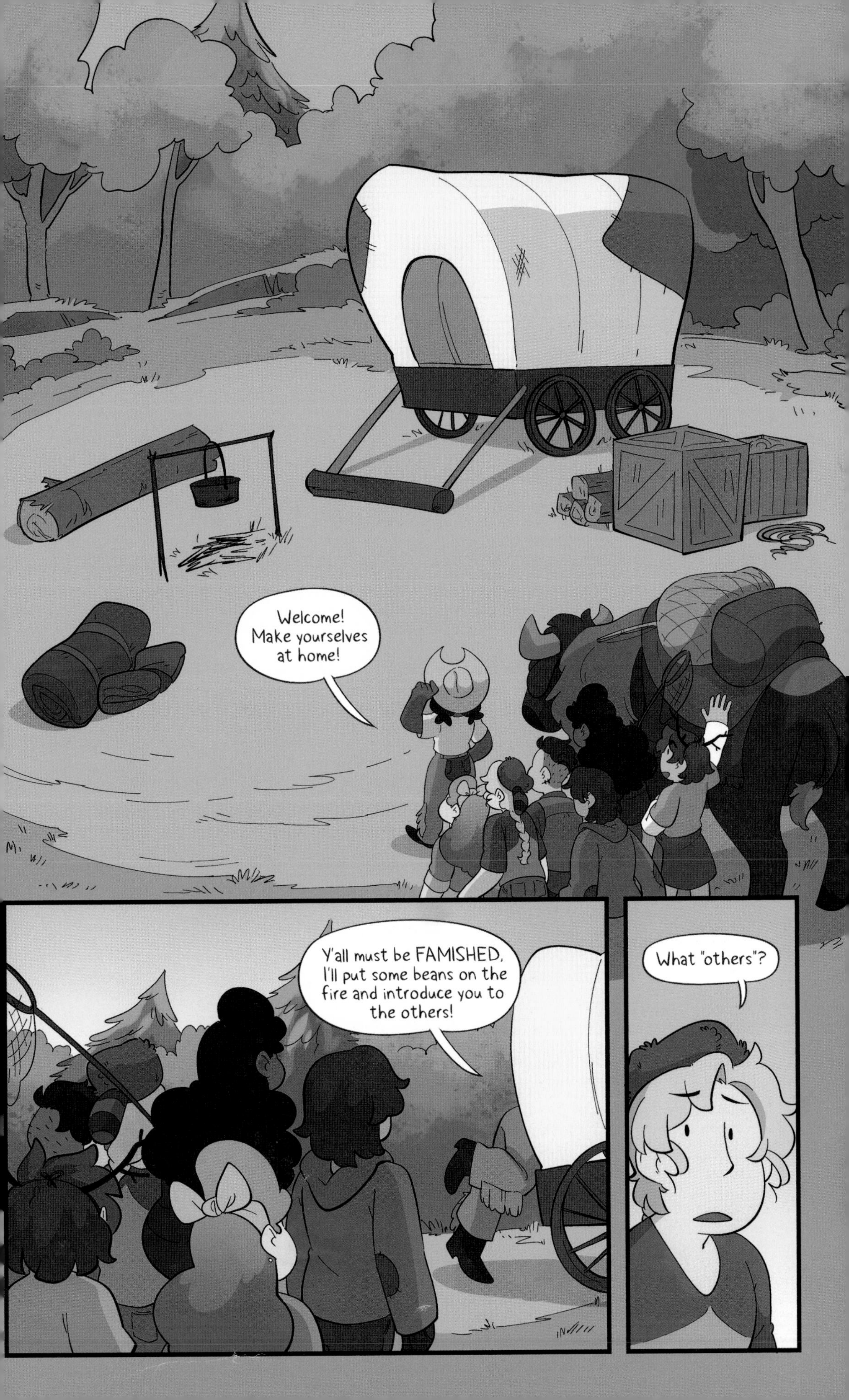
Welcome! Make yourselves at home!
Y'all must be FAMISHED, I'll put some beans on the fire and introduce you to the others!
What "others"?

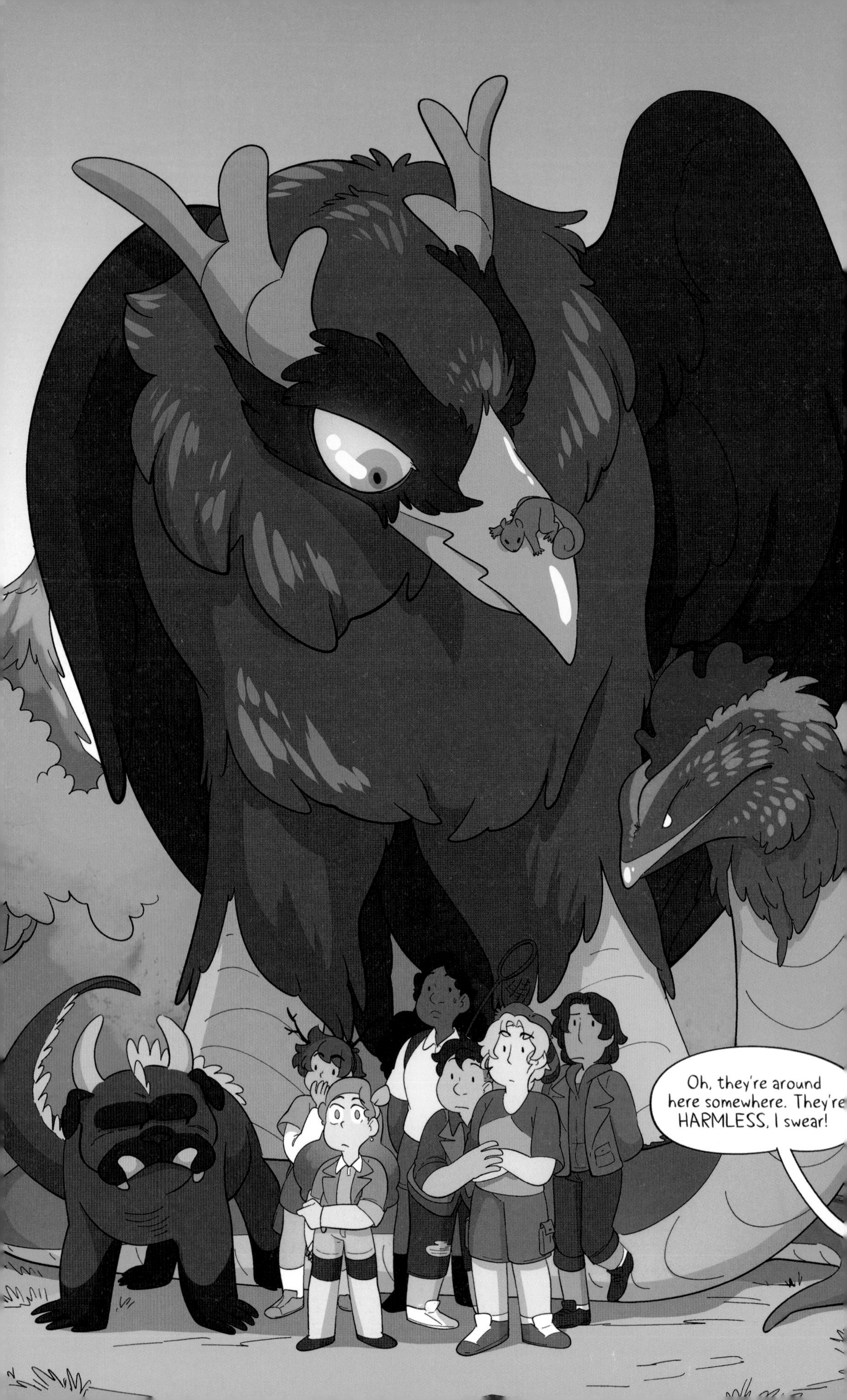
Oh, they're around here somewhere. They're HARMLESS, I swear!

will comr

The ur
It helps
appearar
dress fo
Further
Lumber
to have
part in
Thiskw
Hardc
have
them

THE UNIFORM

should be worn at camp
events when Lumberjanes
n may also be worn at other
ions. It should be worn as a
the uniform dress with
rrect shoes, and stocking or

out grows her uniform or
ng to anoter Lumberjane.
insignia she has
her
her

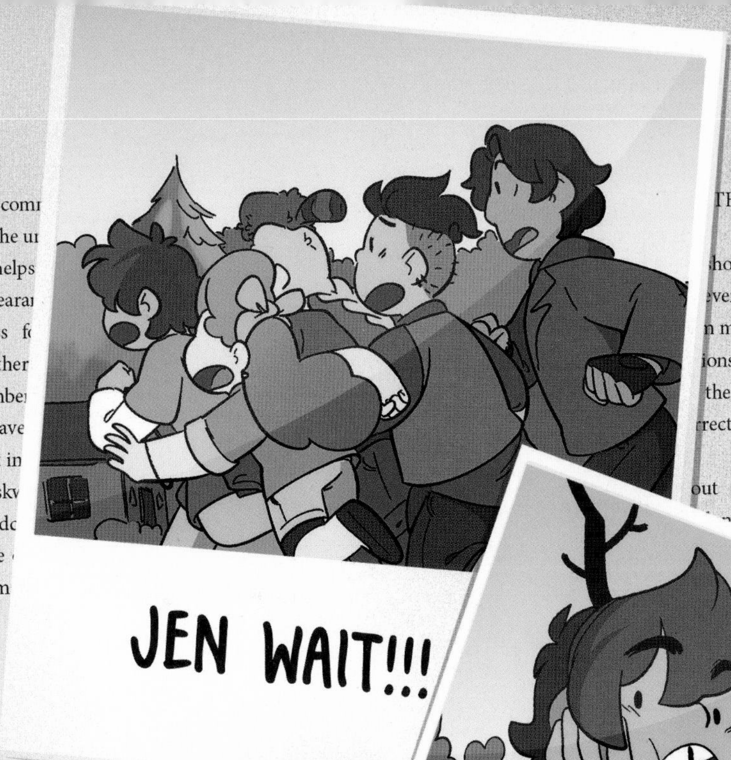
JEN WAIT!!!

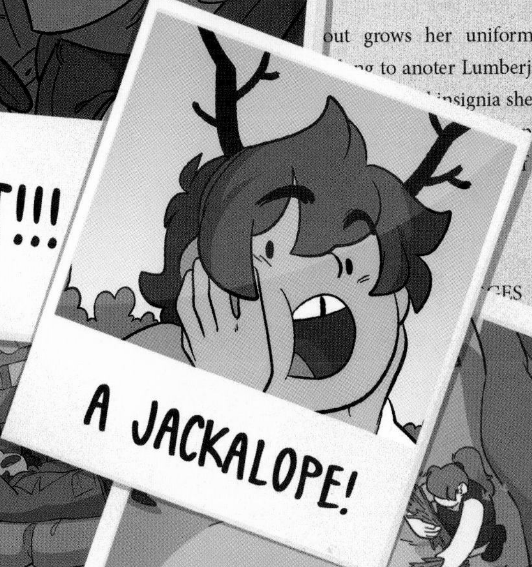
A JACKALOPE!

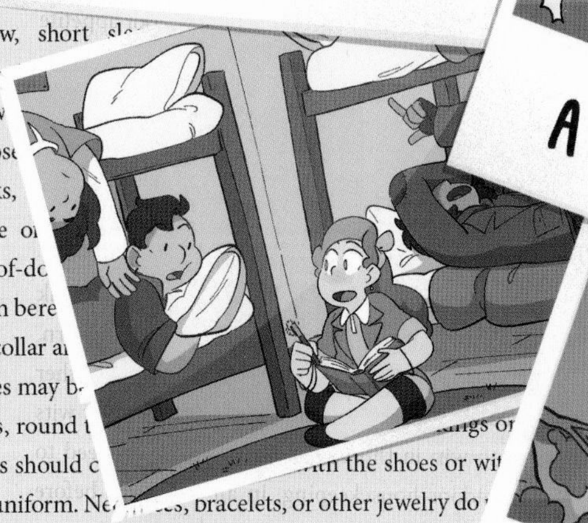

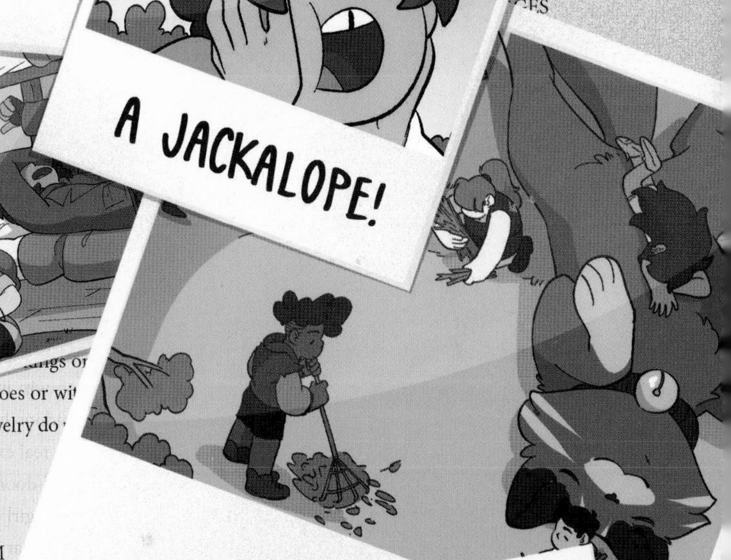

The
yellow, short sl
emb
the w
choose
slacks,
made o
out-of-do
green bere
the collar a
Shoes may b
heels, round t kings or
socks should c with the shoes or wit
the uniform. Ne ces, bracelets, or other jewelry do
belong with a Lumberjane uniform.

HOW TO WEAR THE UNIFORM

To look well in a uniform demands first of uniform be kept in good condition—clean pressed. See that the skirt is the right length for your own height and build, that the belt is adjusted to your waist, that your shoes and stockings are in keeping with the uniform, that you watch your posture and carry yourself with dignity and grace. If the beret is removed indoors, be sure that your hair is neat and kept in place with an insonspicuous clip or ribbon. When you wear a Lumberjane uniform you are identified as a member of this organization and you should be doubly careful to conduct yourself in a way that will show everyone that courtesy and thoughtfullness are part of being a Lumberjane. People are likely to judge a whole nation by the selfishness of a few individuals, to criticize a whole family because of the misconduct of one member, and to feel unkindly toward and organization because of the

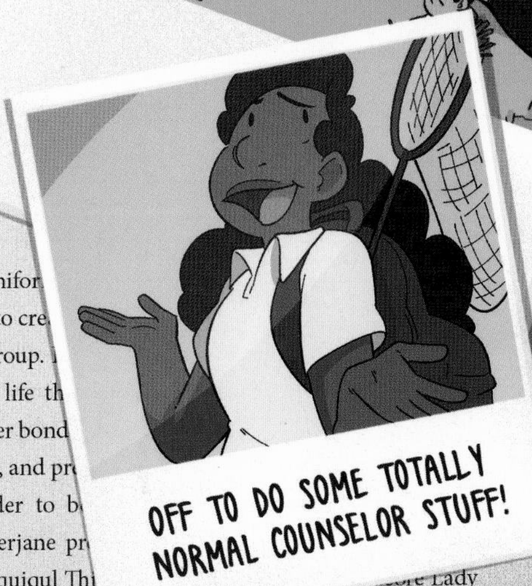
OFF TO DO SOME TOTALLY
NORMAL COUNSELOR STUFF!

The unifor
helps to cre
in a group.
active life th
another bond
future, and pr
in order to b
Lumberjane pr
Penniquiqul Thi ore Lady
Types, but most L will wish to have one. They
can either buy the uniform, or make it themselves from
materials available at the trading post.

LUMBERJANES FIELD MANUAL

CHAPTER
FORTY-SIX

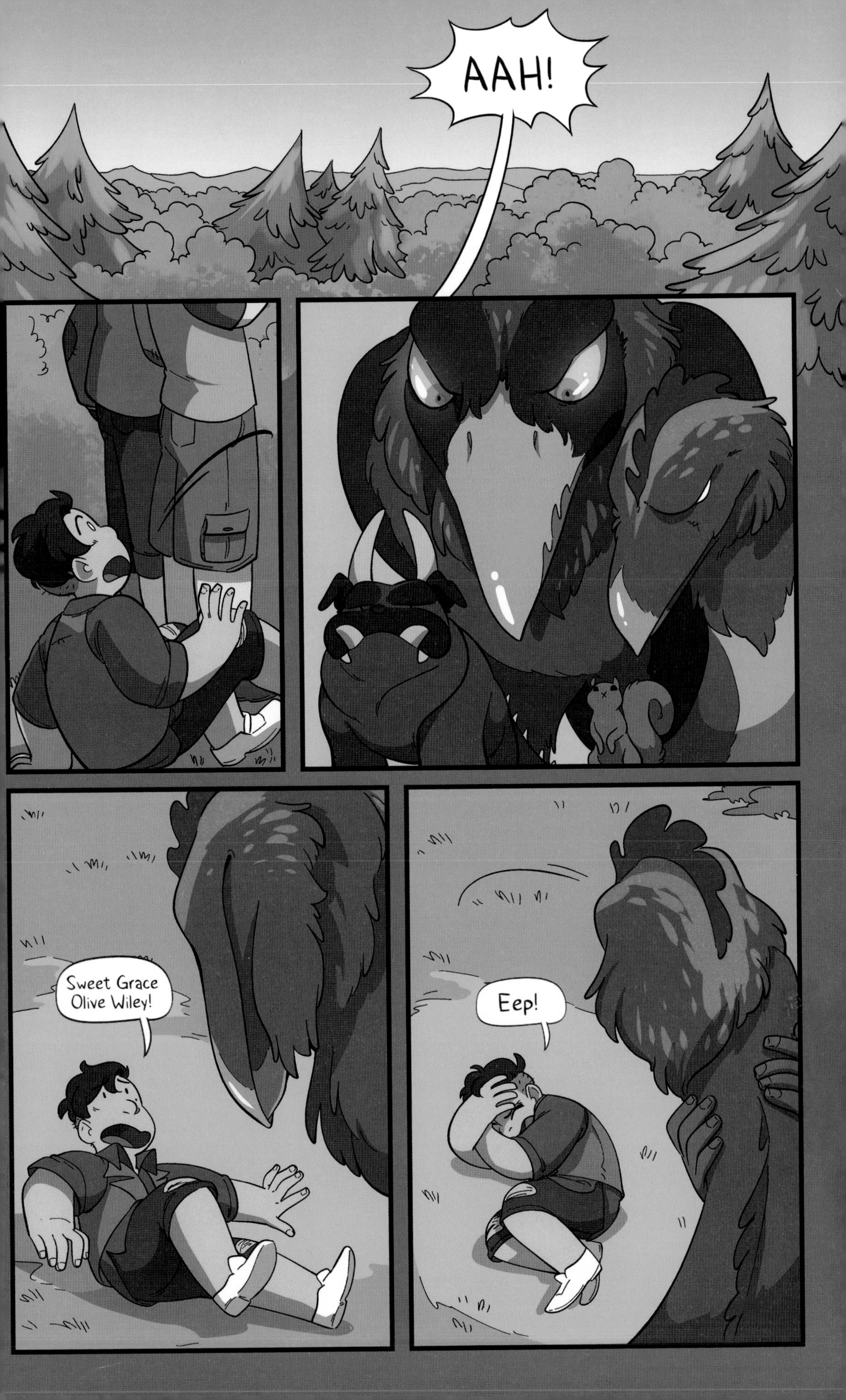
AAH!
Sweet Grace Olive Wiley!
Eep!

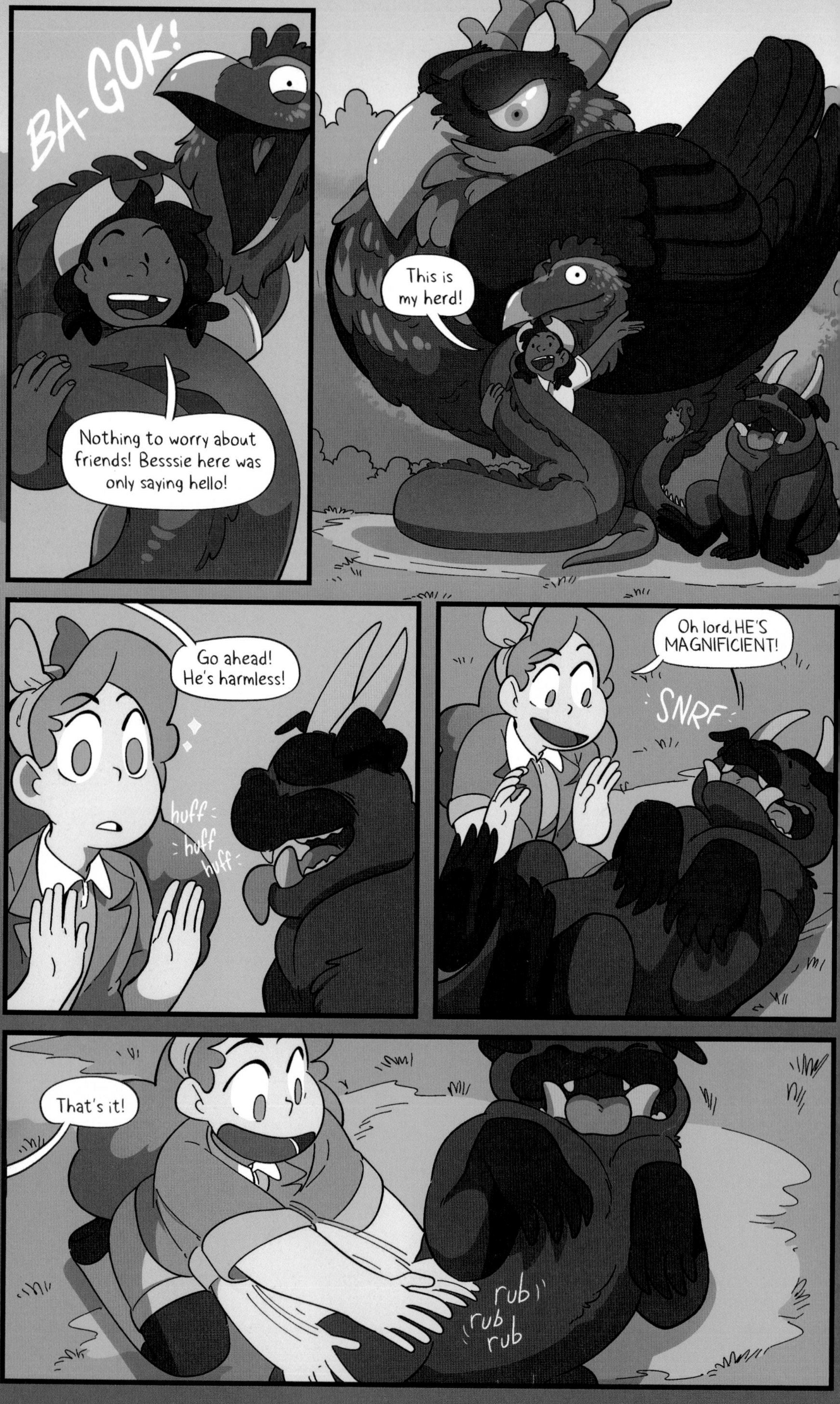
BA-GOK!
Nothing to worry about friends! Besssie here was only saying hello!
This is my herd!
Go ahead! He's harmless!
huff huff huff
Oh lord, HE'S MAGNIFICIENT!
SNRF
That's it!
rub rub rub

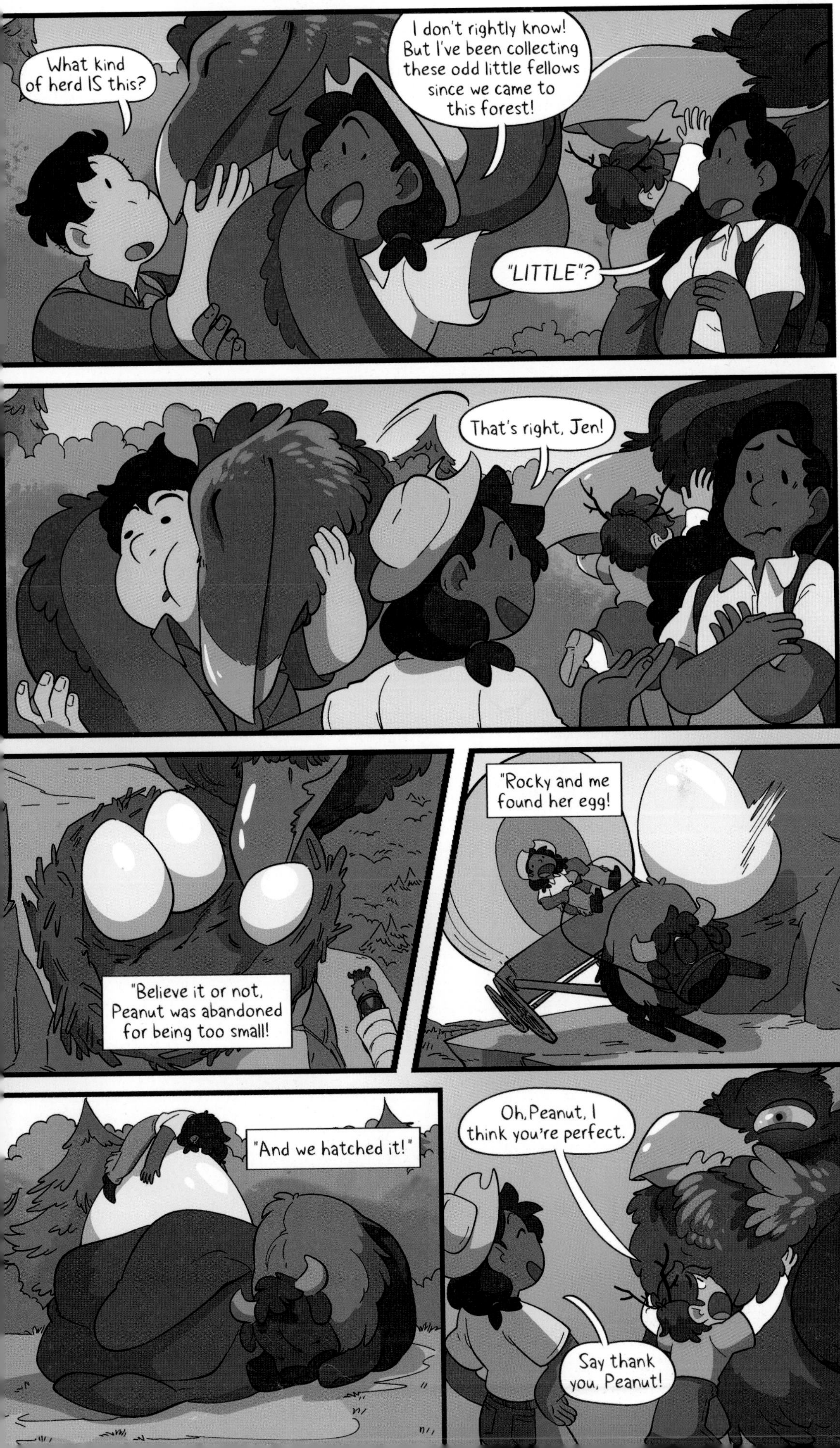
What kind of herd IS this?
I don't rightly know! But I've been collecting these odd little fellows since we came to this forest!
"LITTLE"?
That's right, Jen!
"Believe it or not, Peanut was abandoned for being too small!
"Rocky and me found her egg!
"And we hatched it!"
Oh, Peanut, I think you're perfect.
Say thank you, Peanut!

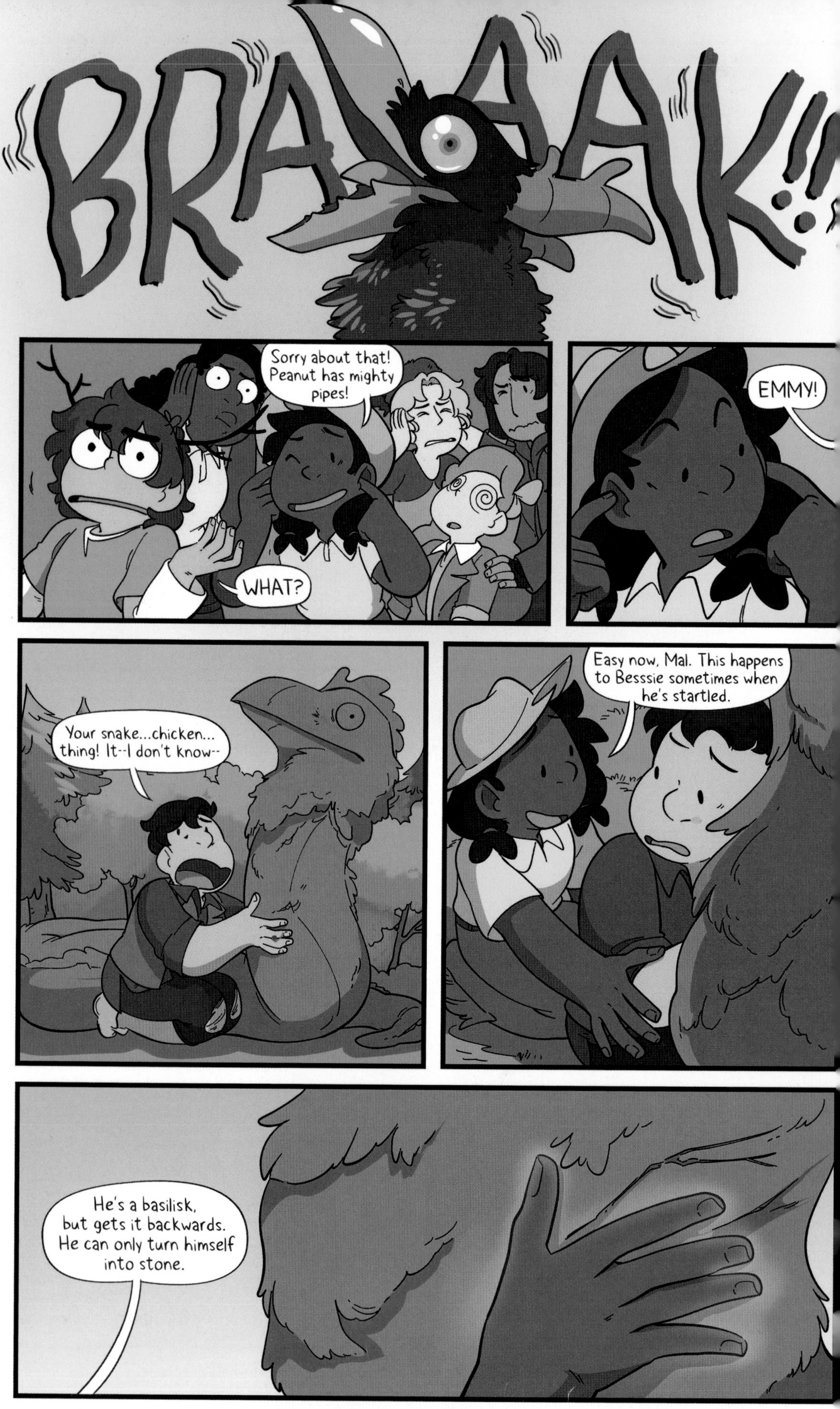
BRAAAK!!!
Sorry about that! Peanut has mighty pipes!
WHAT?
EMMY!
Your snake...chicken... thing! It--I don't know--
Easy now, Mal. This happens to Besssie sometimes when he's startled.
He's a basilisk, but gets it backwards. He can only turn himself into stone.

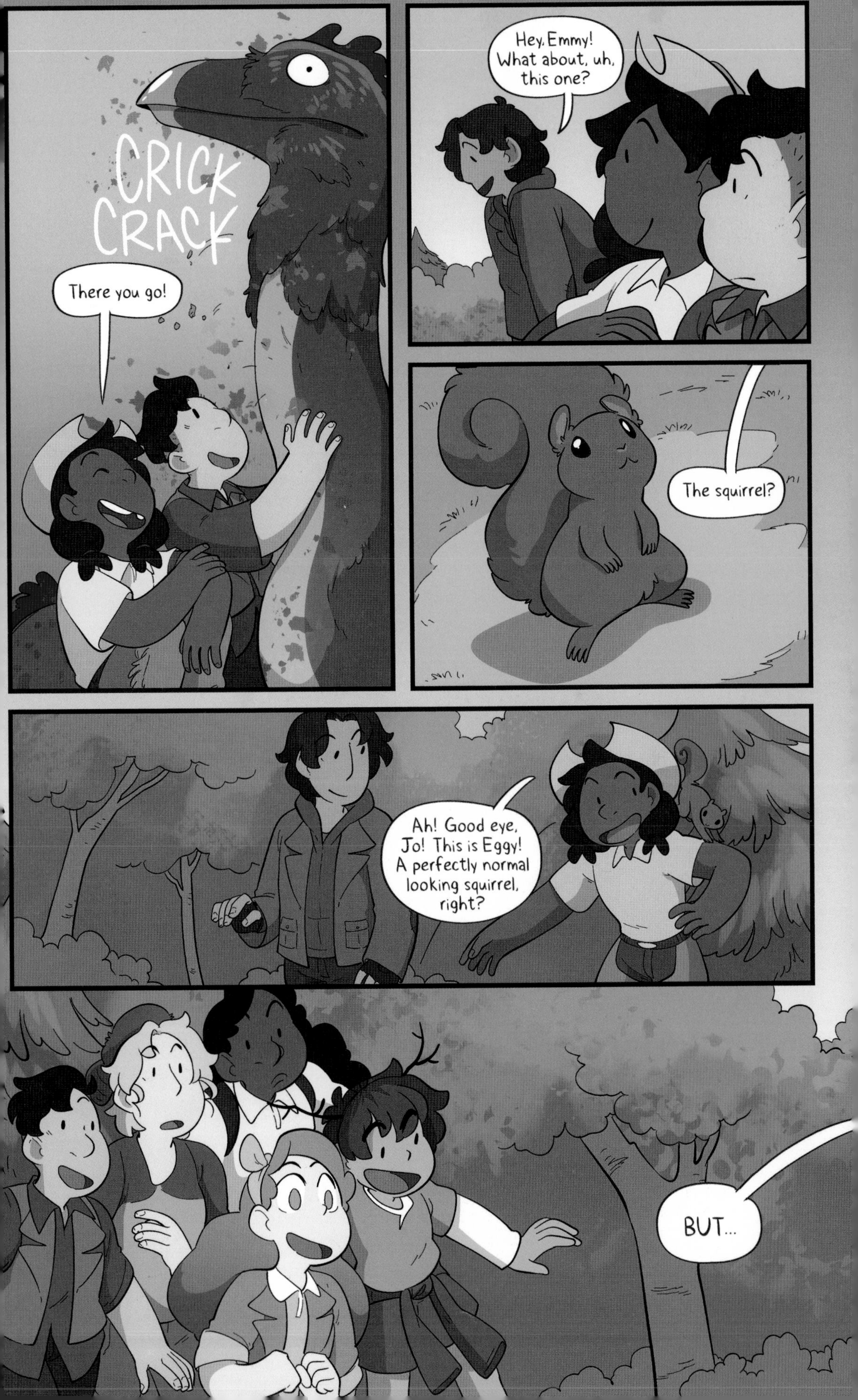
CRICK
CRACK
There you go!
Hey, Emmy! What about, uh, this one?
The squirrel?
Ah! Good eye, Jo! This is Eggy! A perfectly normal looking squirrel, right?
BUT...

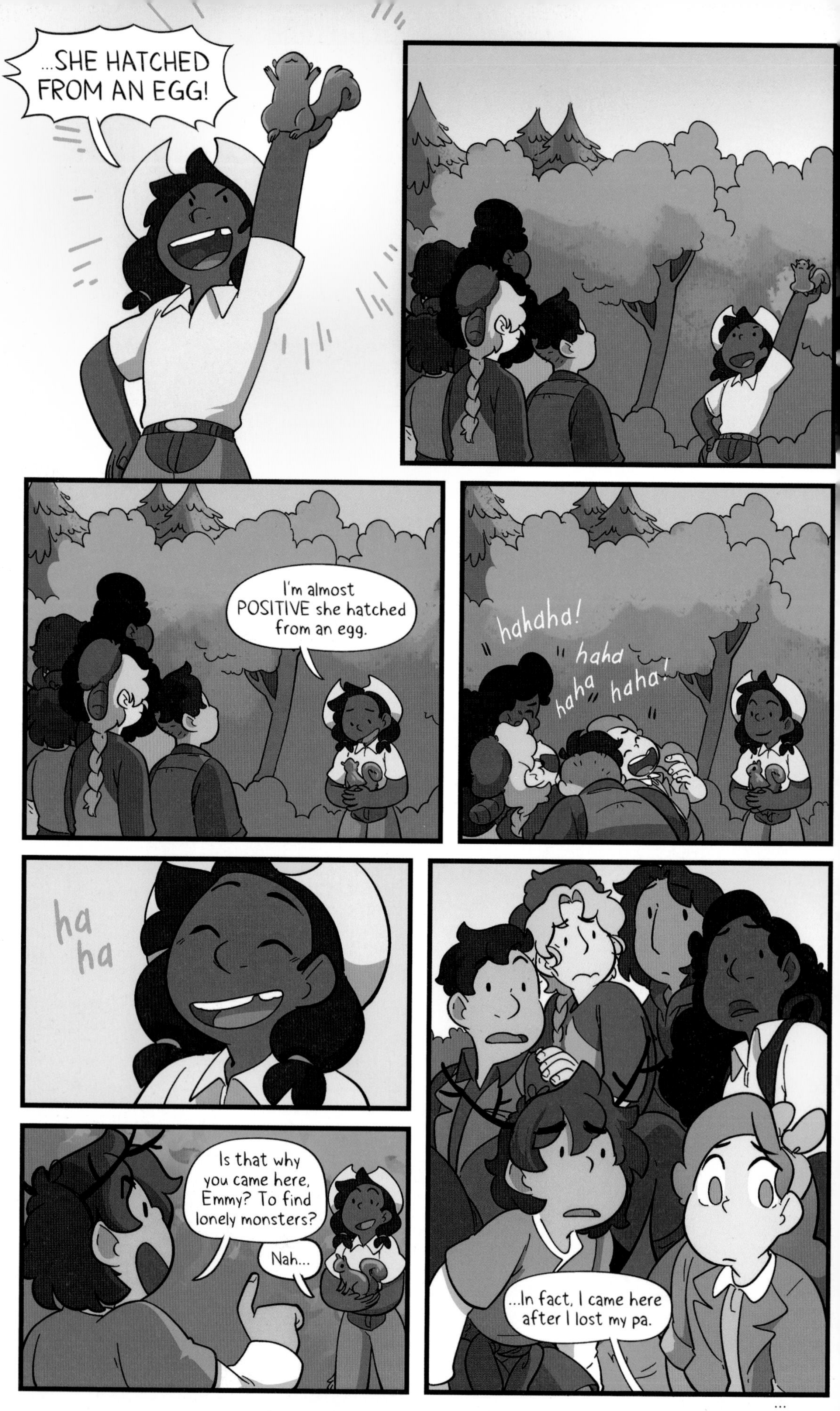
...SHE HATCHED FROM AN EGG!
I'm almost POSITIVE she hatched from an egg.
hahaha!
haha
haha
haha!
ha ha
Is that why you came here, Emmy? To find lonely monsters?
Nah...
...In fact, I came here after I lost my pa.
...

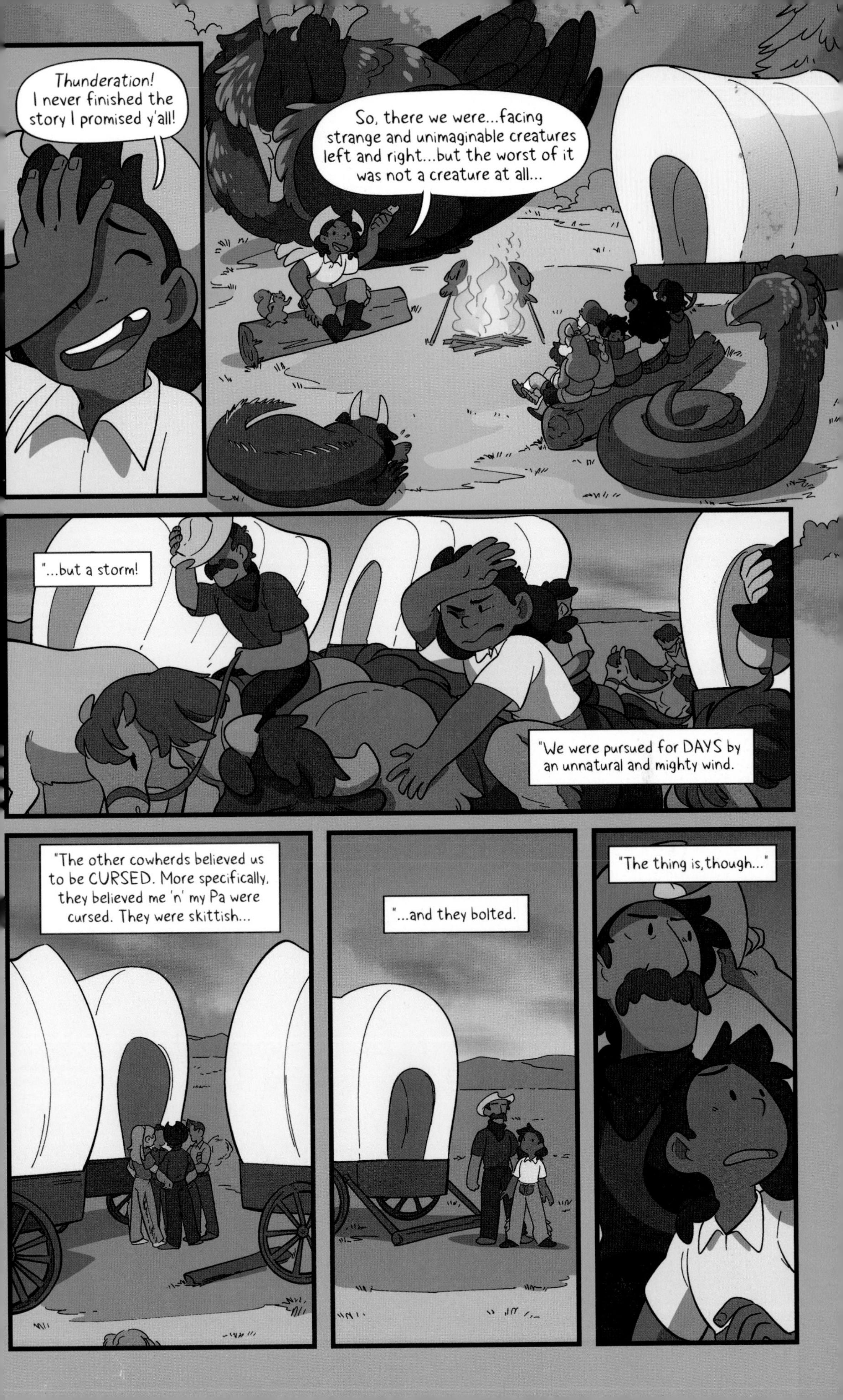
Thunderation! I never finished the story I promised y'all!
So, there we were...facing strange and unimaginable creatures left and right...but the worst of it was not a creature at all...
"...but a storm!
"We were pursued for DAYS by an unnatural and mighty wind.
"The other cowherds believed us to be CURSED. More specifically, they believed me 'n' my Pa were cursed. They were skittish...
"...and they bolted.
"The thing is, though..."

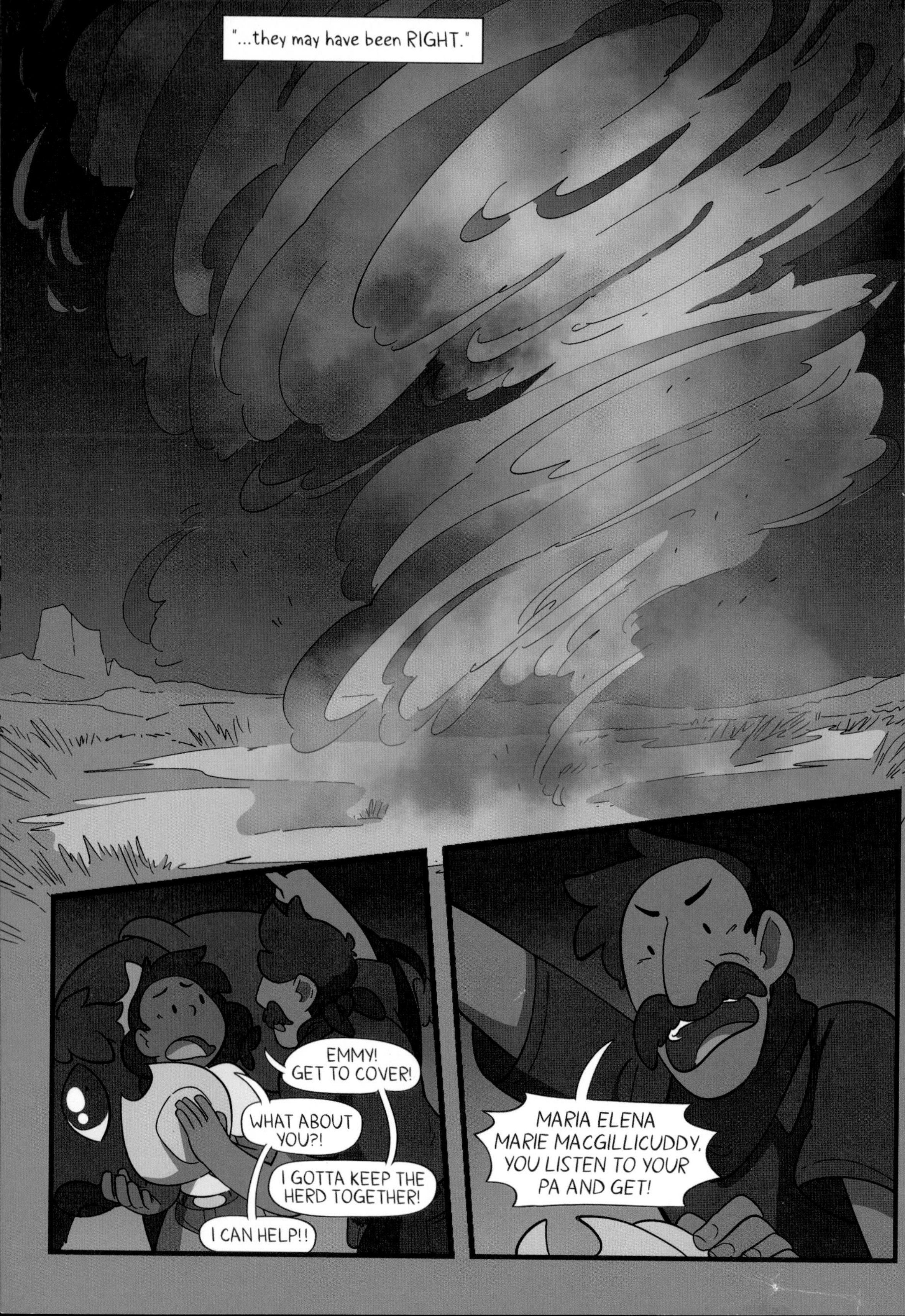
"...they may have been RIGHT."
EMMY! GET TO COVER!
WHAT ABOUT YOU?!
I GOTTA KEEP THE HERD TOGETHER!
I CAN HELP!!
MARIA ELENA MARIE MACGILLICUDDY, YOU LISTEN TO YOUR PA AND GET!

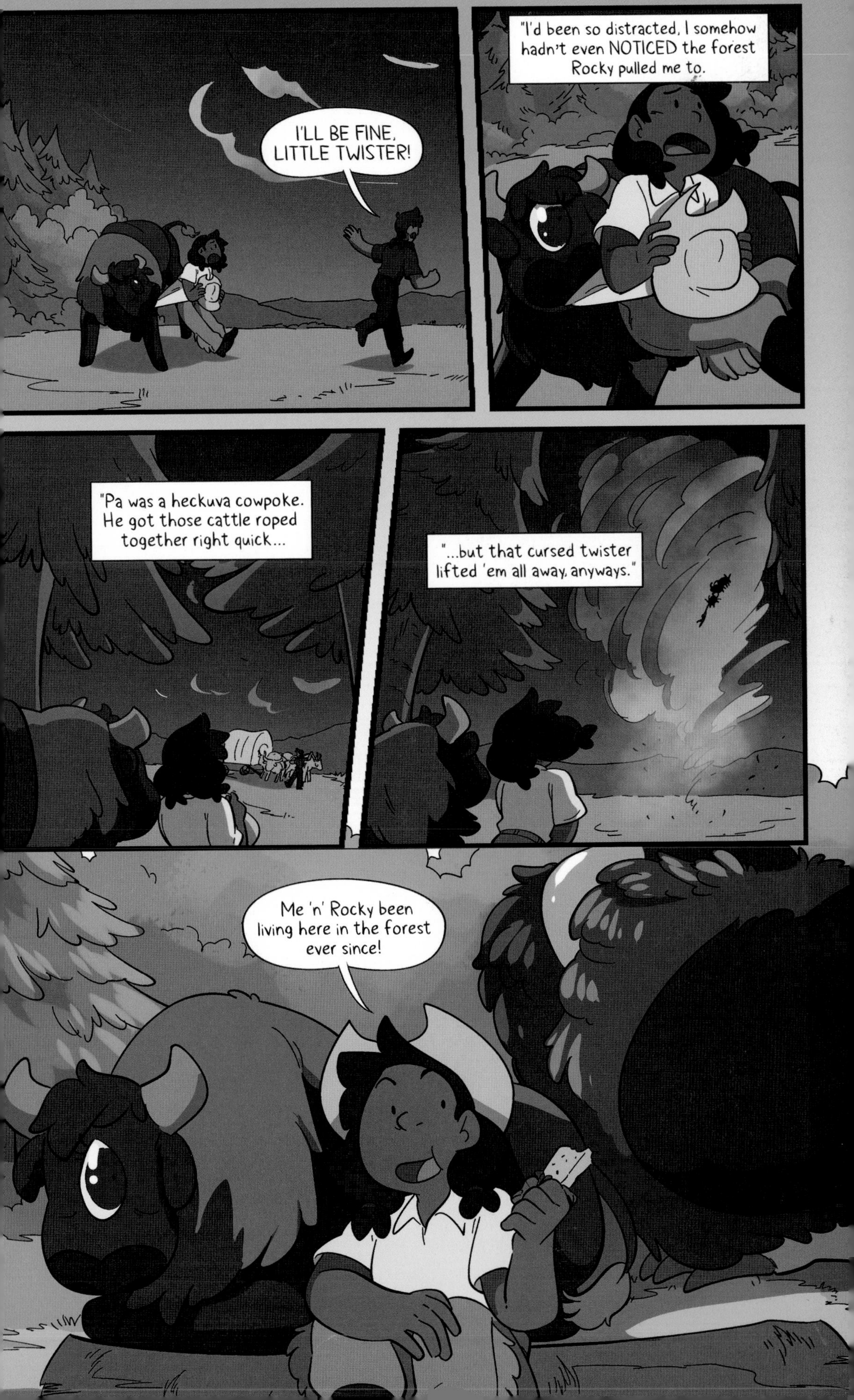
I'LL BE FINE, LITTLE TWISTER!
"I'd been so distracted, I somehow hadn't even NOTICED the forest Rocky pulled me to.
"Pa was a heckuva cowpoke. He got those cattle roped together right quick...
"...but that cursed twister lifted 'em all away, anyways."
Me 'n' Rocky been living here in the forest ever since!

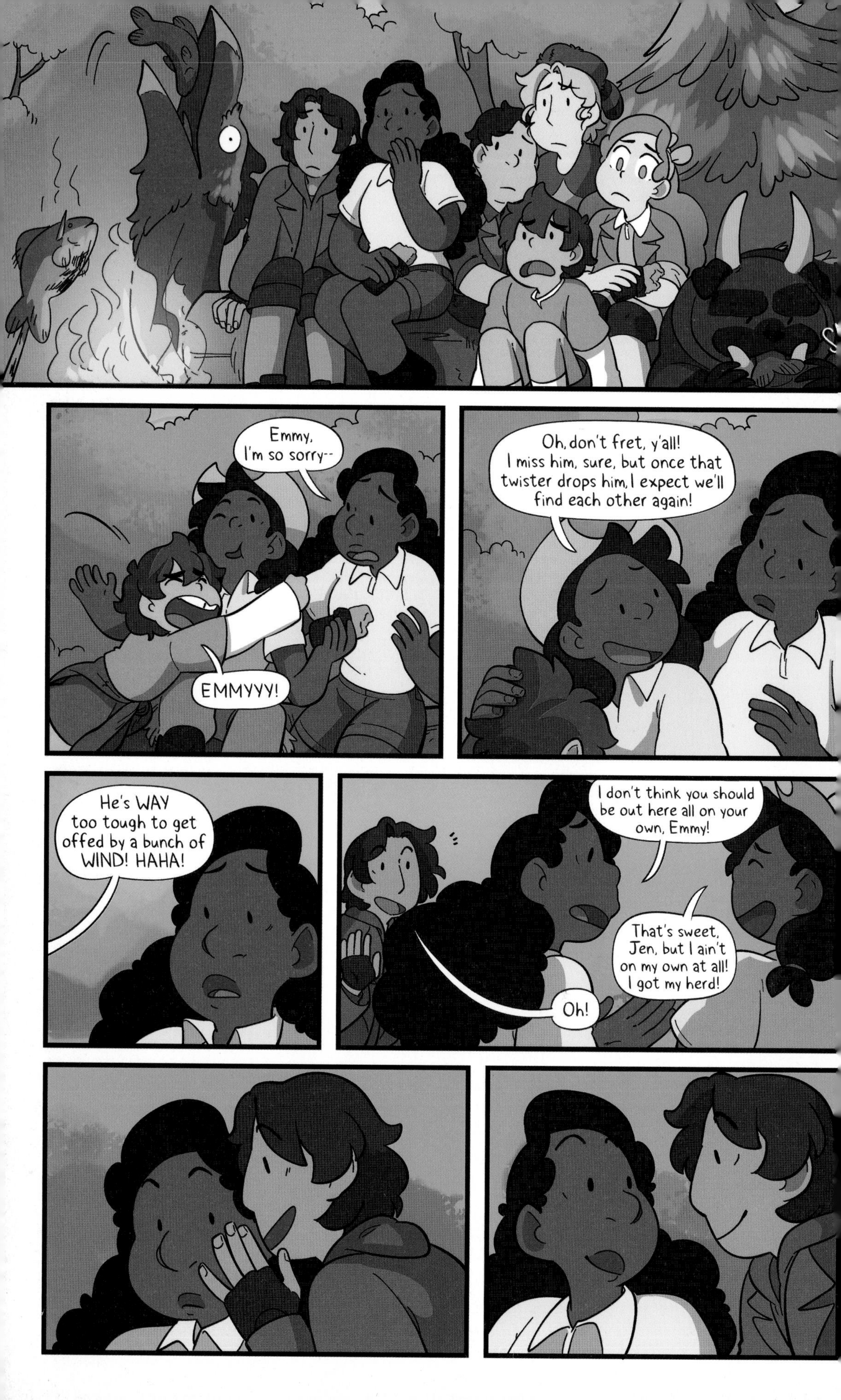
Emmy,
I'm so sorry--
EMMYYY!
Oh, don't fret, y'all!
I miss him, sure, but once that twister drops him, I expect we'll find each other again!
He's WAY too tough to get offed by a bunch of WIND! HAHA!
I don't think you should be out here all on your own, Emmy!
That's sweet, Jen, but I ain't on my own at all! I got my herd!
Oh!

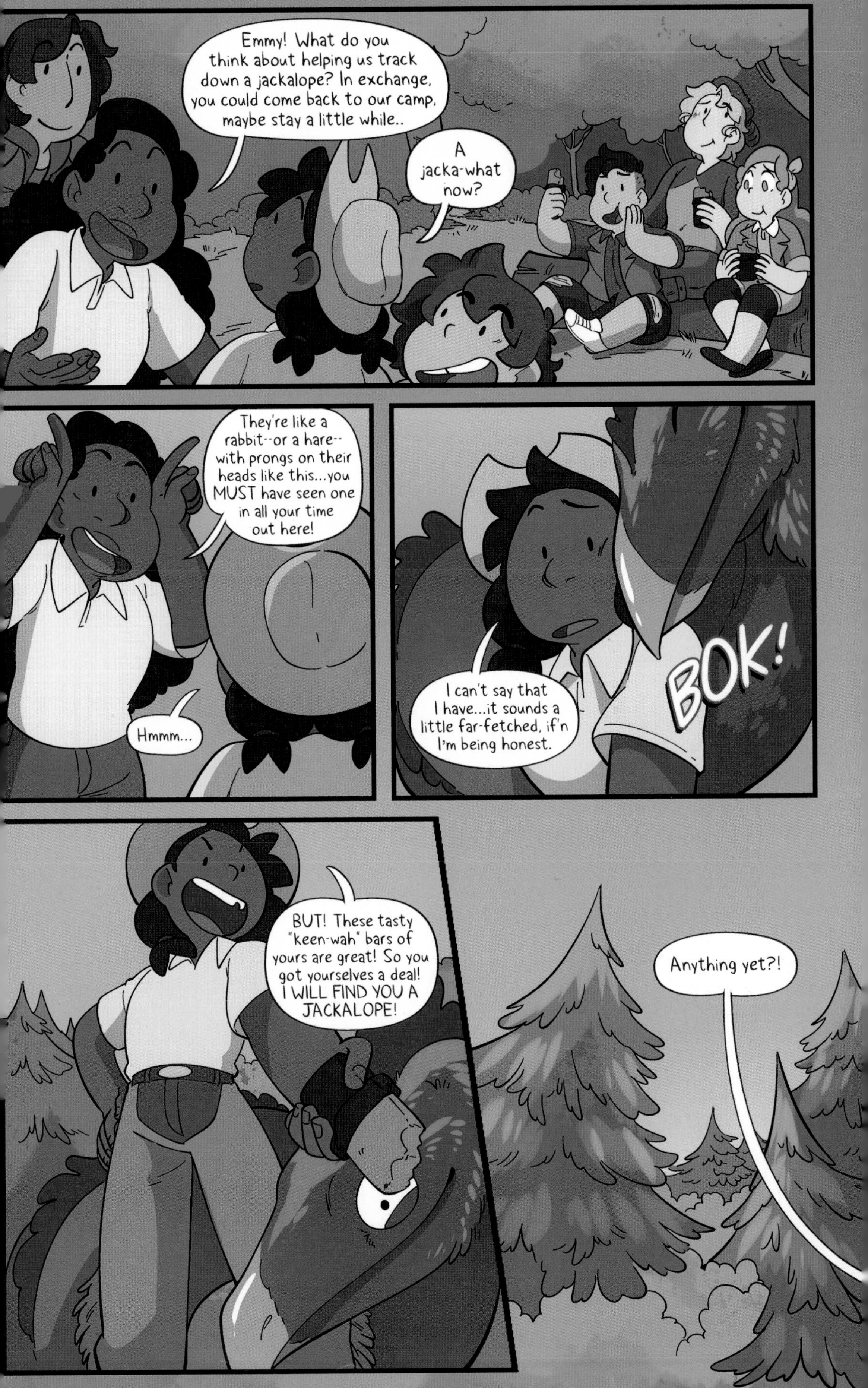
Emmy! What do you think about helping us track down a jackalope? In exchange, you could come back to our camp, maybe stay a little while..
A jacka-what now?
They're like a rabbit--or a hare--with prongs on their heads like this...you MUST have seen one in all your time out here!
Hmmm...
I can't say that I have...it sounds a little far-fetched, if'n I'm being honest.
BOK!
BUT! These tasty "keen-wah" bars of yours are great! So you got yourselves a deal! I WILL FIND YOU A JACKALOPE!
Anything yet?!

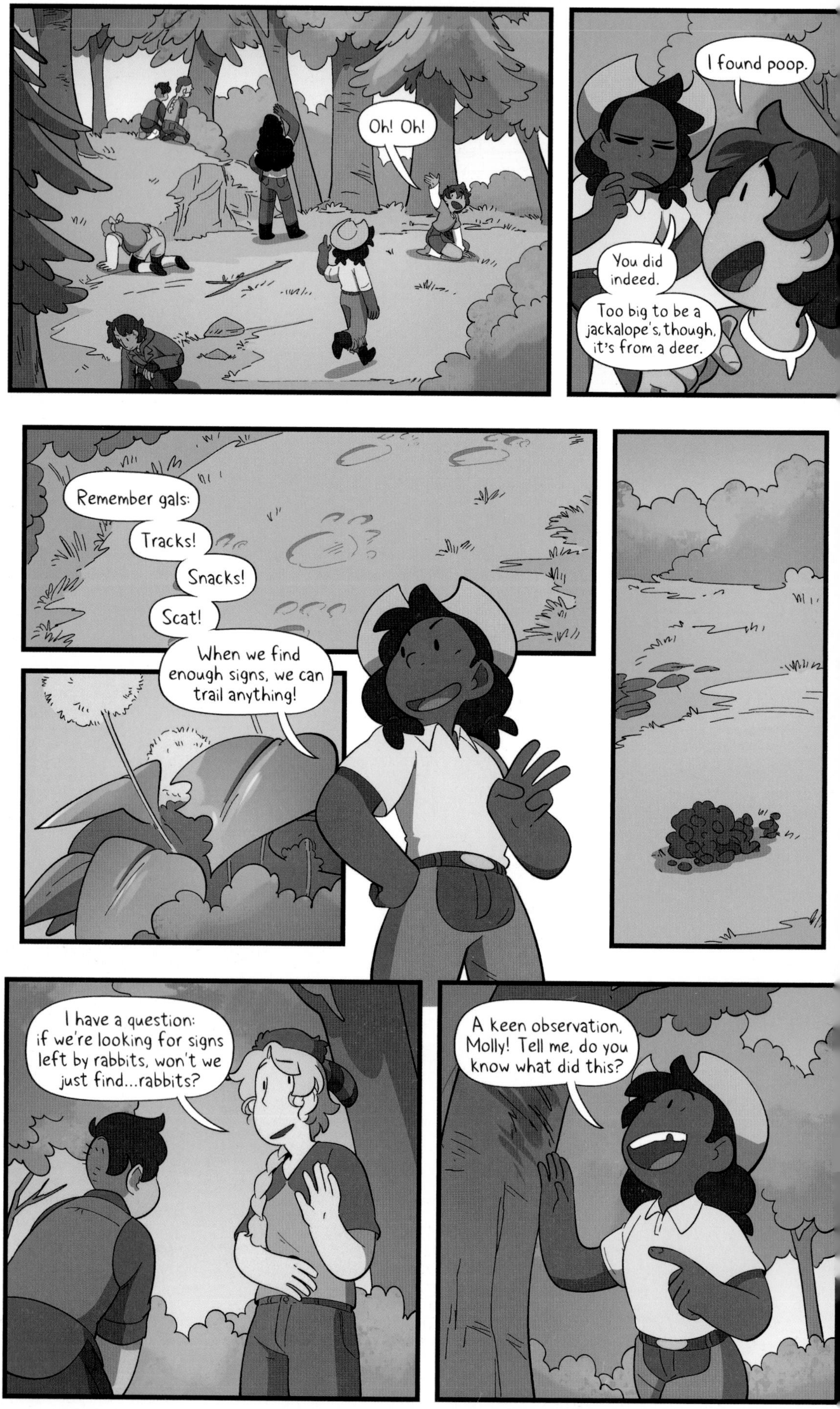
Oh! Oh!
I found poop.
You did indeed.
Too big to be a jackalope's, though, it's from a deer.
Remember gals:
Tracks!
Snacks!
Scat!
When we find enough signs, we can trail anything!
I have a question: if we're looking for signs left by rabbits, won't we just find...rabbits?
A keen observation, Molly! Tell me, do you know what did this?

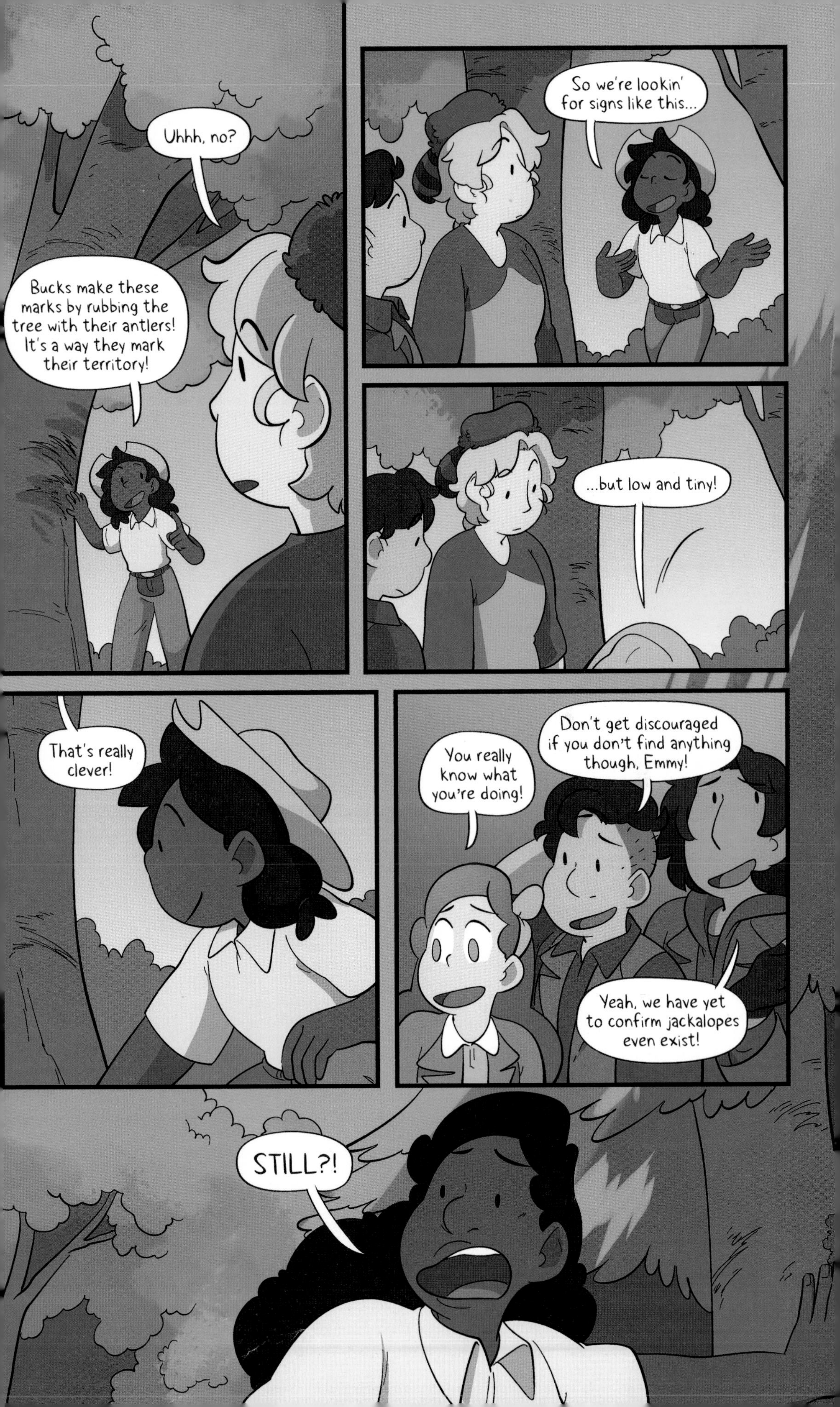
Uhhh, no?
So we're lookin' for signs like this...
Bucks make these marks by rubbing the tree with their antlers! It's a way they mark their territory!
...but low and tiny!
That's really clever!
Don't get discouraged if you don't find anything though, Emmy!
You really know what you're doing!
Yeah, we have yet to confirm jackalopes even exist!
STILL?!

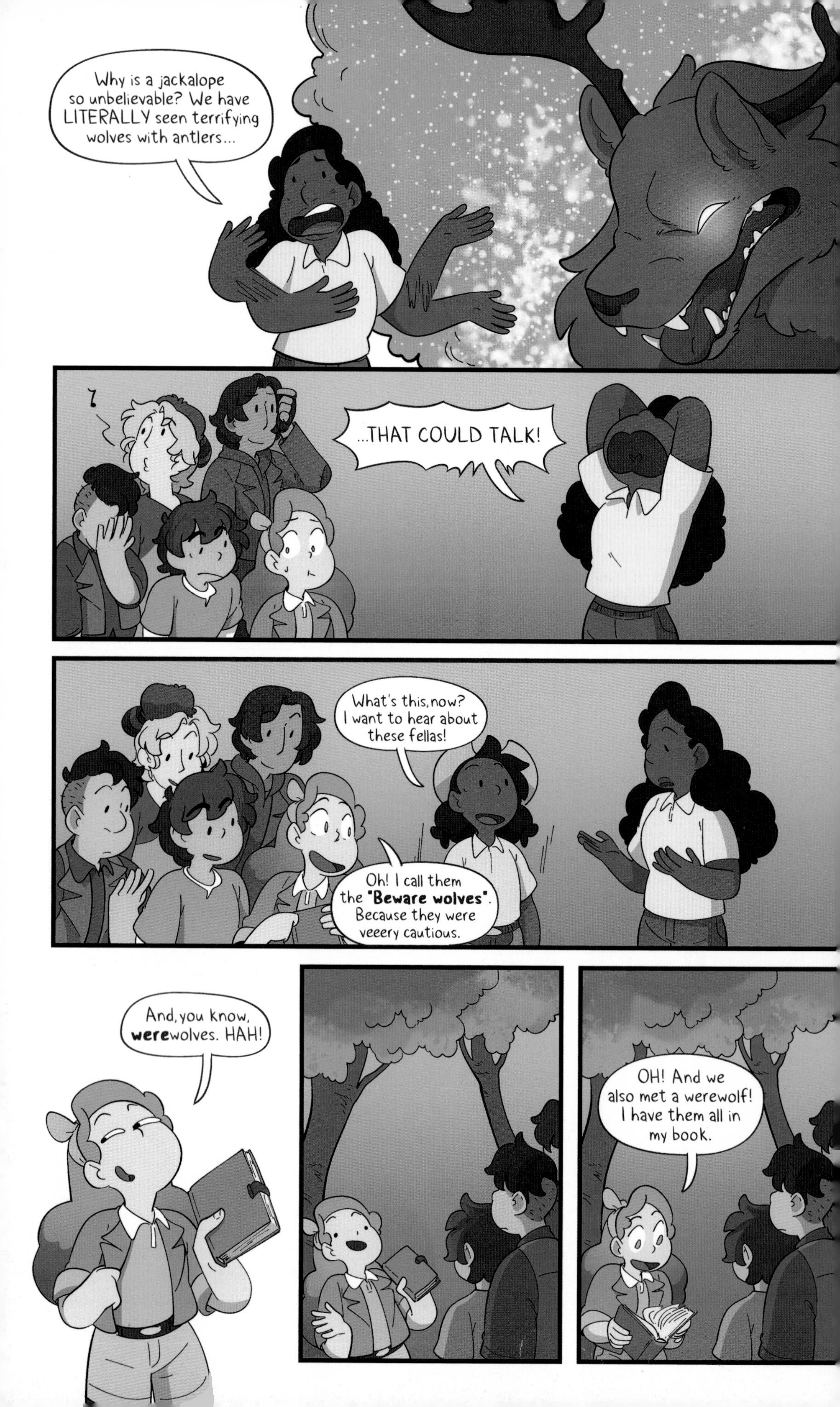
Why is a jackalope so unbelievable? We have LITERALLY seen terrifying wolves with antlers...
...THAT COULD TALK!
What's this, now? I want to hear about these fellas!
Oh! I call them the **"Beware wolves"**. Because they were veeery cautious.
And, you know, **were**wolves. HAH!
OH! And we also met a werewolf! I have them all in my book.

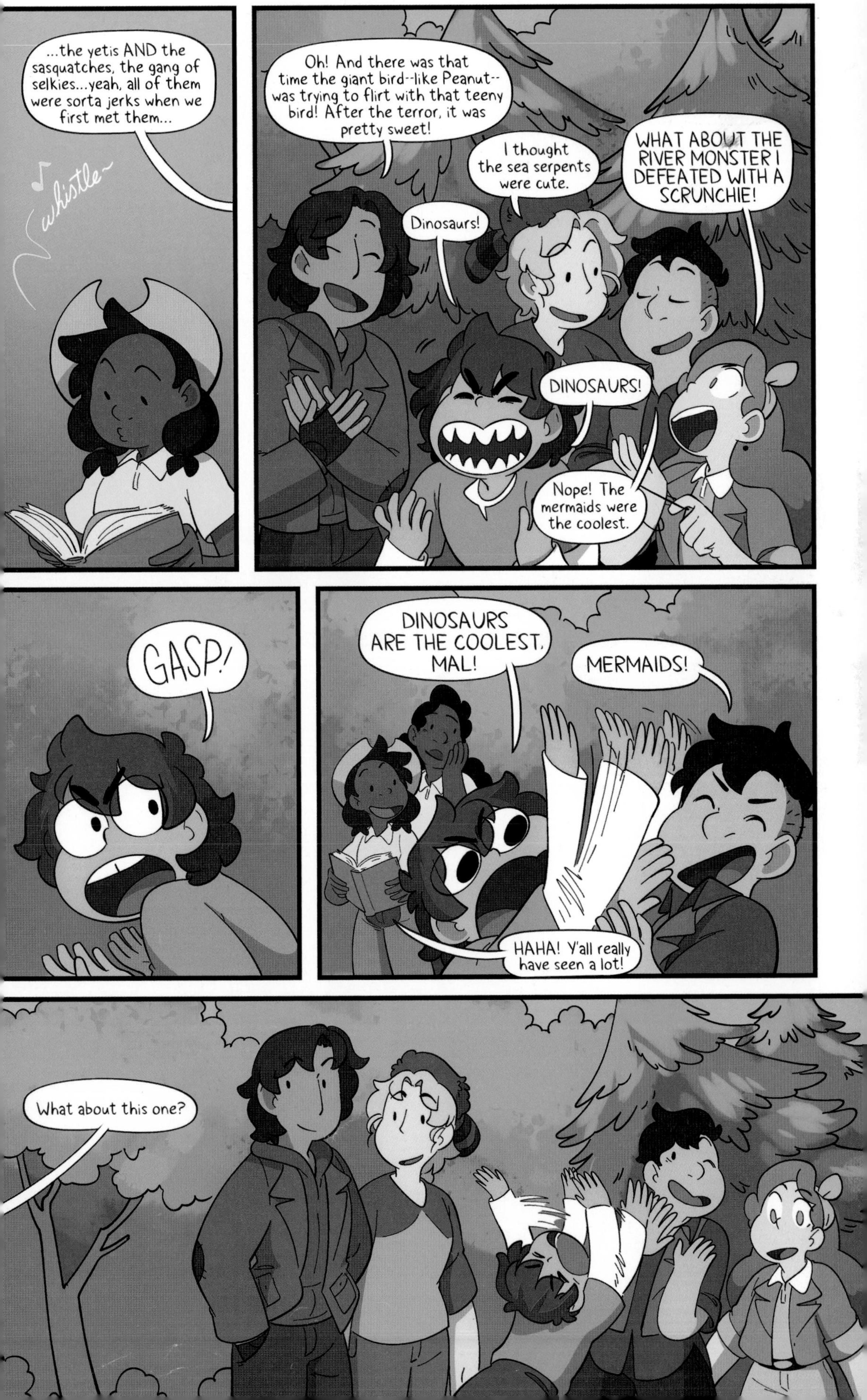
...the yetis AND the sasquatches, the gang of selkies...yeah, all of them were sorta jerks when we first met them...
whistle~
Oh! And there was that time the giant bird--like Peanut--was trying to flirt with that teeny bird! After the terror, it was pretty sweet!
I thought the sea serpents were cute.
WHAT ABOUT THE RIVER MONSTER I DEFEATED WITH A SCRUNCHIE!
Dinosaurs!
DINOSAURS!
Nope! The mermaids were the coolest.
GASP!
DINOSAURS ARE THE COOLEST, MAL!
MERMAIDS!
HAHA! Y'all really have seen a lot!
What about this one?

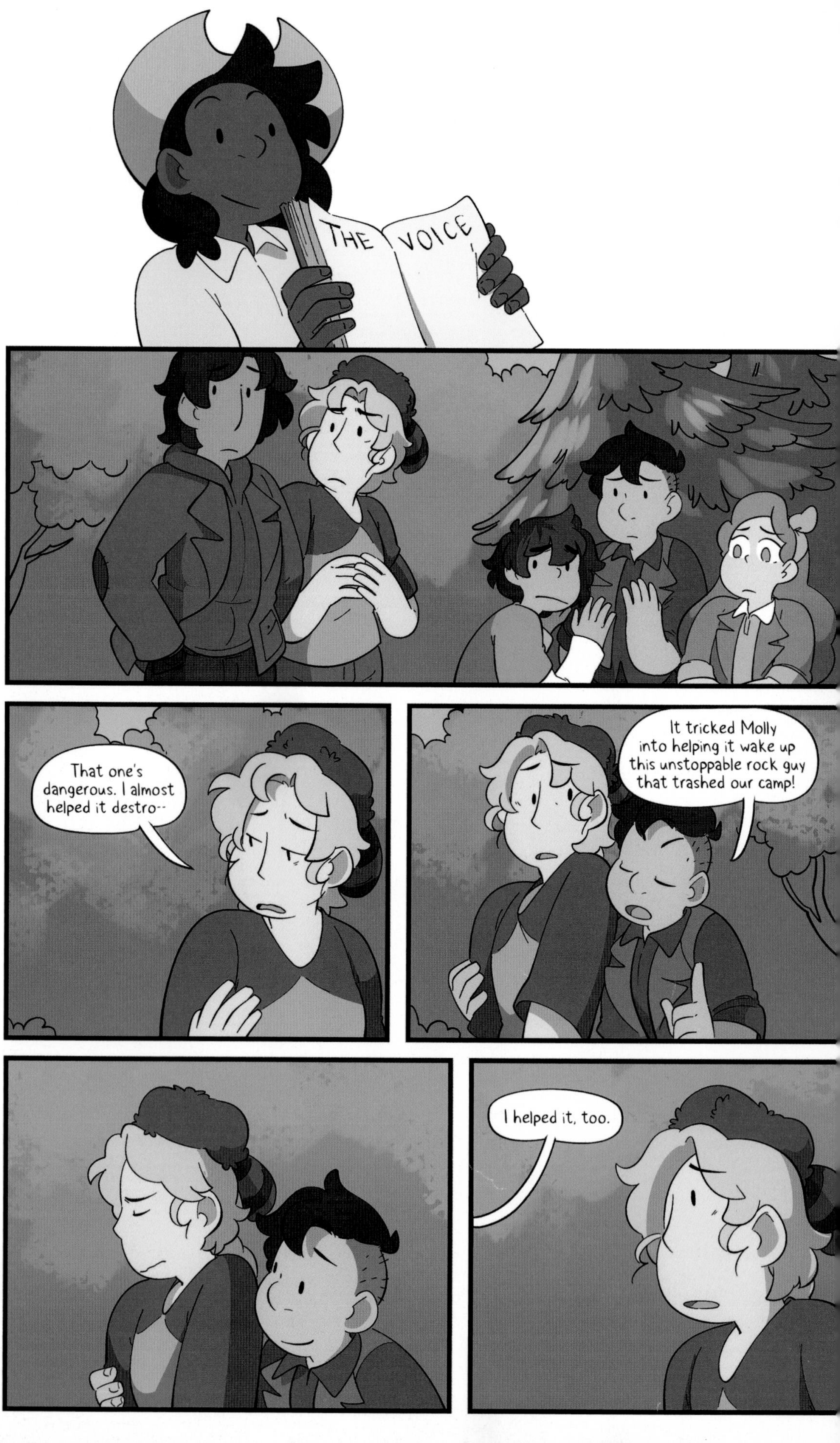
THE VOICE
That one's dangerous. I almost helped it destro--
It tricked Molly into helping it wake up this unstoppable rock guy that trashed our camp!
I helped it, too.

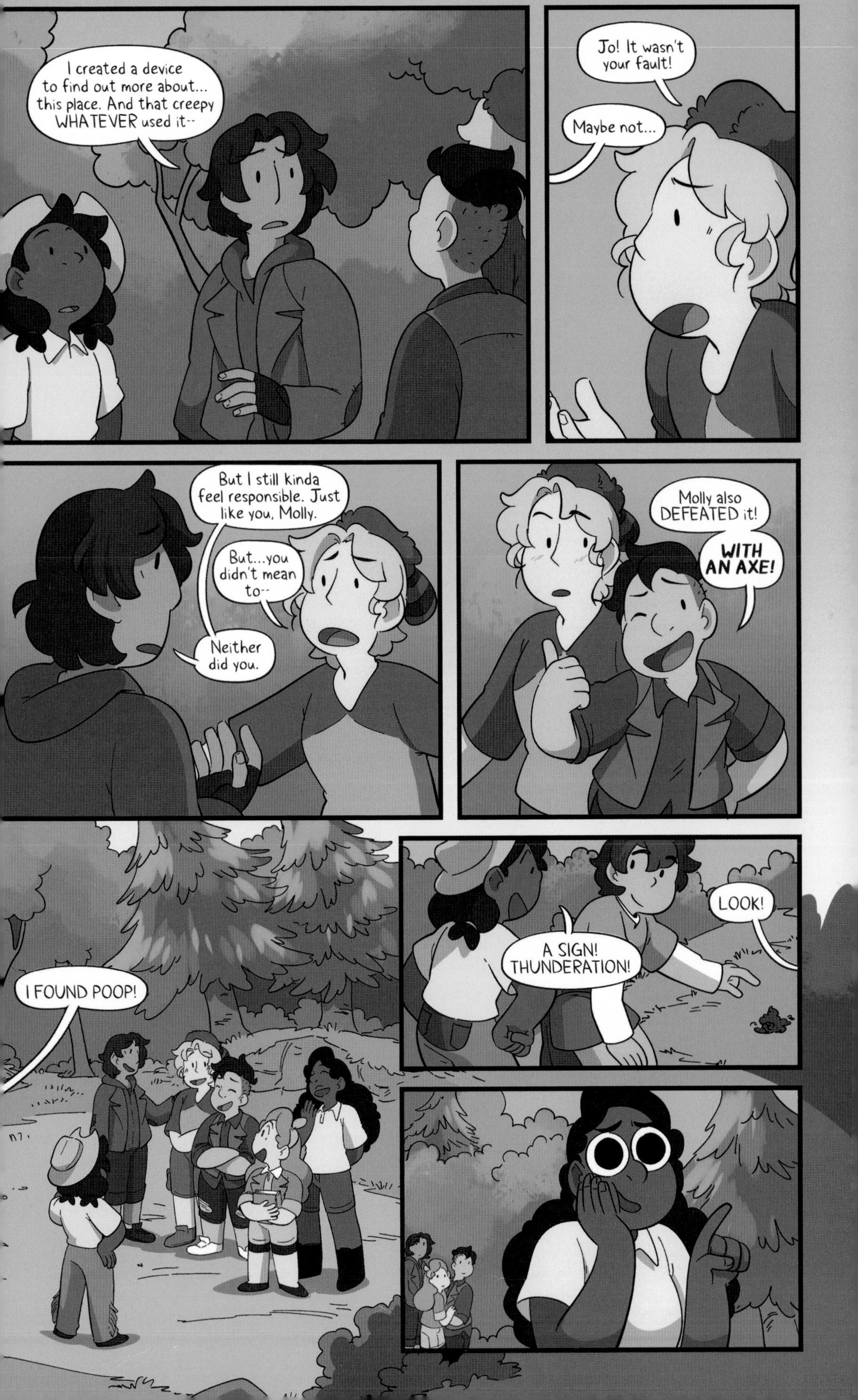
I created a device to find out more about... this place. And that creepy WHATEVER used it--
Jo! It wasn't your fault!
Maybe not...
But I still kinda feel responsible. Just like you, Molly.
But...you didn't mean to--
Neither did you.
Molly also DEFEATED it!
WITH AN AXE!
I FOUND POOP!
LOOK!
A SIGN! THUNDERATION!

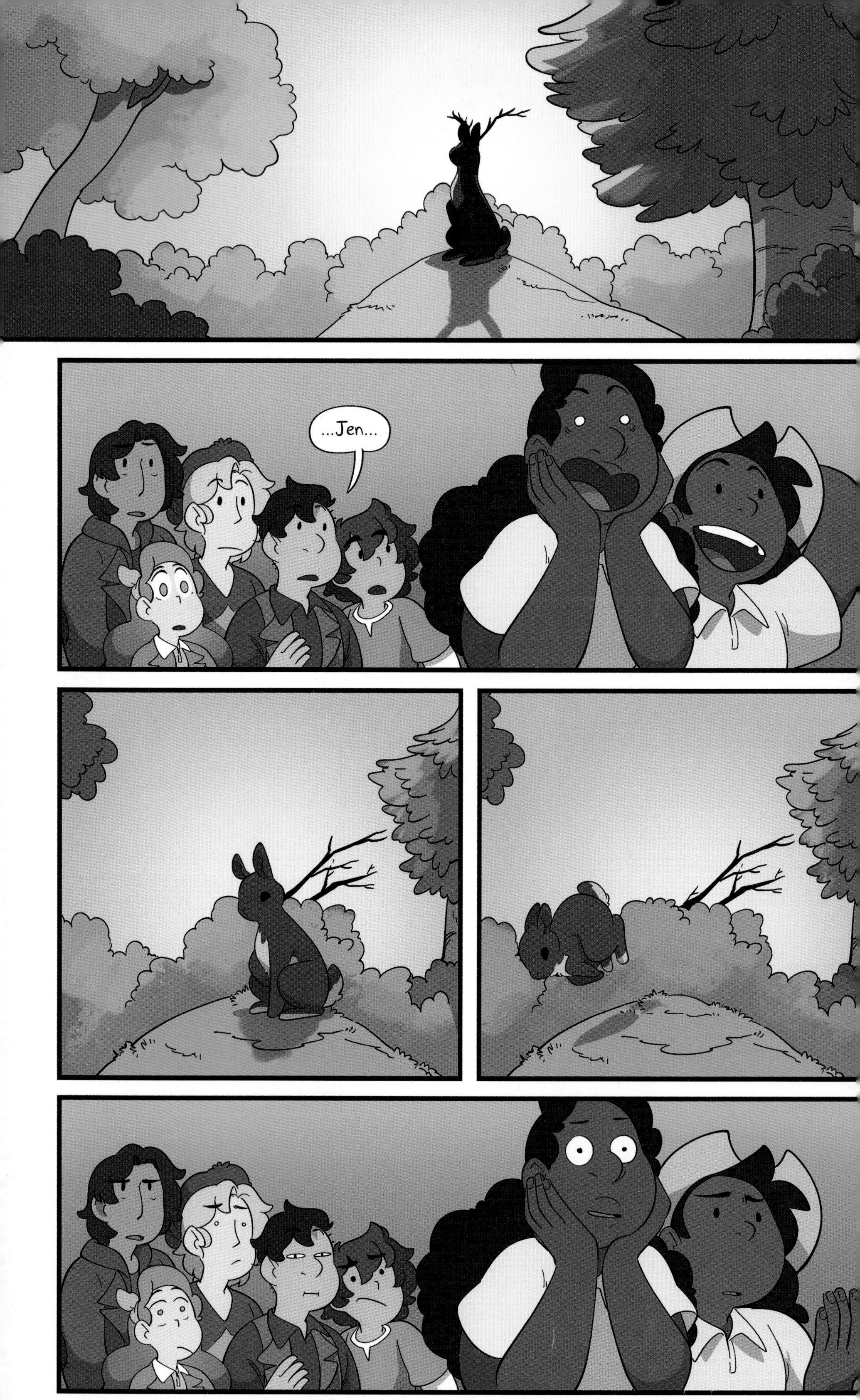
...Jen...

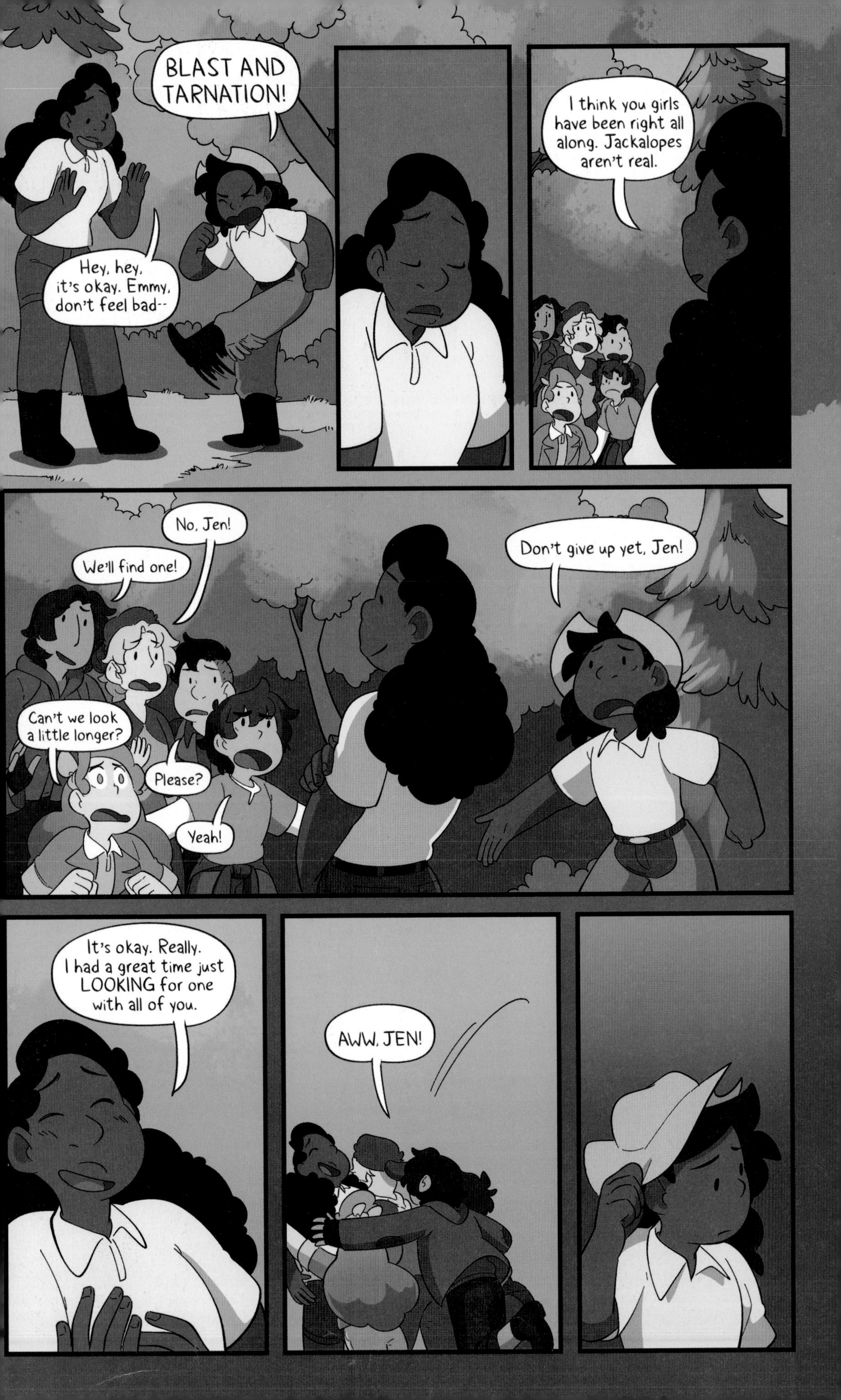
BLAST AND TARNATION!
Hey, hey, it's okay. Emmy, don't feel bad--
I think you girls have been right all along. Jackalopes aren't real.
No, Jen!
We'll find one!
Don't give up yet, Jen!
Can't we look a little longer?
Please?
Yeah!
It's okay. Really. I had a great time just LOOKING for one with all of you.
AWW, JEN!

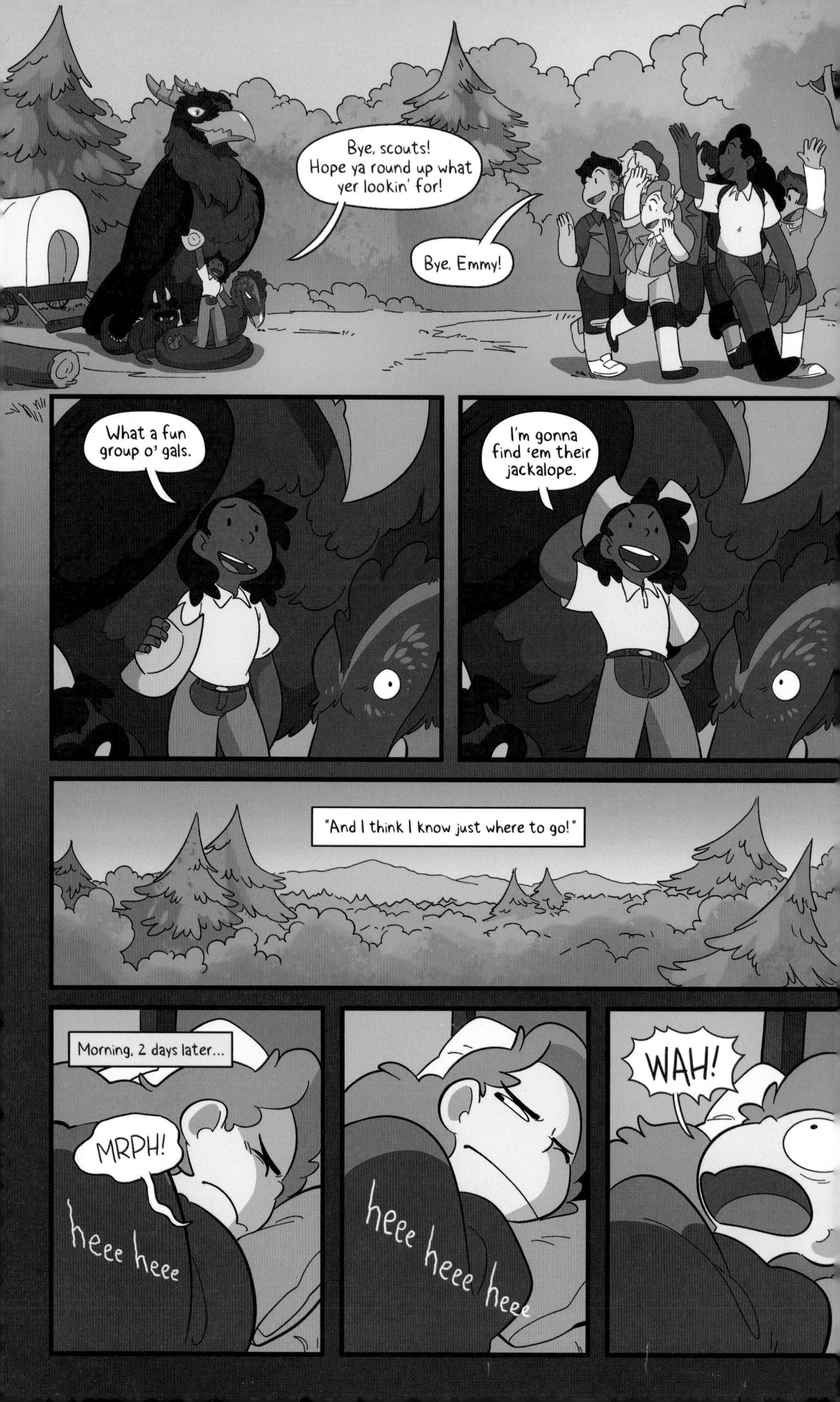

Bye, scouts! Hope ya round up what yer lookin' for!
Bye, Emmy!
What a fun group o' gals.
I'm gonna find 'em their jackalope.
"And I think I know just where to go!"
Morning, 2 days later...
MRPH!
heee heee
heee heee heee
WAH!

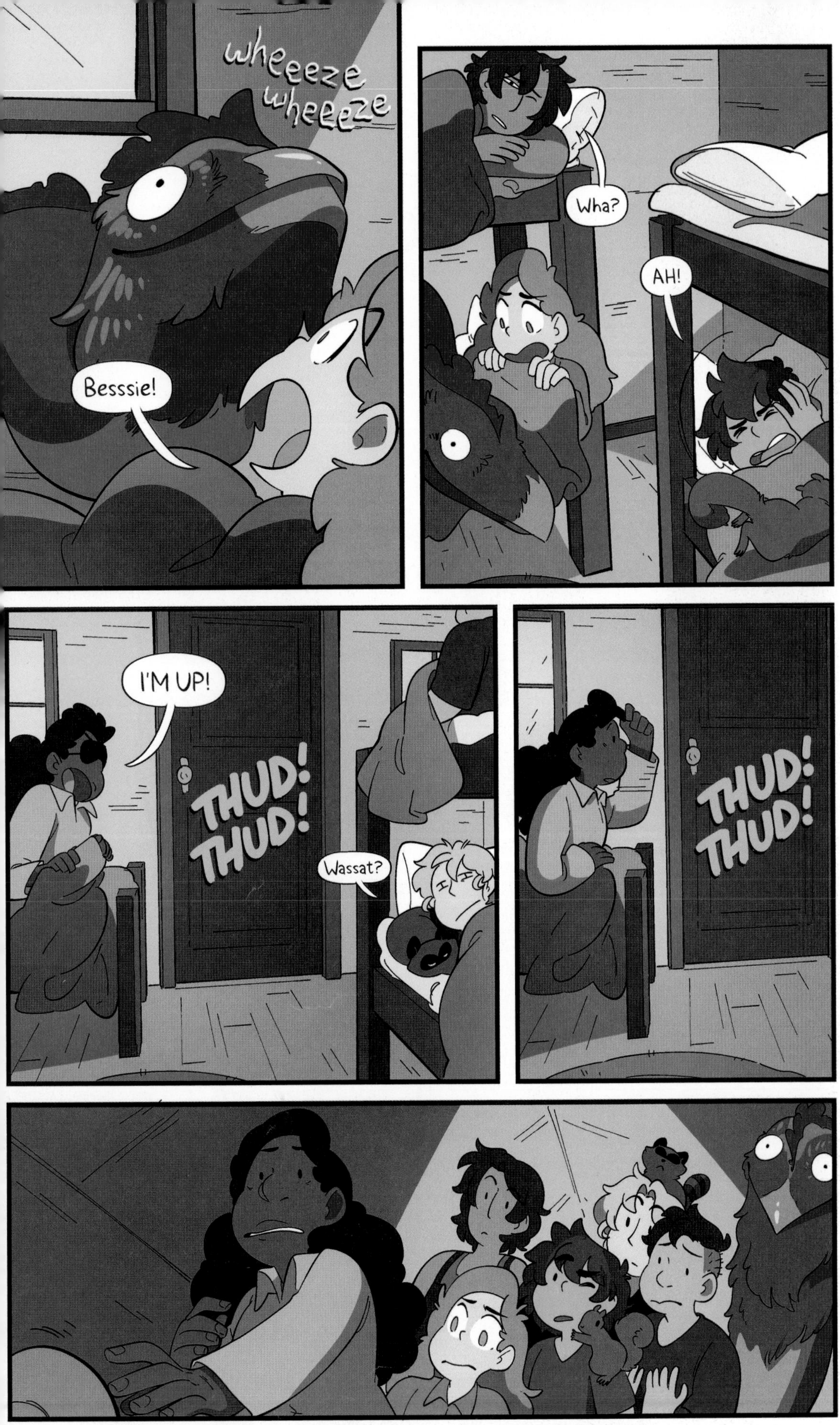
wheeeze
wheeeze
Besssie!
Wha?
AH!
I'M UP!
THUD!
THUD!
Wassat?
THUD!
THUD!

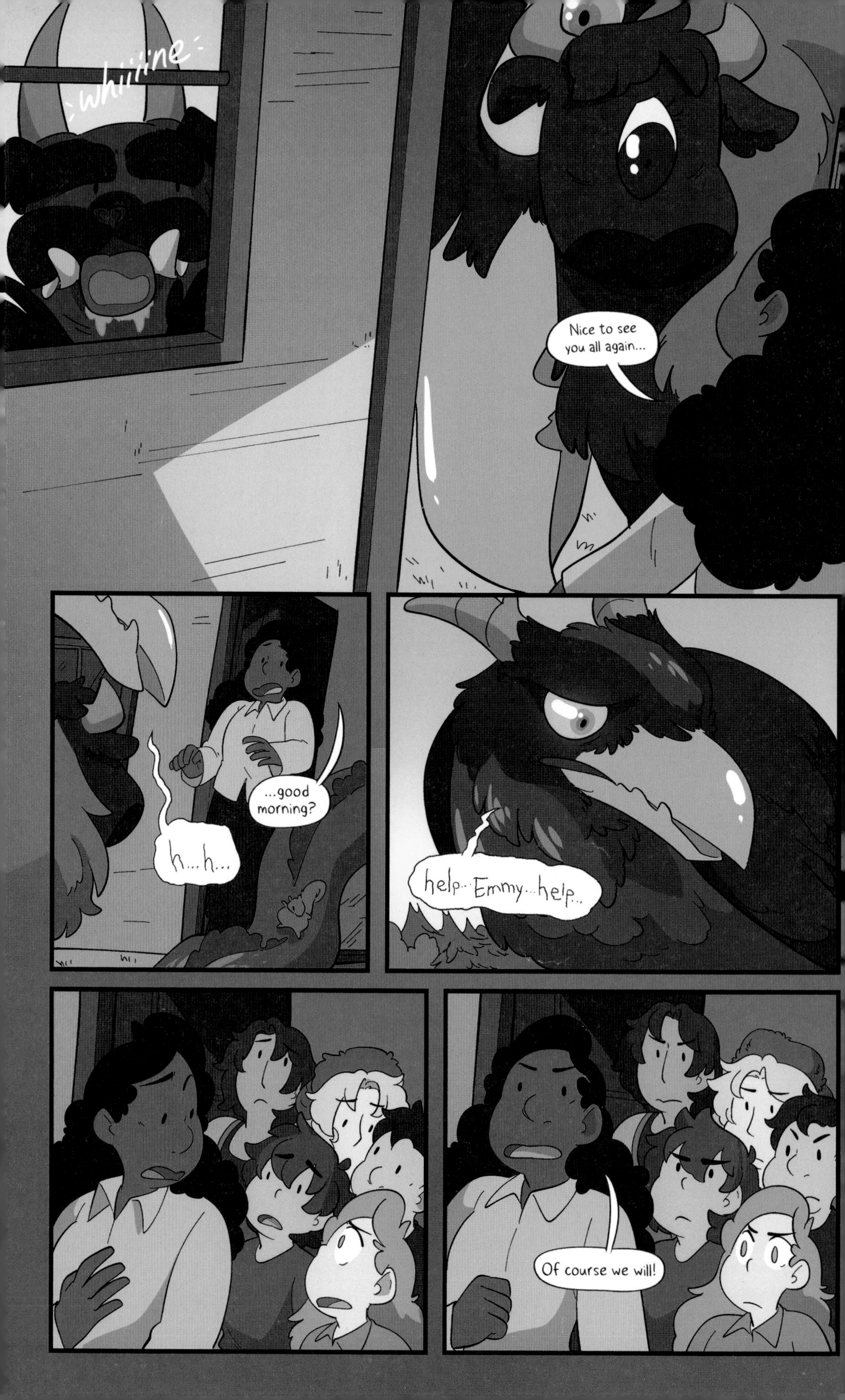
whiiiine
Nice to see you all again...
...good morning?
h...h...
help...Emmy...help...
Of course we will!

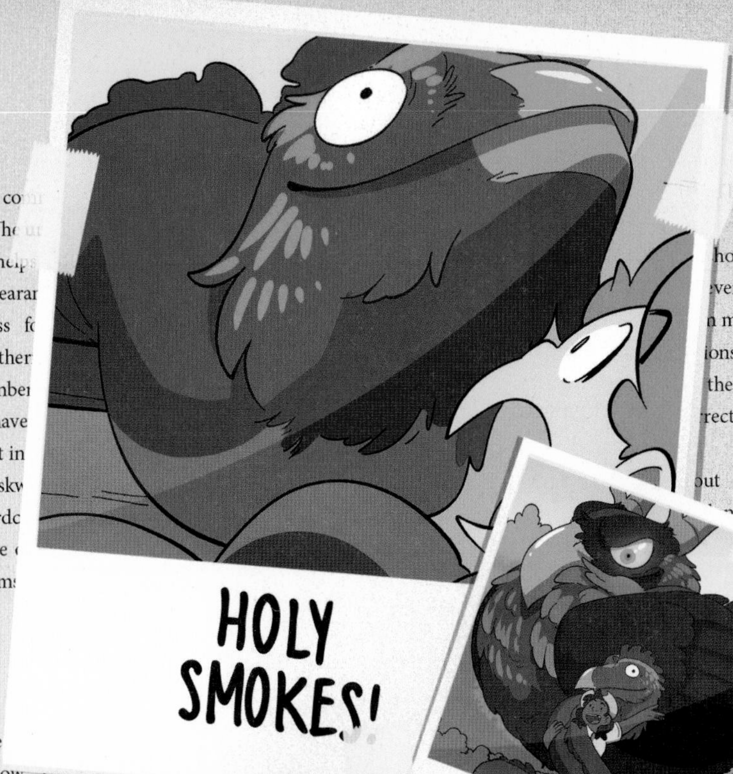
HOLY
SMOKES!

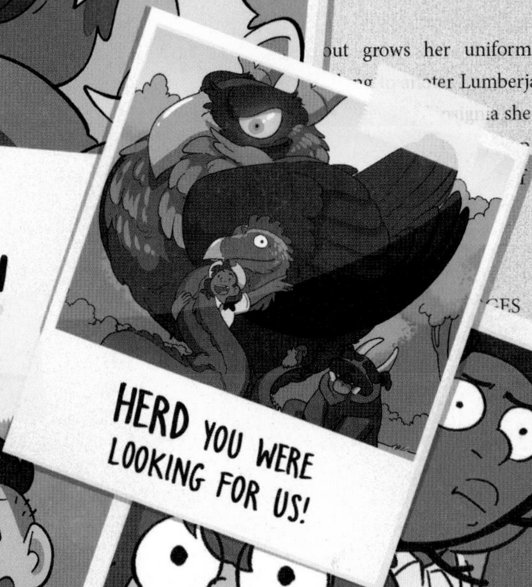
HERD YOU WERE
LOOKING FOR US!

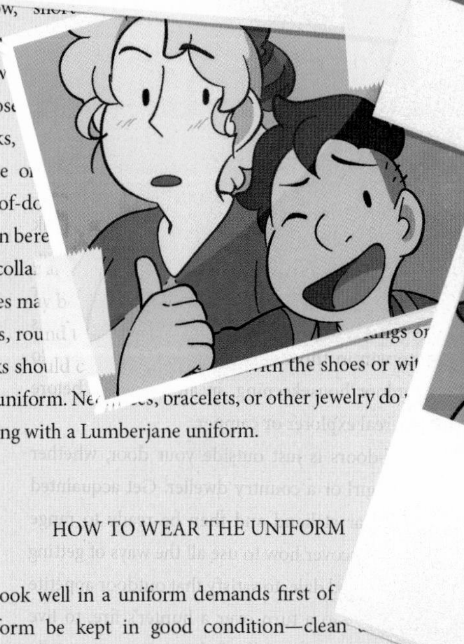

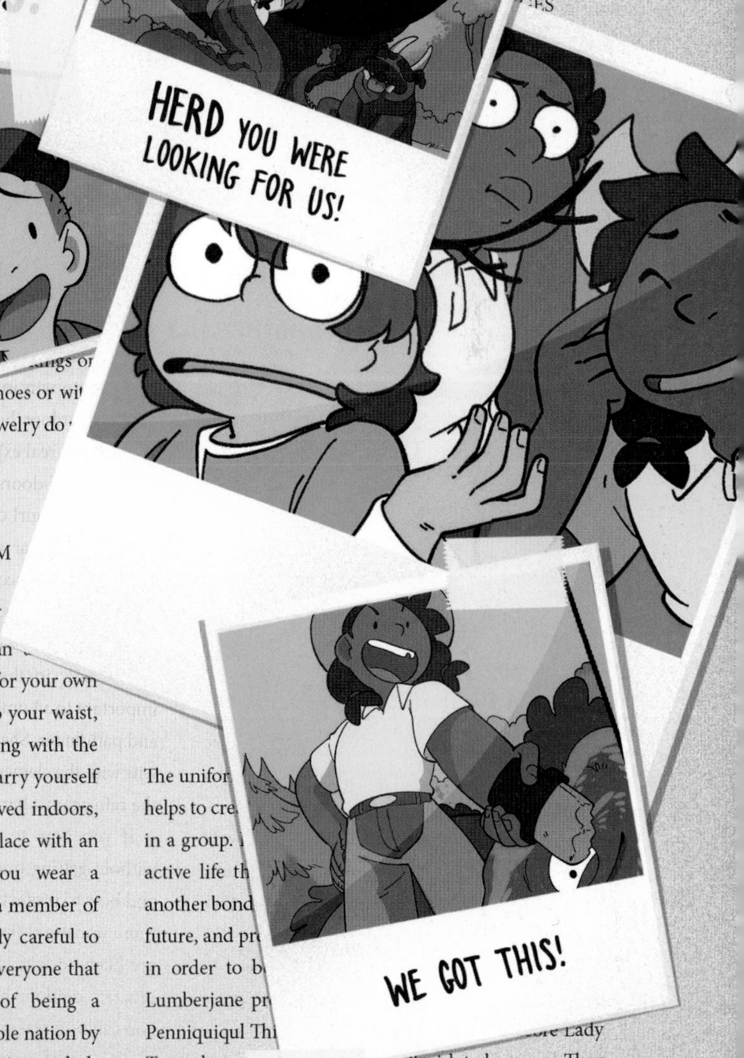
WE GOT THIS!

will co…
The u… It help… appearan… dress fo… Further… Lumber… to have… part in… Thiskw… Hardc… have … thems…

…HE UNIFORM

…hould be worn at camp …vents when Lumberjanes …n may also be worn at other …ions. It should be worn as a … the uniform dress with …rrect shoes, and stocking or

…out grows her uniform or …ng to another Lumberjane. …ia she has … her … her

…GES

The … yellow, … emb… the w… choos… slacks, … made o… out-of-do… green bere… the colla… Shoes ma… heels, rou… …kings or socks shou… …with the shoes or wit… the uniform. Ne… …es, bracelets, or other jewelry do… belong with a Lumberjane uniform.

HOW TO WEAR THE UNIFORM

To look well in a uniform demands first of … uniform be kept in good condition—clean … pressed. See that the skirt is the right length for your own height and build, that the belt is adjusted to your waist, that your shoes and stockings are in keeping with the uniform, that you watch your posture and carry yourself with dignity and grace. If the beret is removed indoors, be sure that your hair is neat and kept in place with an insonspicuous clip or ribbon. When you wear a Lumberjane uniform you are identified as a member of this organization and you should be doubly careful to conduct yourself in a way that will show everyone that courtesy and thoughtfullness are part of being a Lumberjane. People are likely to judge a whole nation by the selfishness of a few individuals, to criticize a whole family because of the misconduct of one member, and to feel unkindly toward and organization because of the

The unifor… helps to cre… in a group. … active life th… another bond… future, and pr… in order to b… Lumberjane pr… Penniquiqul Thi… …ore Lady Types, but m… …will wish to have one. They can either bu… …, or make it themselves from materials available at the trading post.

LUMBERJANES FIELD MANUAL

CHAPTER FORTY-SEVEN

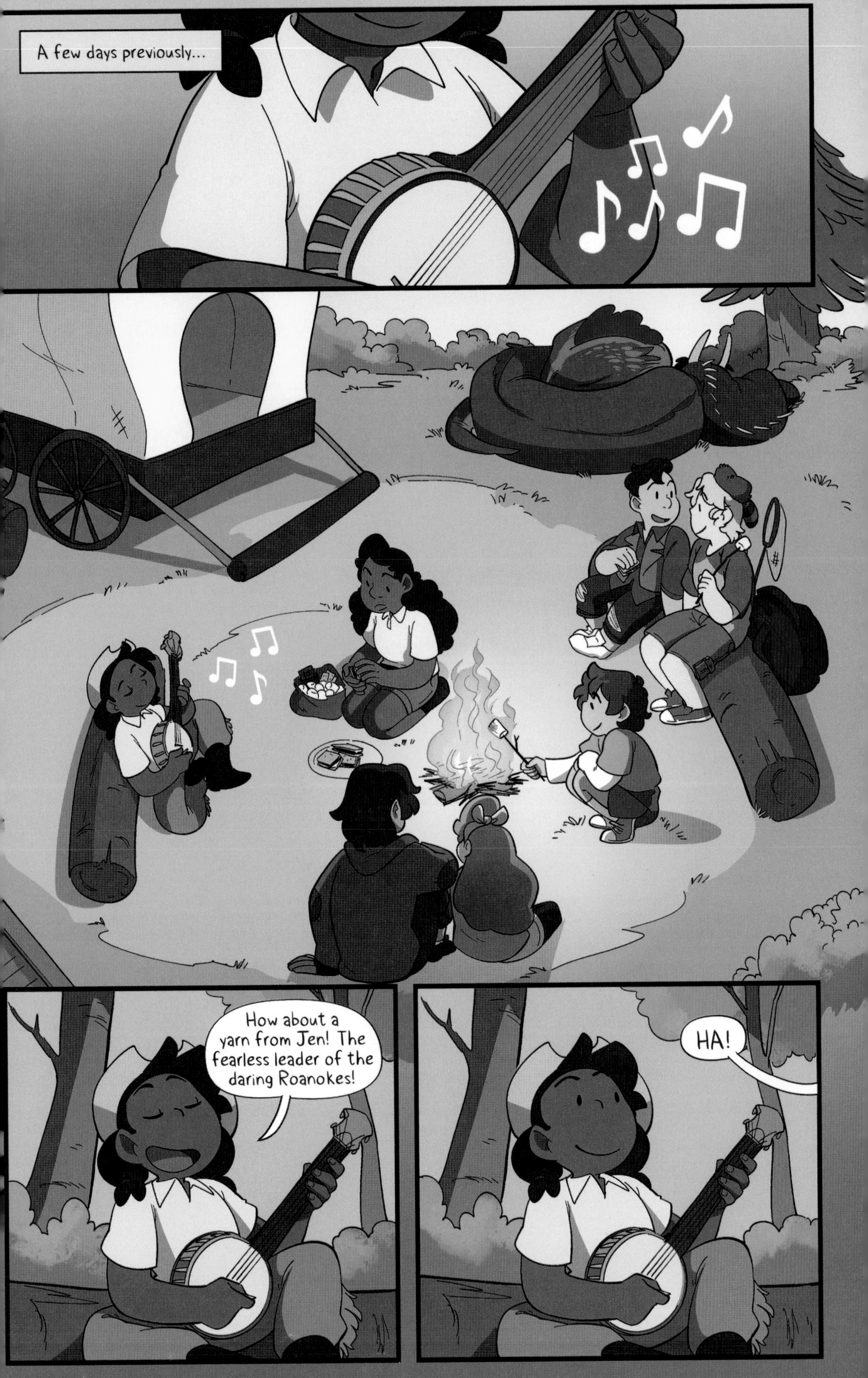
A few days previously...
How about a yarn from Jen! The fearless leader of the daring Roanokes!
HA!

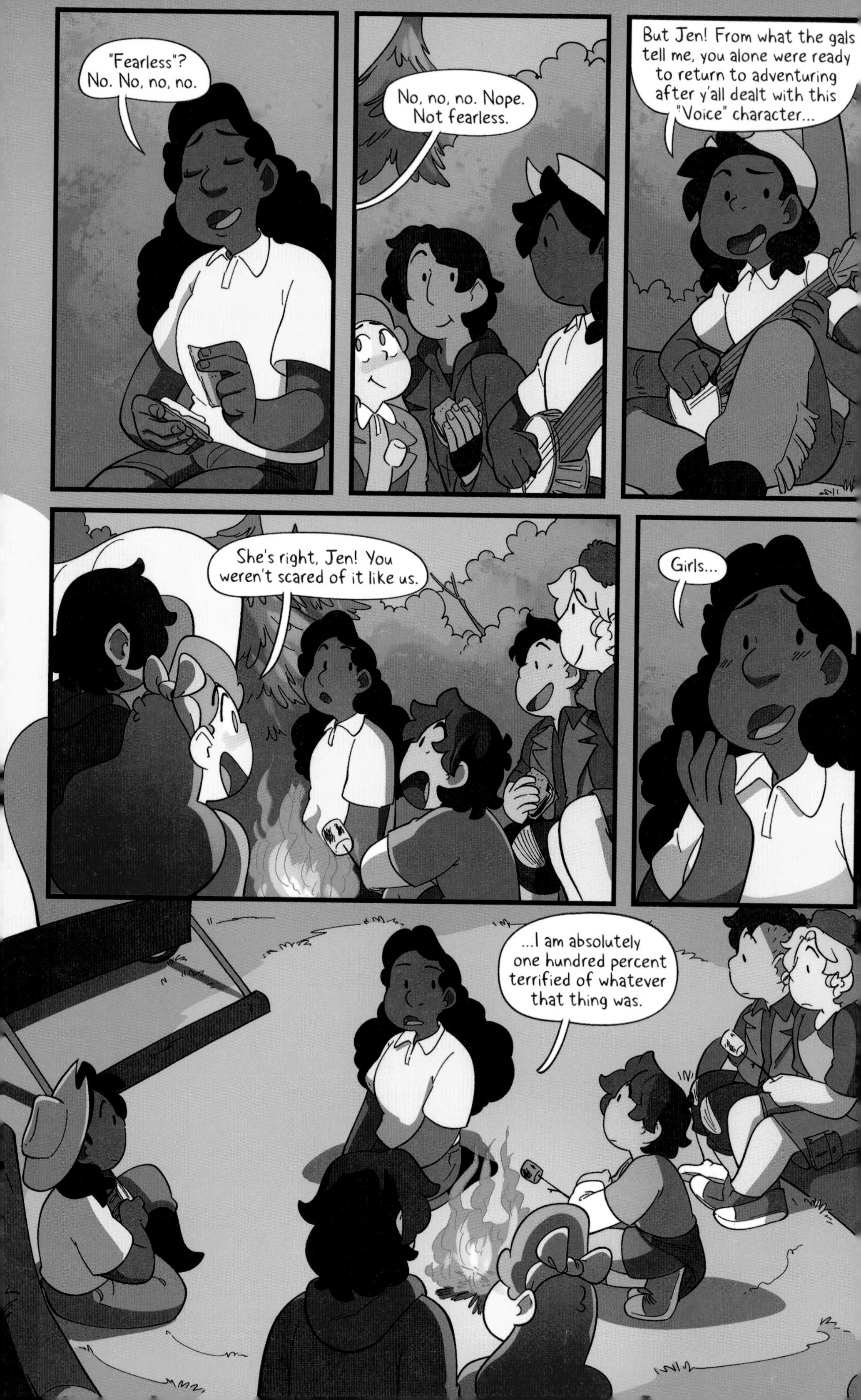

"Fearless"? No. No, no, no.
No, no, no. Nope. Not fearless.
But Jen! From what the gals tell me, you alone were ready to return to adventuring after y'all dealt with this "Voice" character...
She's right, Jen! You weren't scared of it like us.
Girls...
...I am absolutely one hundred percent terrified of whatever that thing was.

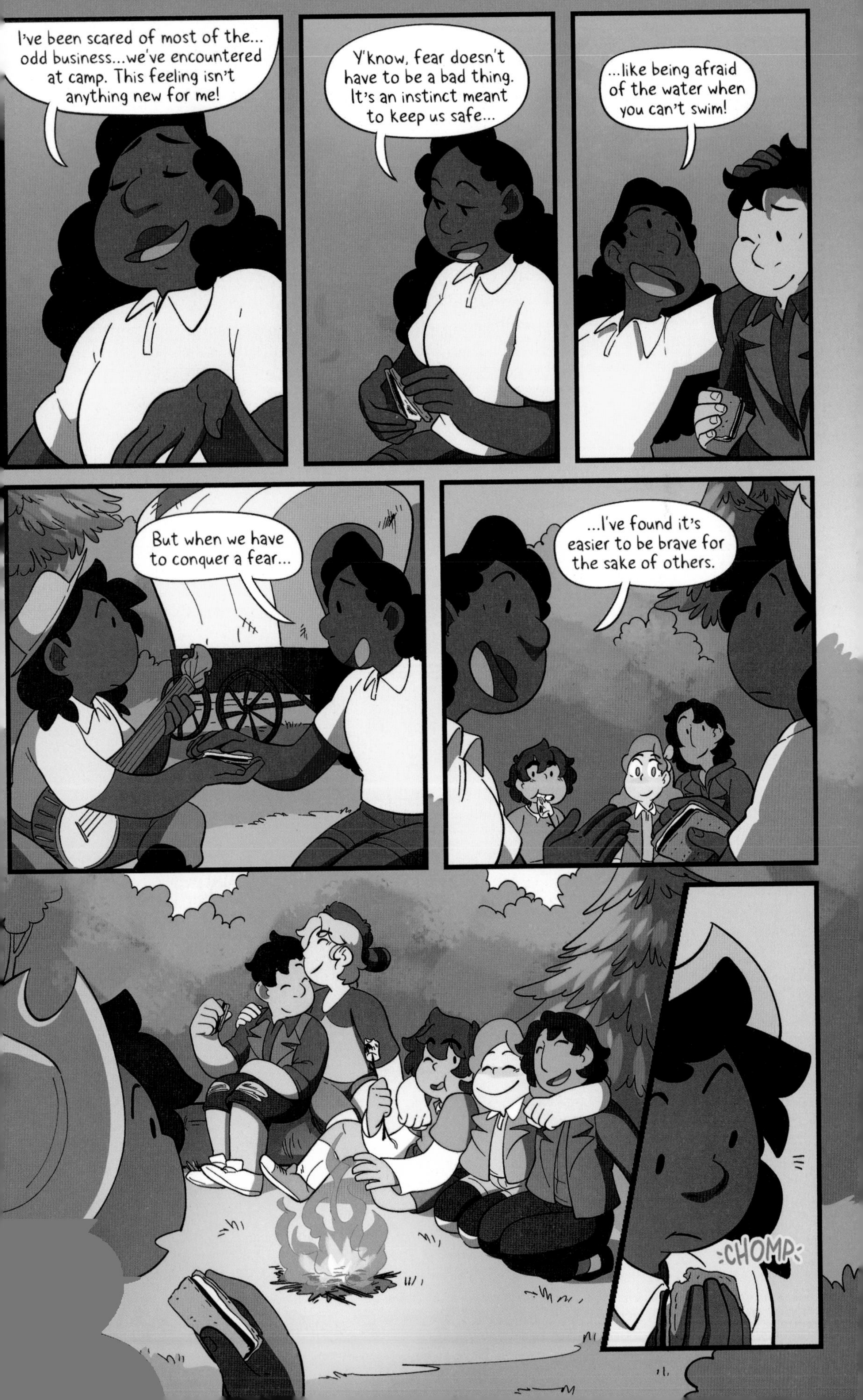
I've been scared of most of the... odd business...we've encountered at camp. This feeling isn't anything new for me!
Y'know, fear doesn't have to be a bad thing. It's an instinct meant to keep us safe...
...like being afraid of the water when you can't swim!
But when we have to conquer a fear...
...I've found it's easier to be brave for the sake of others.
CHOMP

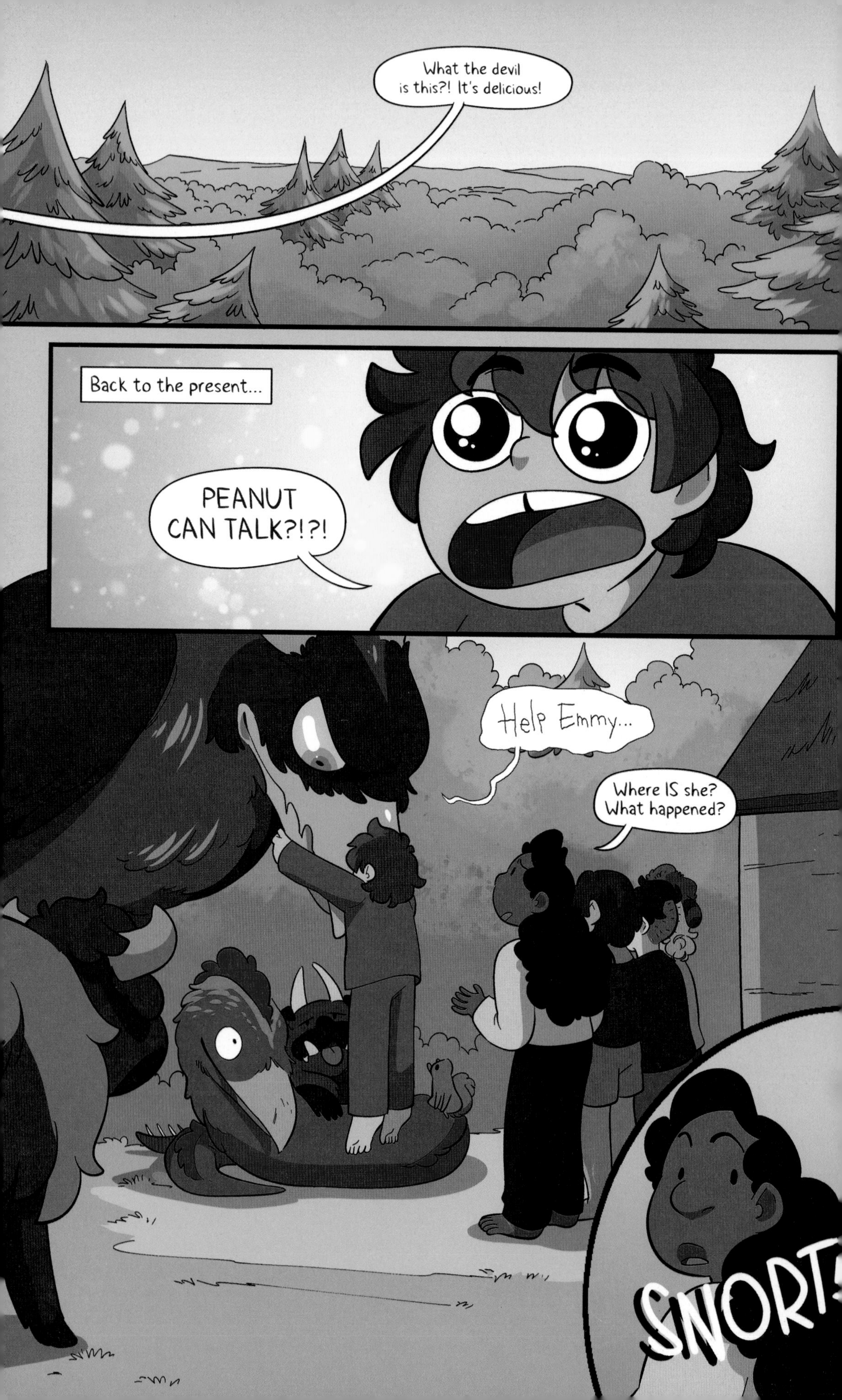
What the devil is this?! It's delicious!
Back to the present...
PEANUT CAN TALK?!?!
Help Emmy...
Where IS she? What happened?
SNORT!

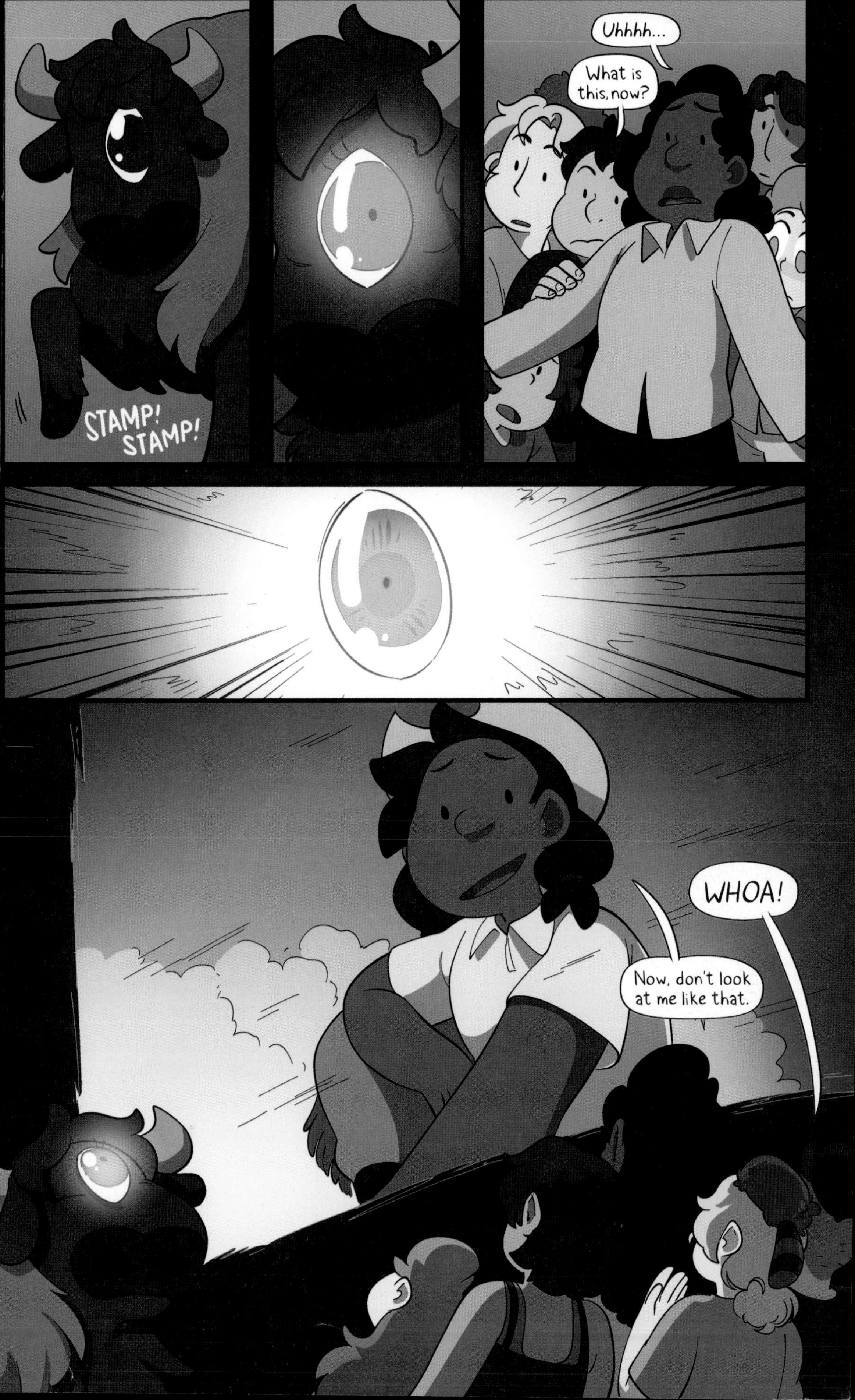
STAMP!
STAMP!
Uhhhh...
What is this, now?
WHOA!
Now, don't look at me like that.

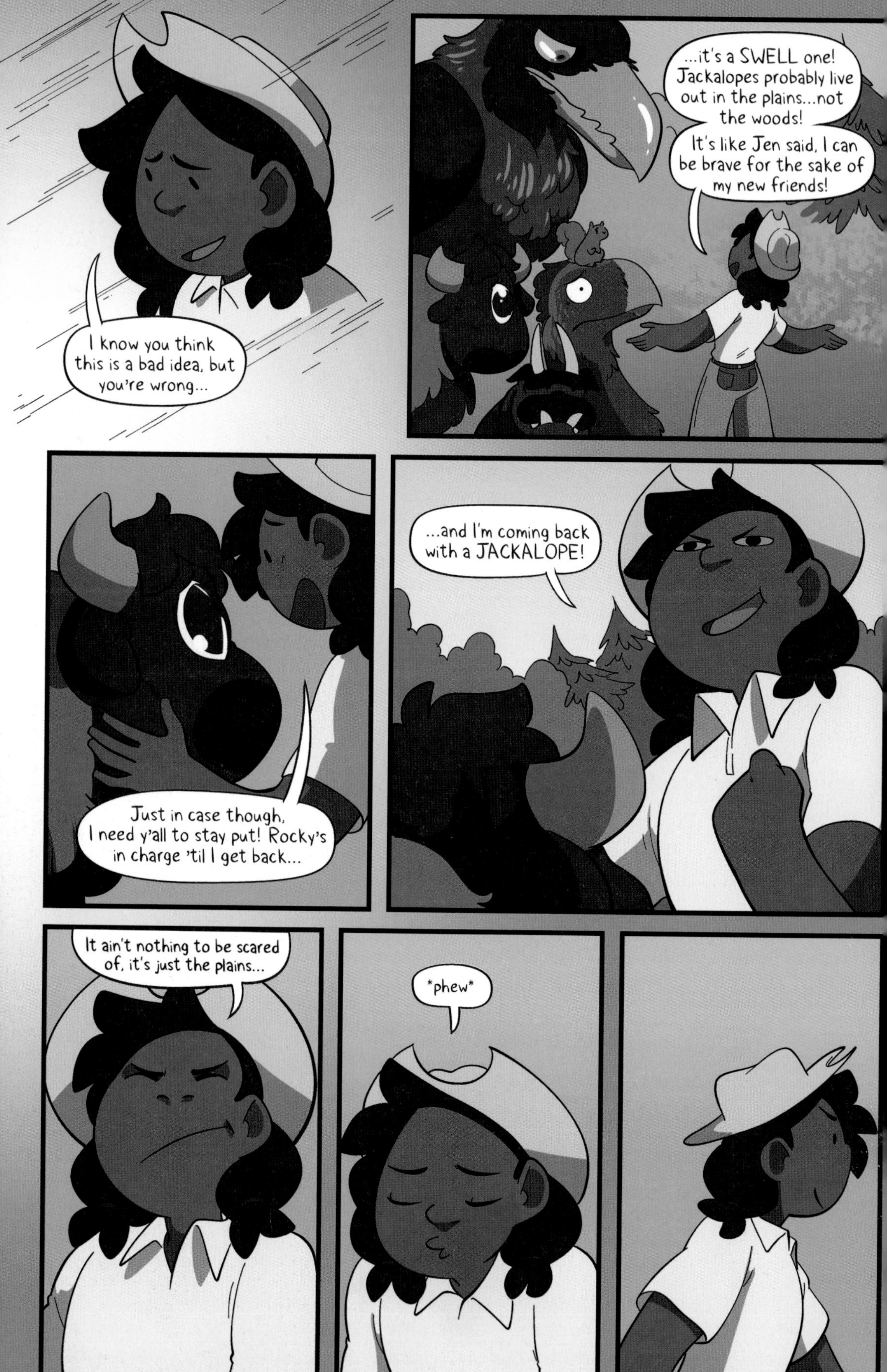
I know you think this is a bad idea, but you're wrong...
...it's a SWELL one! Jackalopes probably live out in the plains...not the woods!
It's like Jen said, I can be brave for the sake of my new friends!
Just in case though, I need y'all to stay put! Rocky's in charge 'til I get back...
...and I'm coming back with a JACKALOPE!
It ain't nothing to be scared of, it's just the plains...
phew

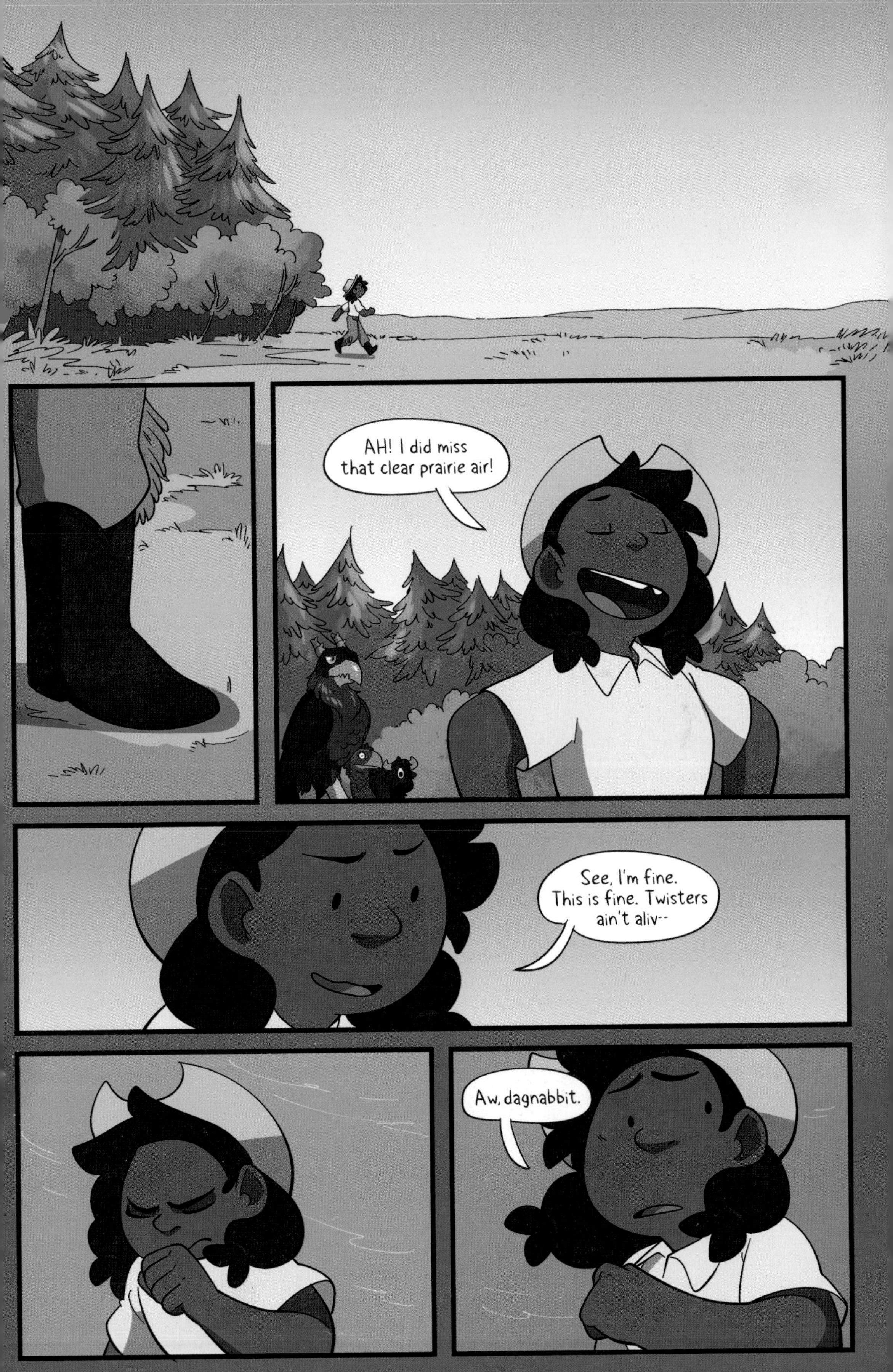
AH! I did miss that clear prairie air!
See, I'm fine. This is fine. Twisters ain't aliv--
Aw, dagnabbit.

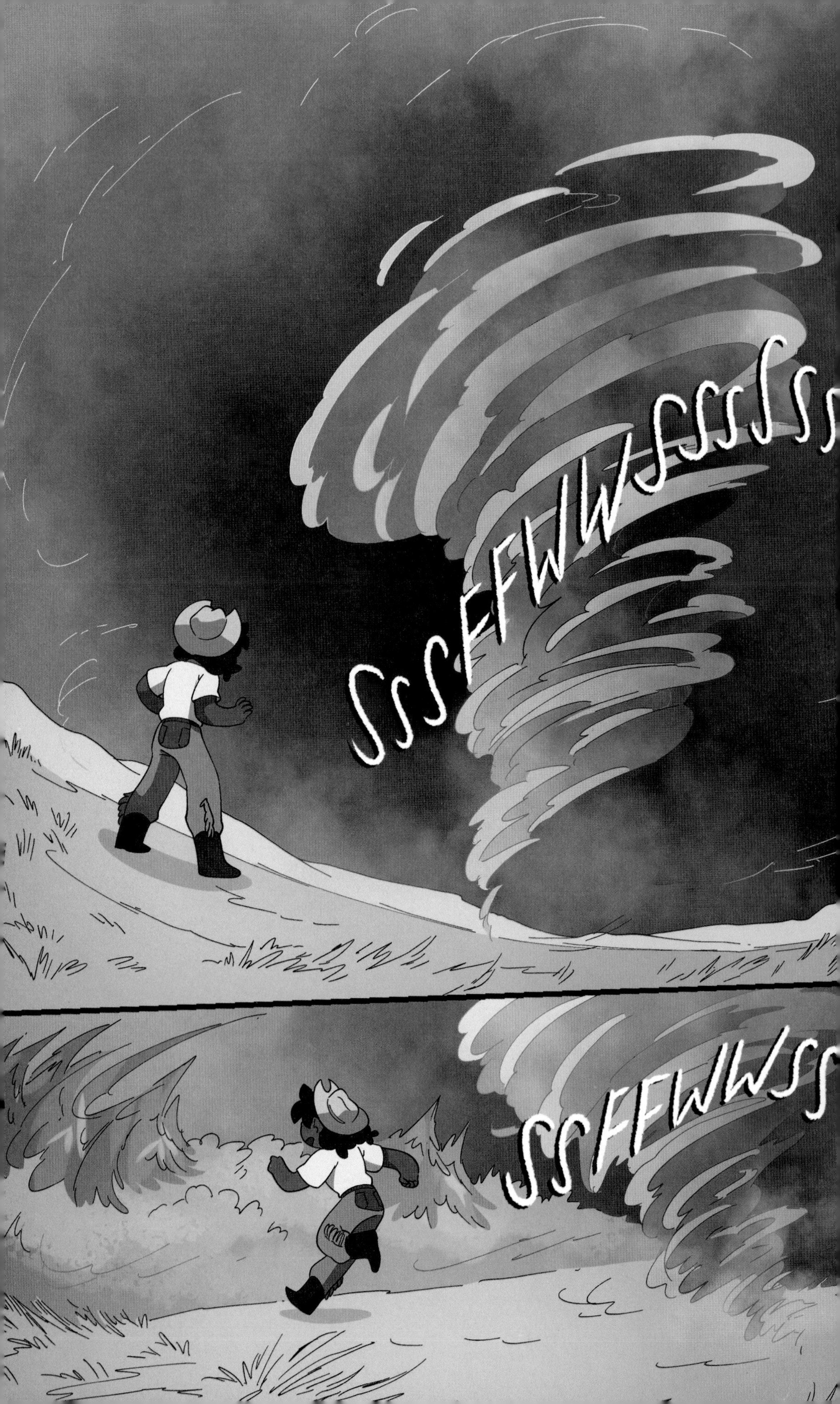
SSSFFWWSSSSSS
SSFFWWSS

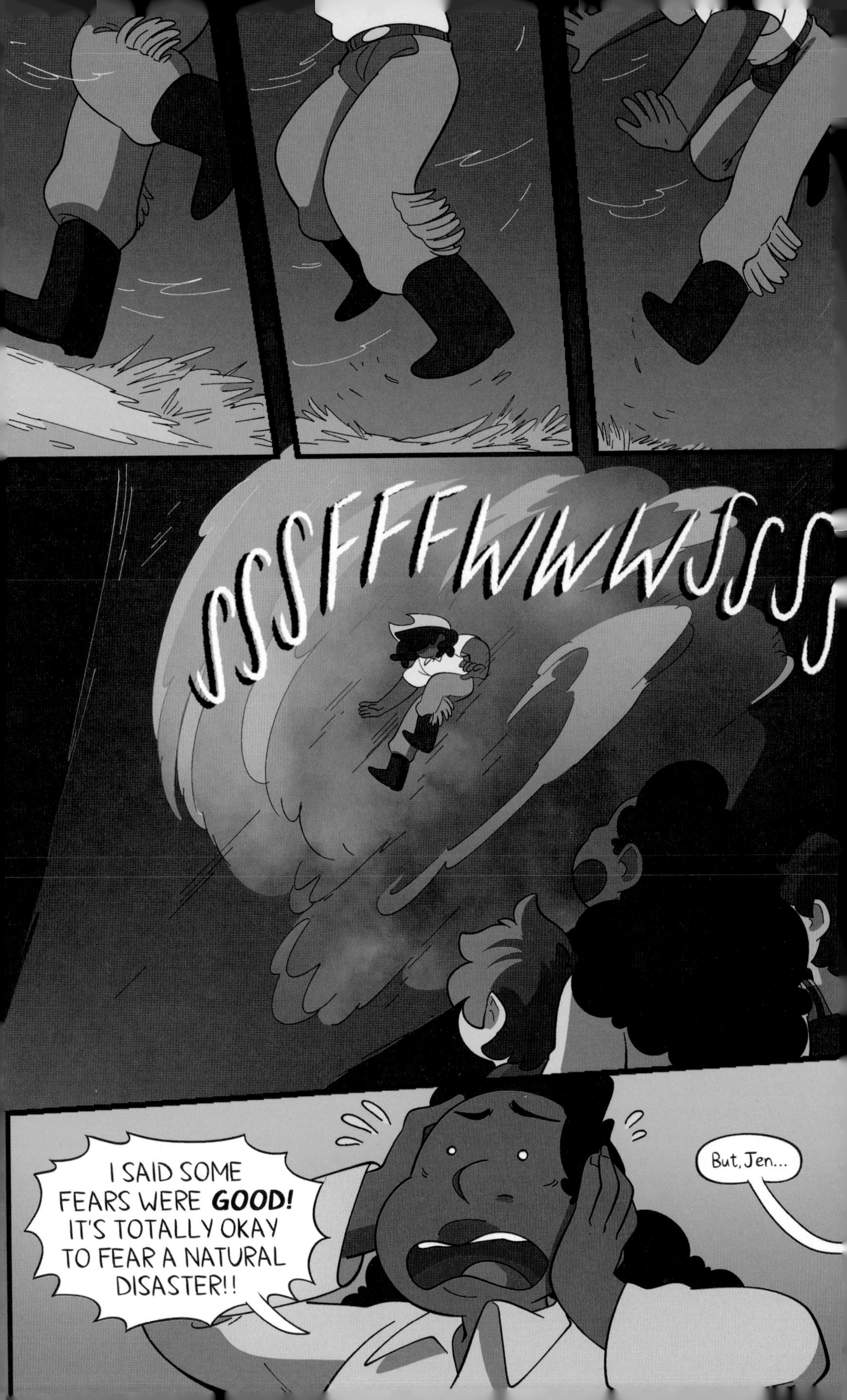
SSSFFFWWWSSS
I SAID SOME FEARS WERE **GOOD!** IT'S TOTALLY OKAY TO FEAR A NATURAL DISASTER!!
But, Jen...

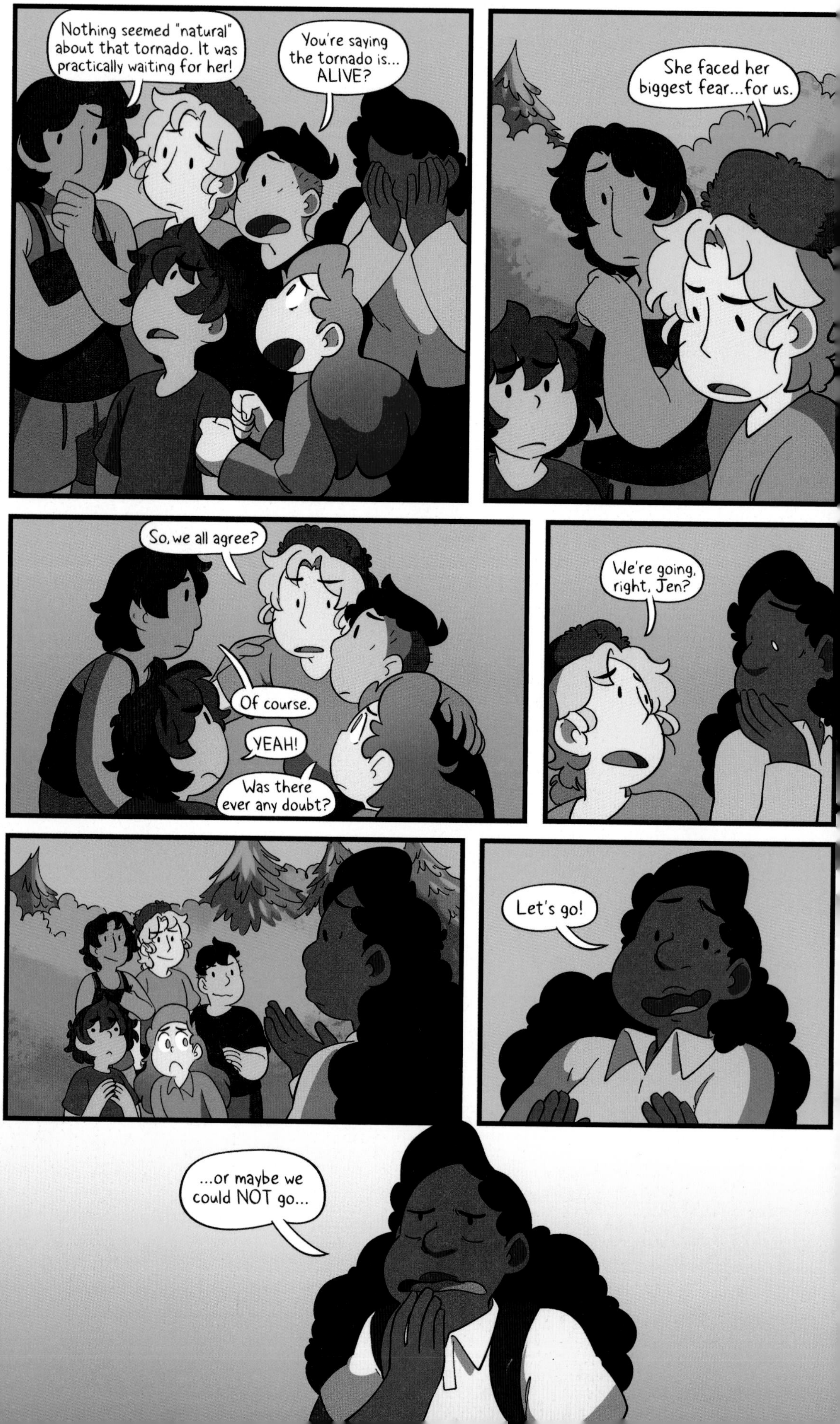

Nothing seemed "natural" about that tornado. It was practically waiting for her!
You're saying the tornado is... ALIVE?
She faced her biggest fear...for us.
So, we all agree?
Of course.
YEAH!
Was there ever any doubt?
We're going, right, Jen?
Let's go!
...or maybe we could NOT go...

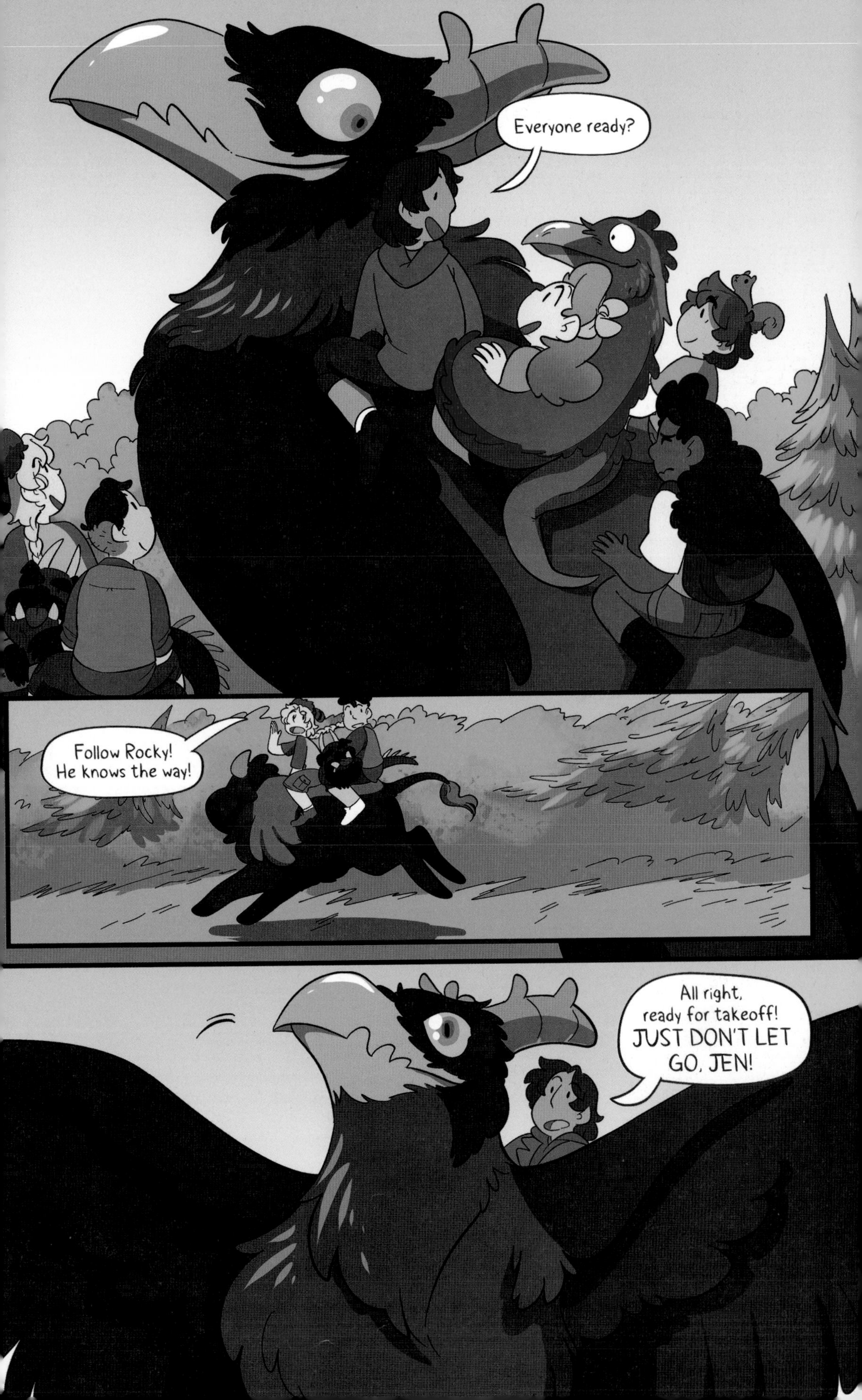
Everyone ready?
Follow Rocky! He knows the way!
All right, ready for takeoff! JUST DON'T LET GO, JEN!

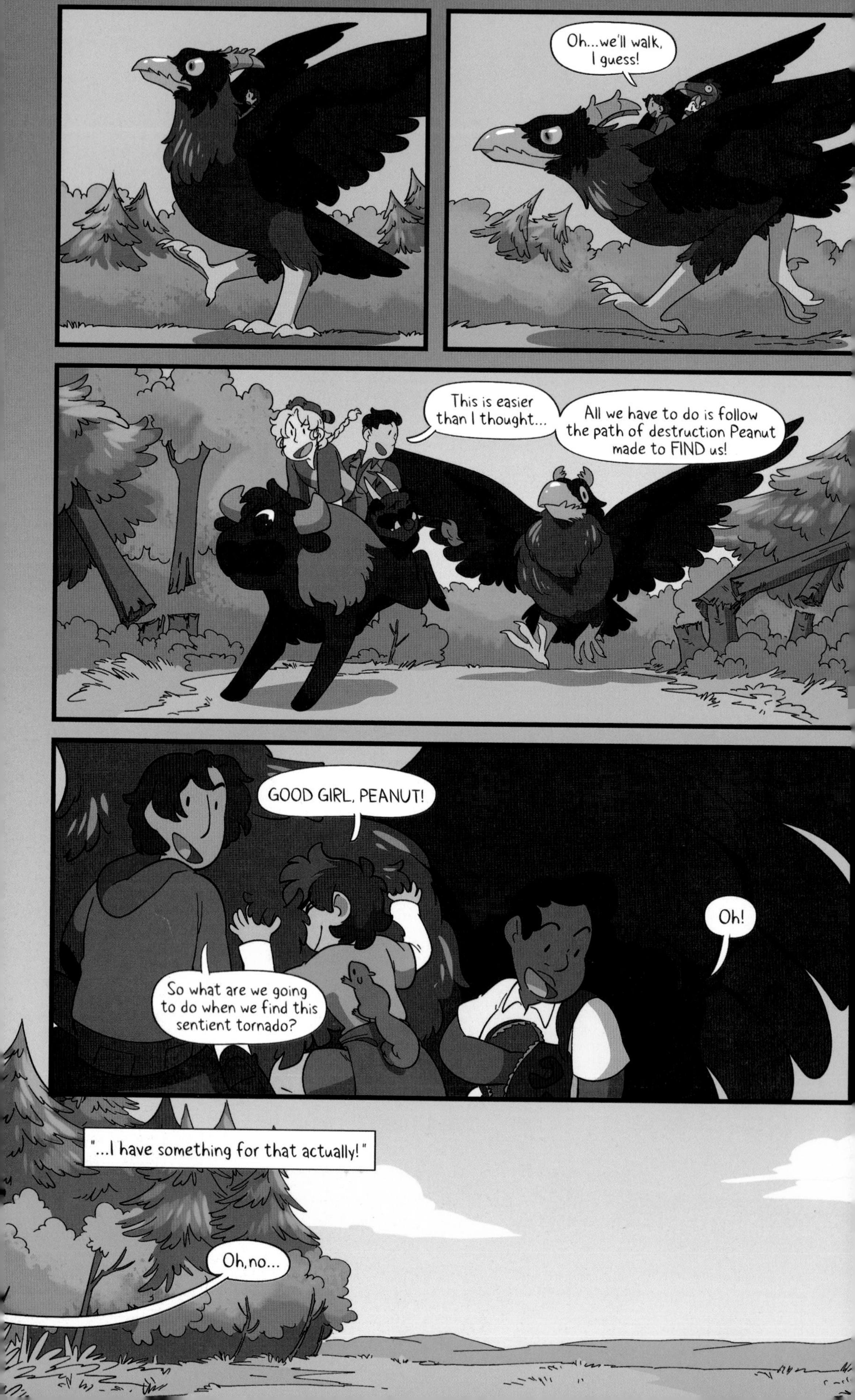
Oh...we'll walk, I guess!
This is easier than I thought...
All we have to do is follow the path of destruction Peanut made to FIND us!
GOOD GIRL, PEANUT!
So what are we going to do when we find this sentient tornado?
Oh!
"...I have something for that actually!"
Oh, no...

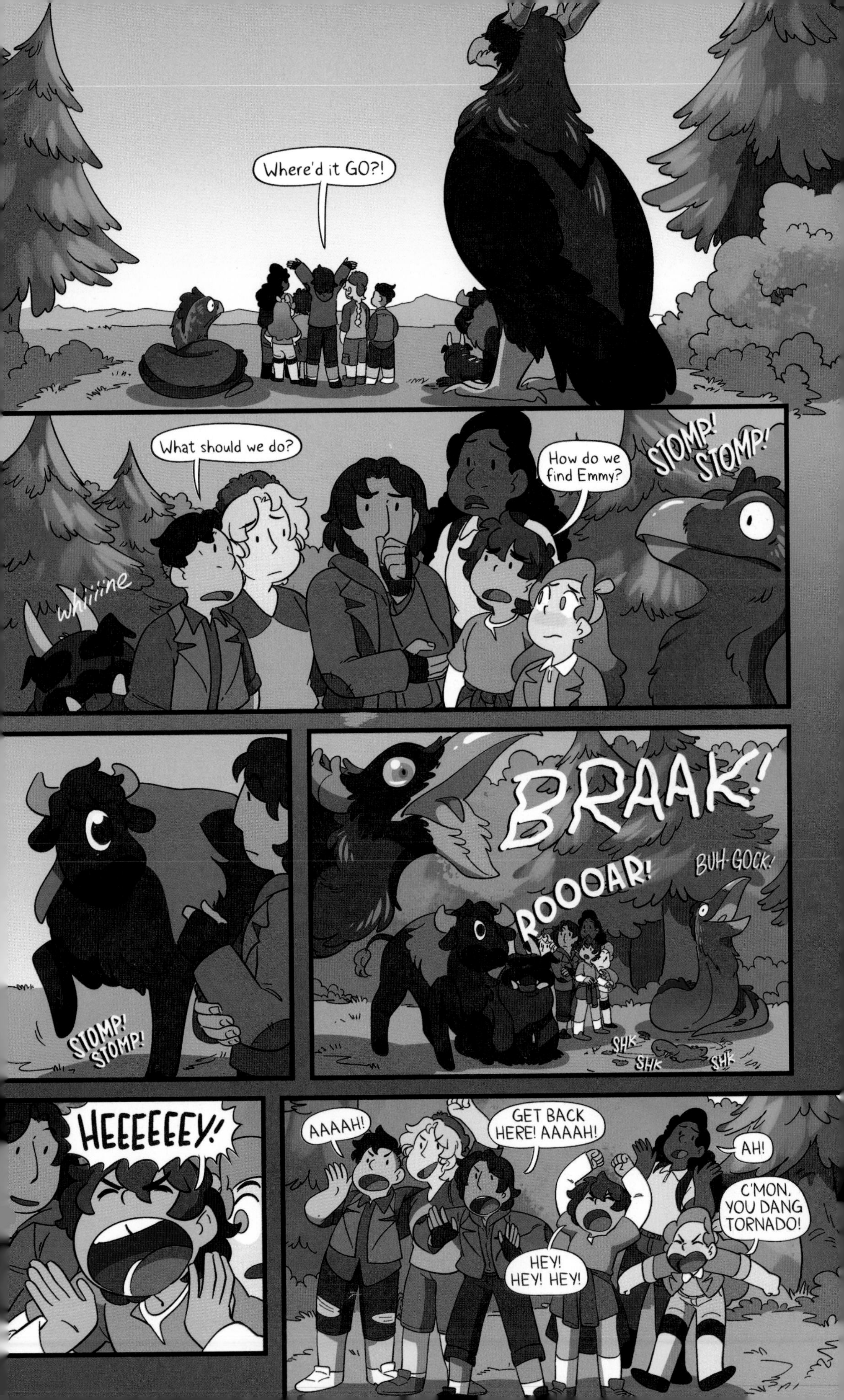
Where'd it GO?!
What should we do?
How do we find Emmy?
STOMP! STOMP!
whiiiine
STOMP! STOMP!
BRAAK!
ROOOAR!
BUH-GOCK!
SHK SHK SHK
HEEEEEEY!
AAAAH!
GET BACK HERE! AAAAH!
AH!
C'MON, YOU DANG TORNADO!
HEY! HEY! HEY!

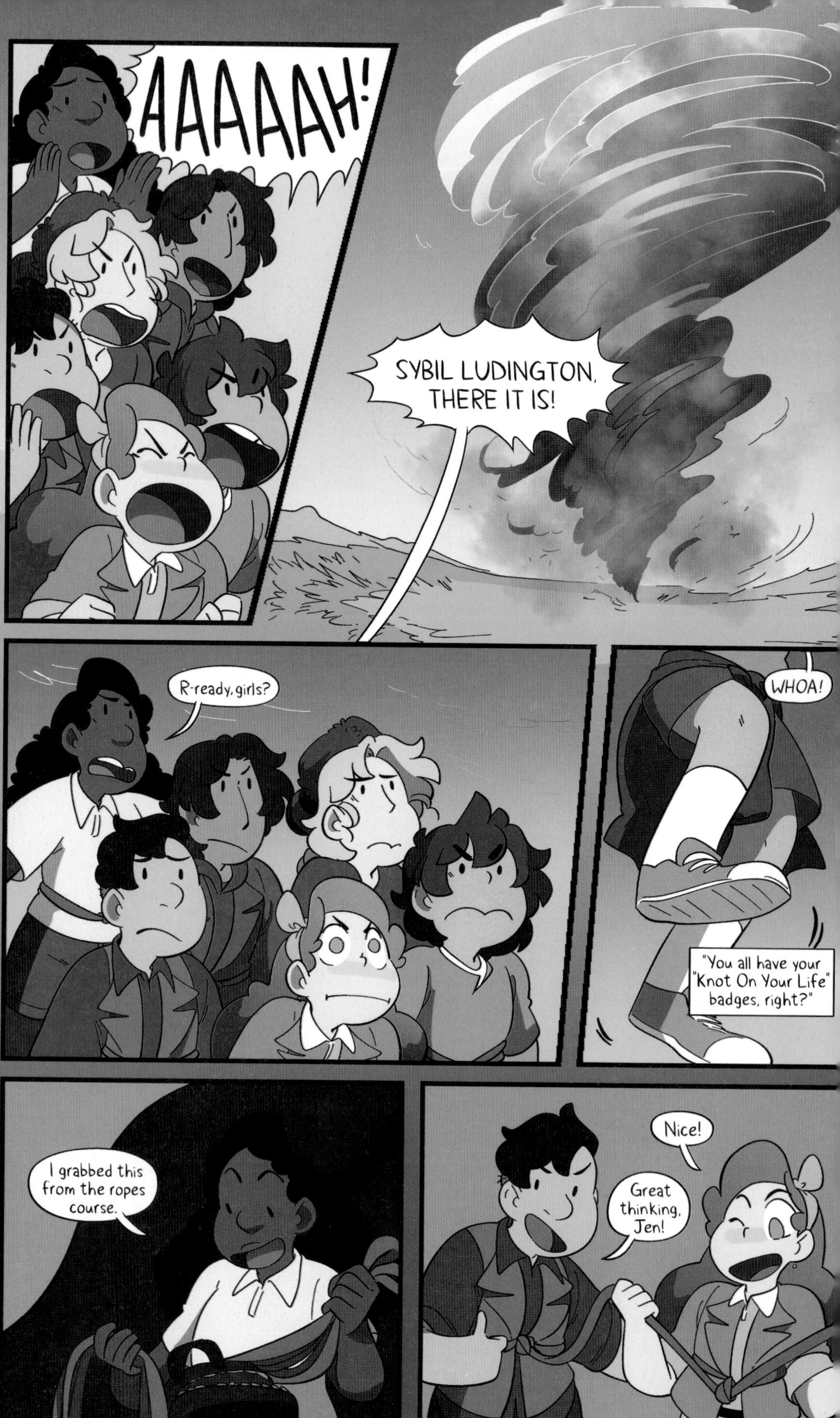
AAAAAH!
SYBIL LUDINGTON, THERE IT IS!
R-ready, girls?
WHOA!
"You all have your "Knot On Your Life" badges, right?"
I grabbed this from the ropes course.
Nice!
Great thinking, Jen!

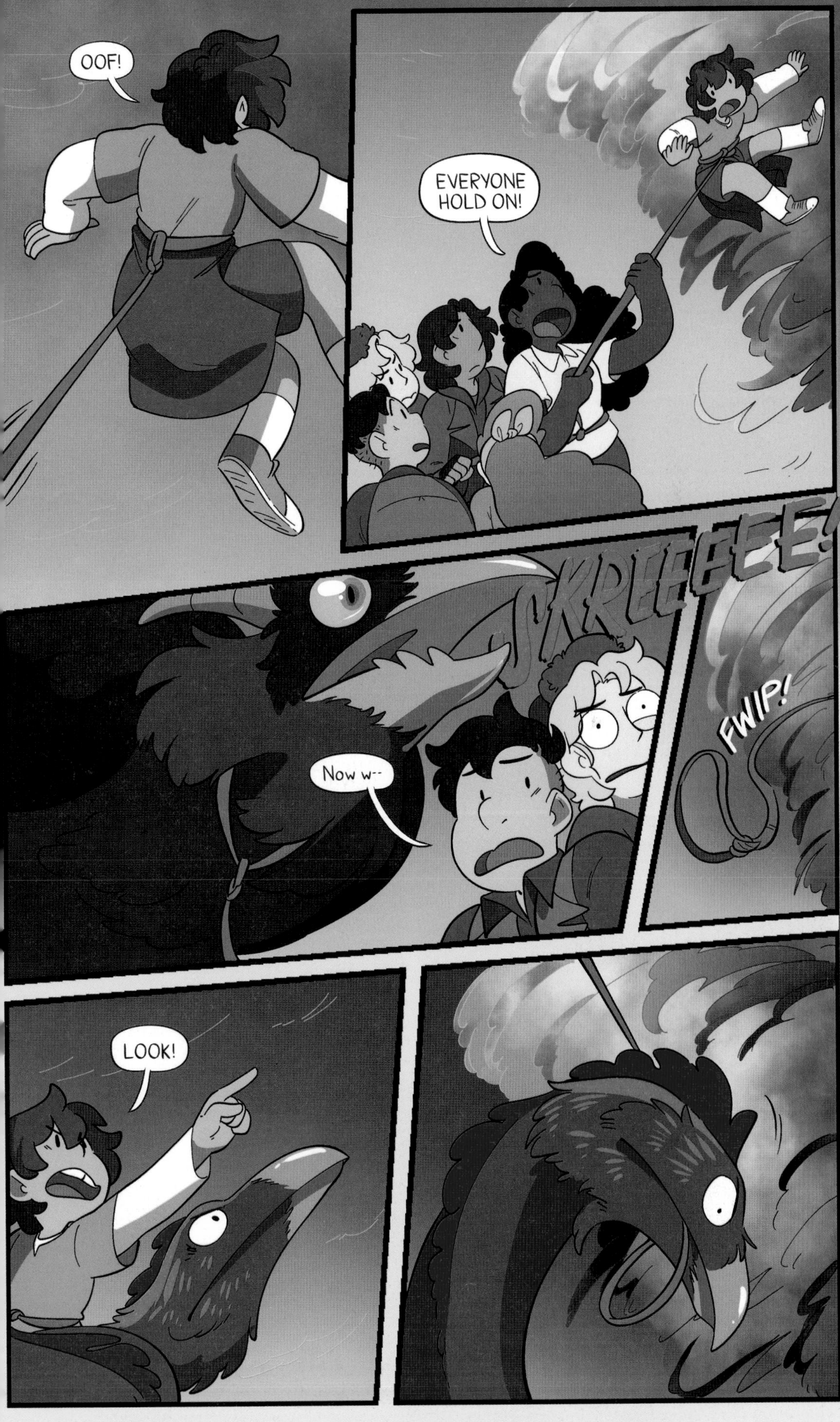
OOF!
EVERYONE HOLD ON!
SKREEEEEE!
Now w--
FWIP!
LOOK!

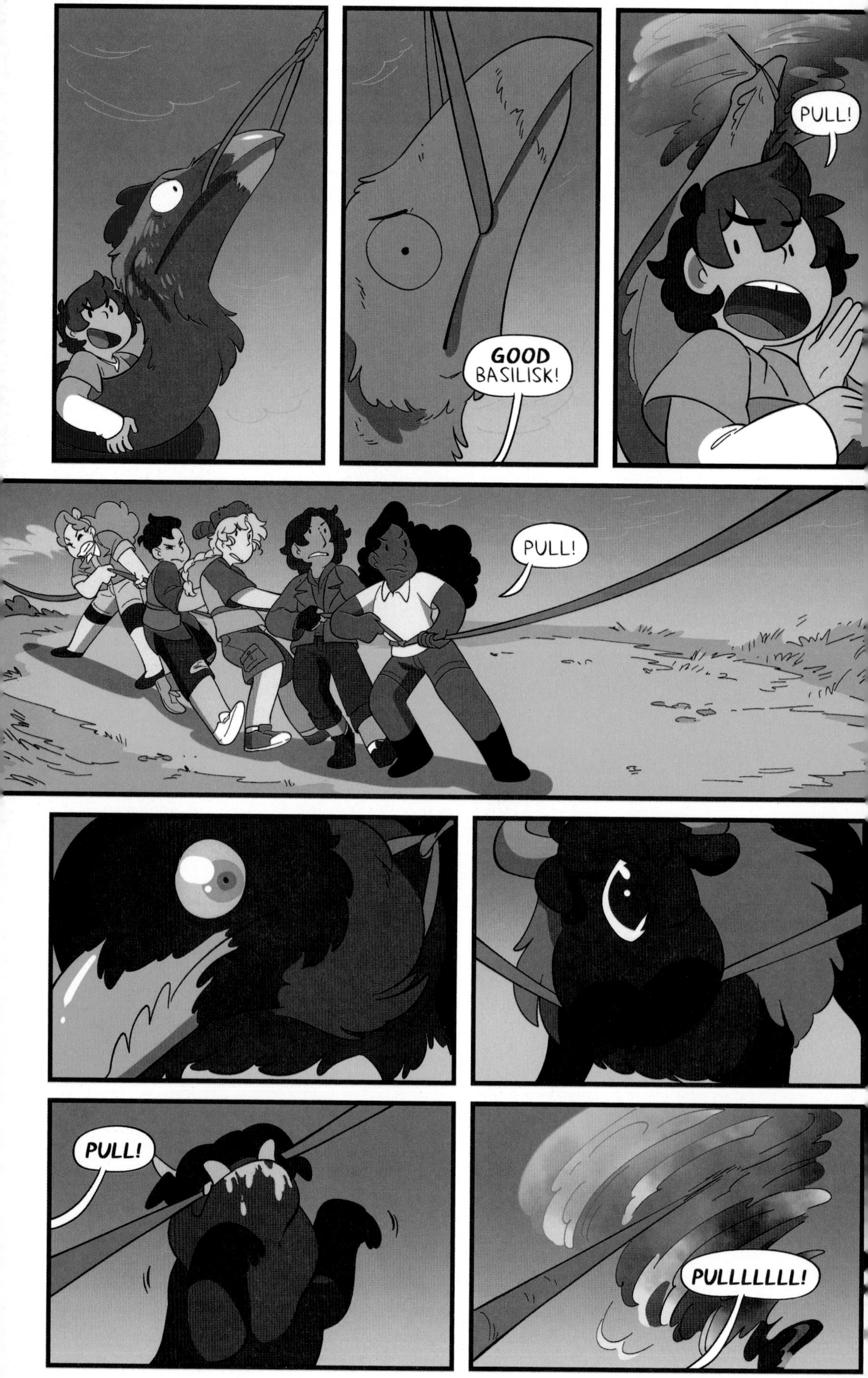
GOOD BASILISK!
PULL!
PULL!
PULL!
PULLLLLLLL!

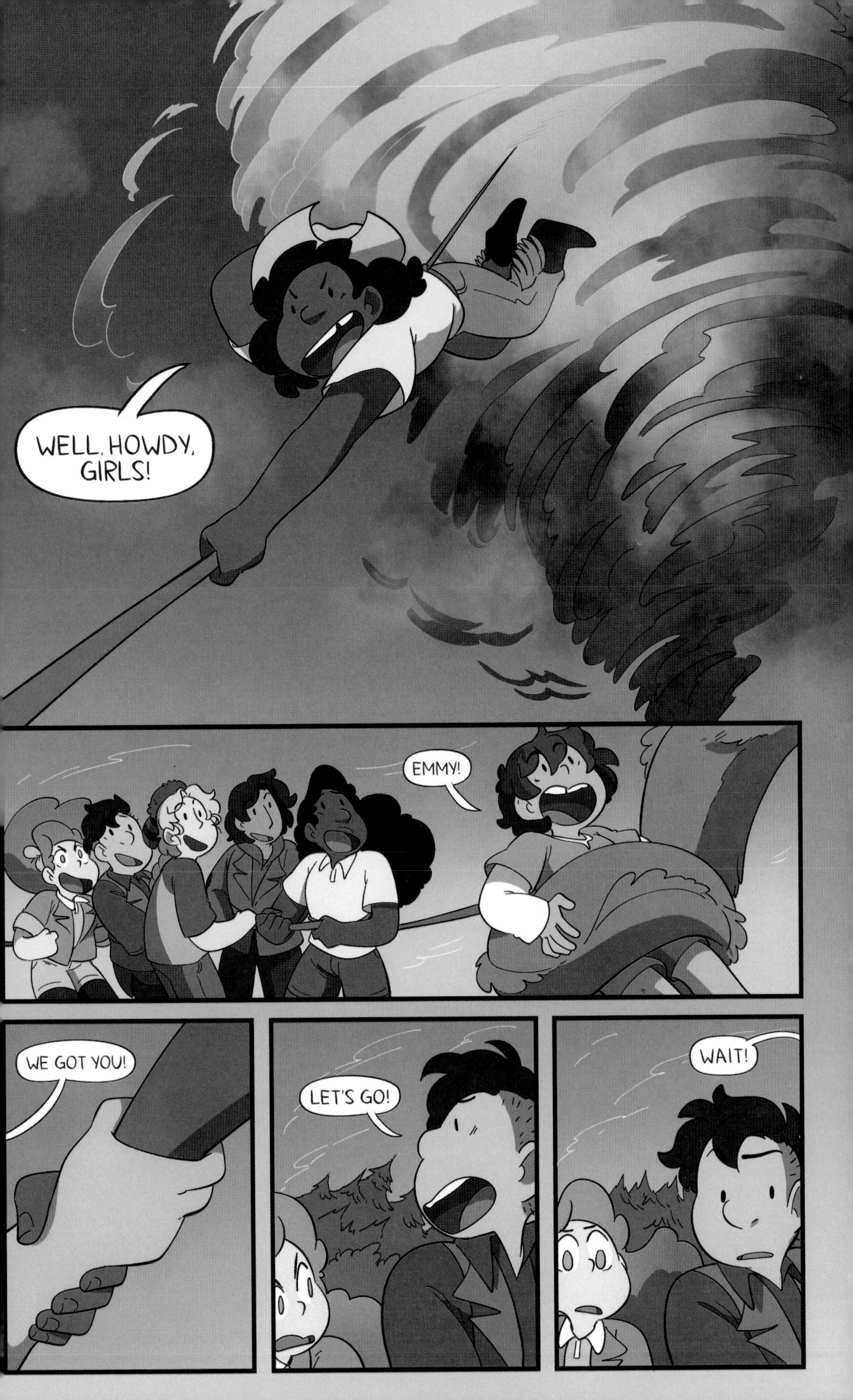
WELL, HOWDY, GIRLS!
EMMY!
WE GOT YOU!
LET'S GO!
WAIT!

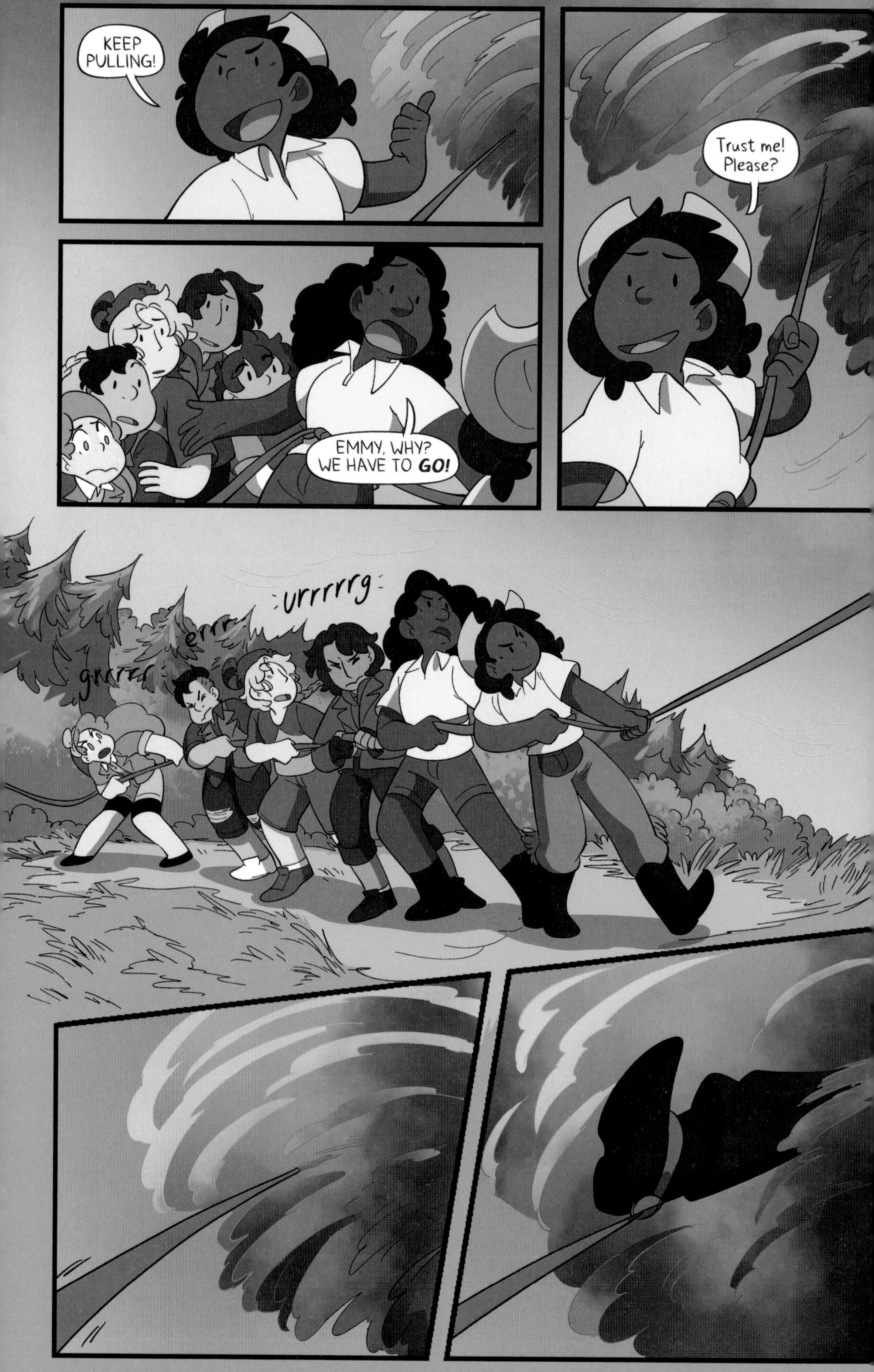
KEEP PULLING!
Trust me! Please?
EMMY, WHY? WE HAVE TO GO!
urrrrrg
errr
grrrrr

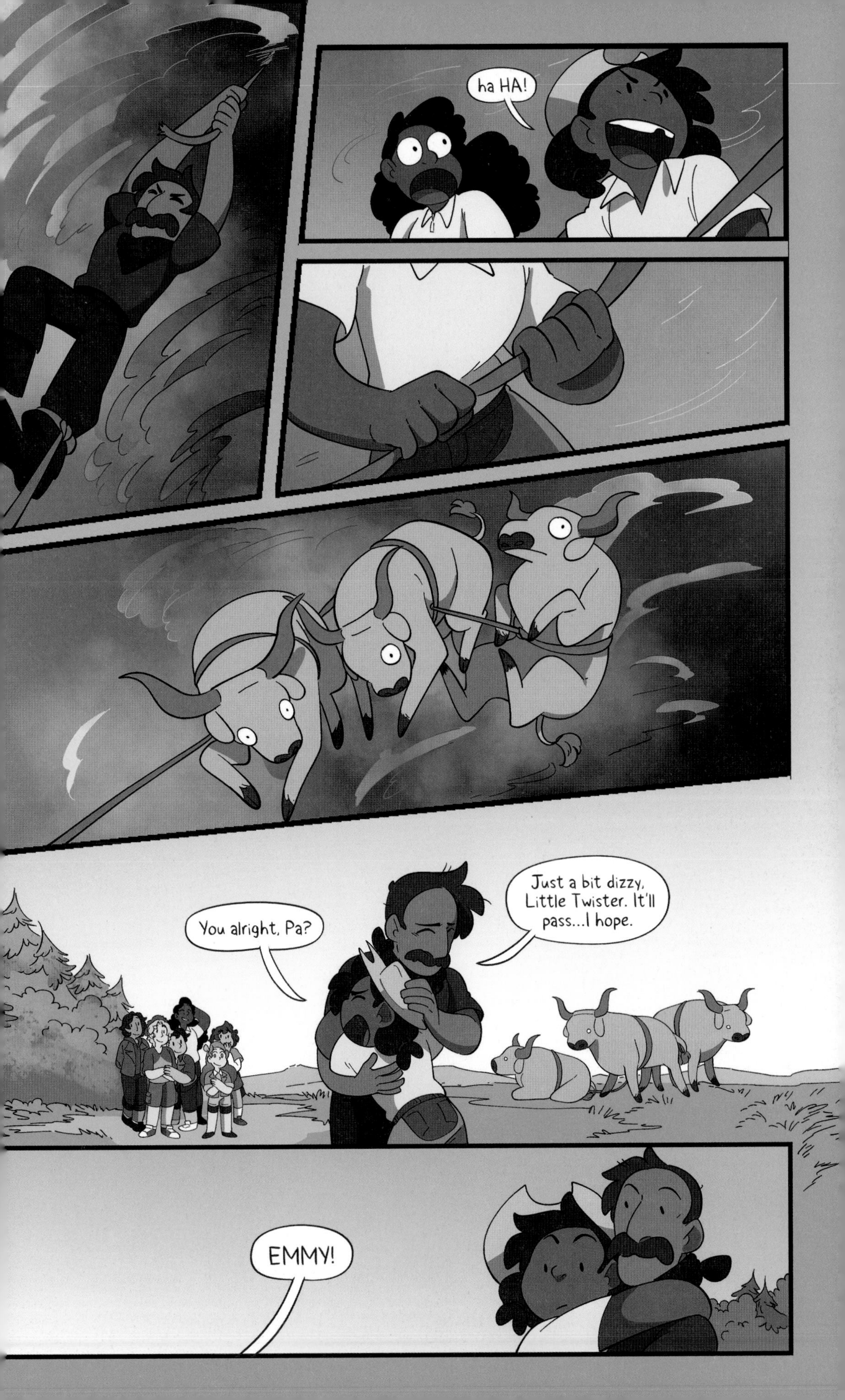

ha HA!
You alright, Pa?
Just a bit dizzy, Little Twister. It'll pass...I hope.
EMMY!

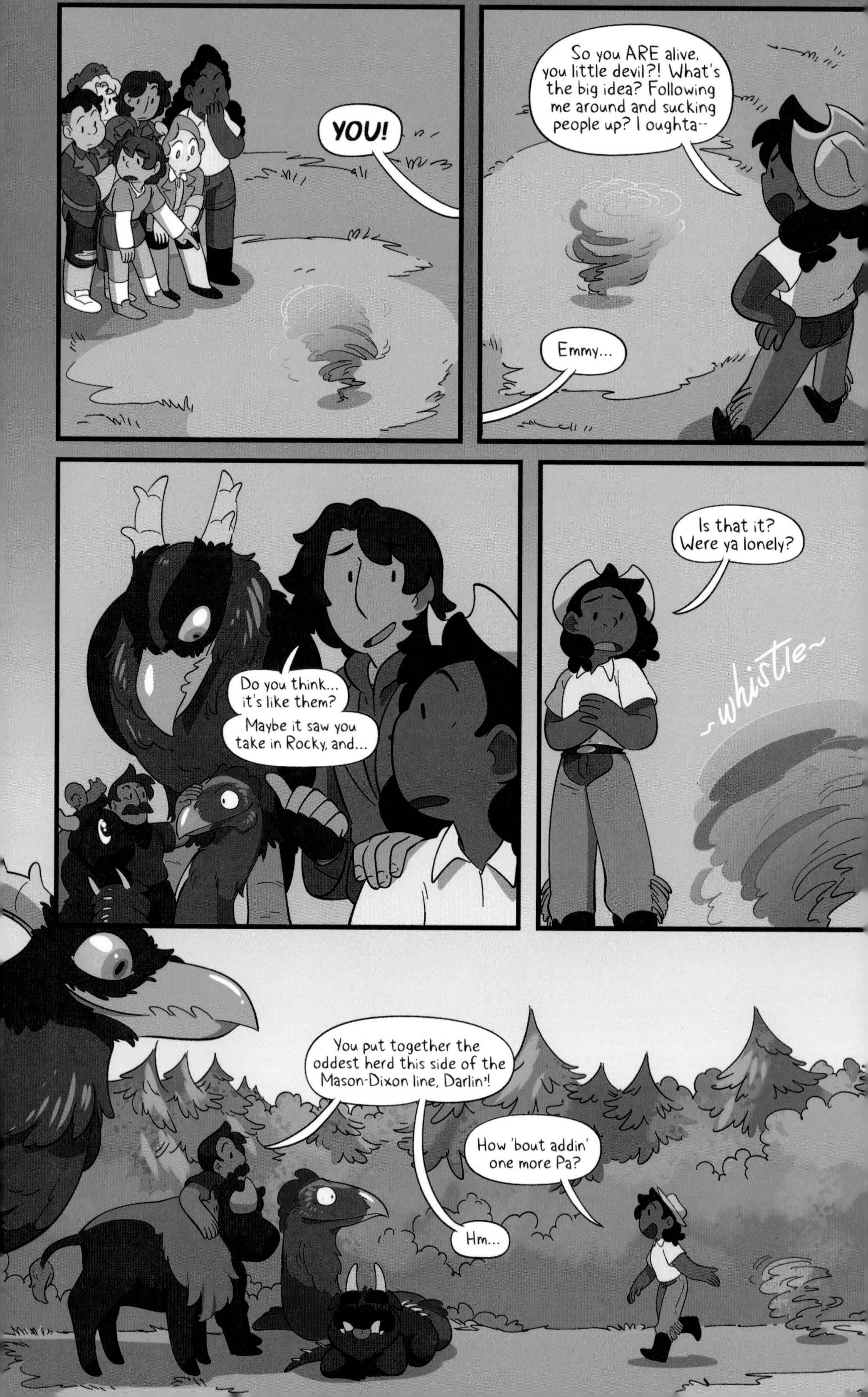
YOU!
So you ARE alive, you little devil?! What's the big idea? Following me around and sucking people up? I oughta--
Emmy...
Do you think... it's like them?
Maybe it saw you take in Rocky, and...
Is that it? Were ya lonely?
~whistle~
You put together the oddest herd this side of the Mason-Dixon line, Darlin'!
How 'bout addin' one more Pa?
Hm...

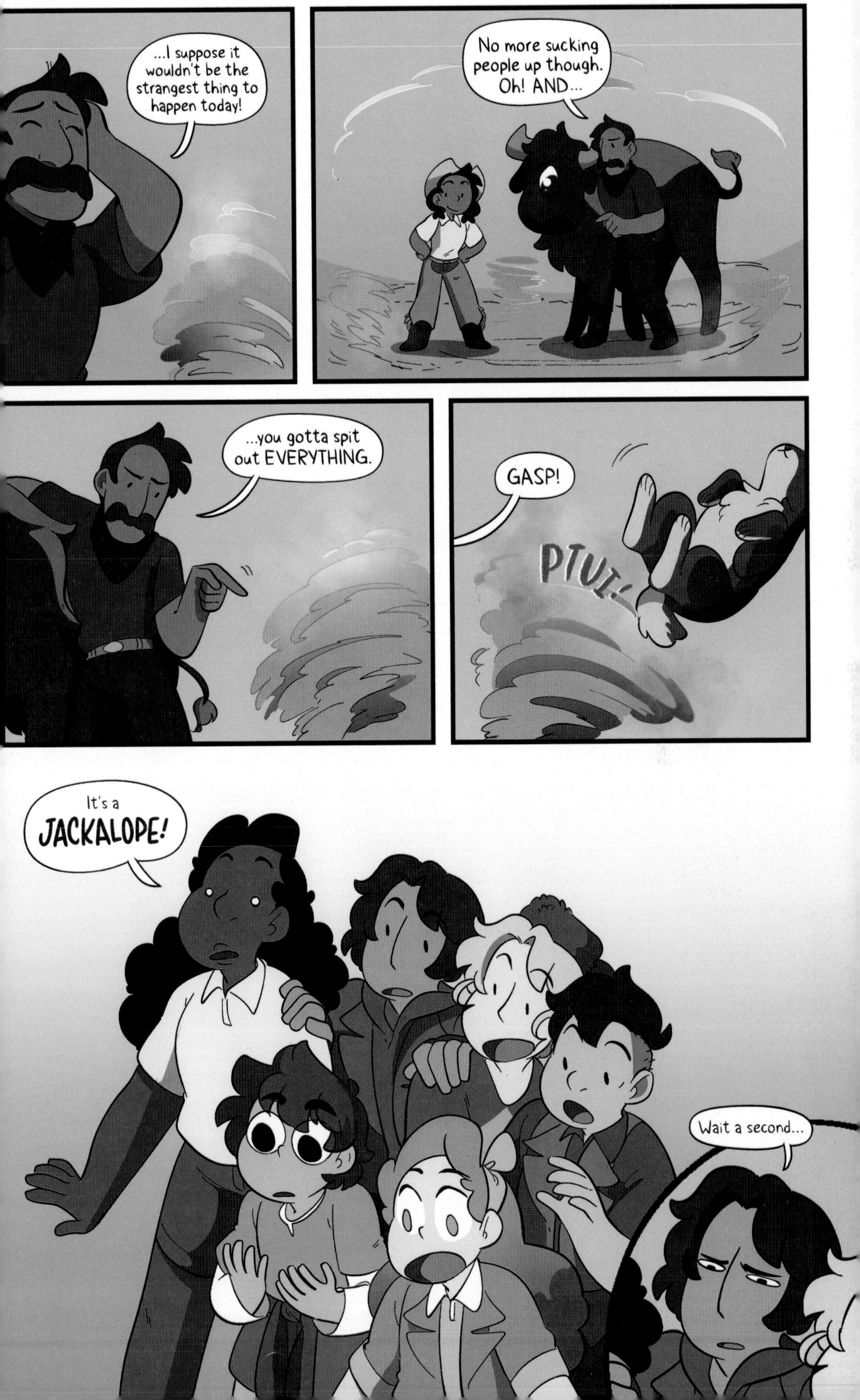

...I suppose it wouldn't be the strangest thing to happen today!
No more sucking people up though. Oh! AND...
...you gotta spit out EVERYTHING.
GASP!
PTUI!
It's a JACKALOPE!
Wait a second...

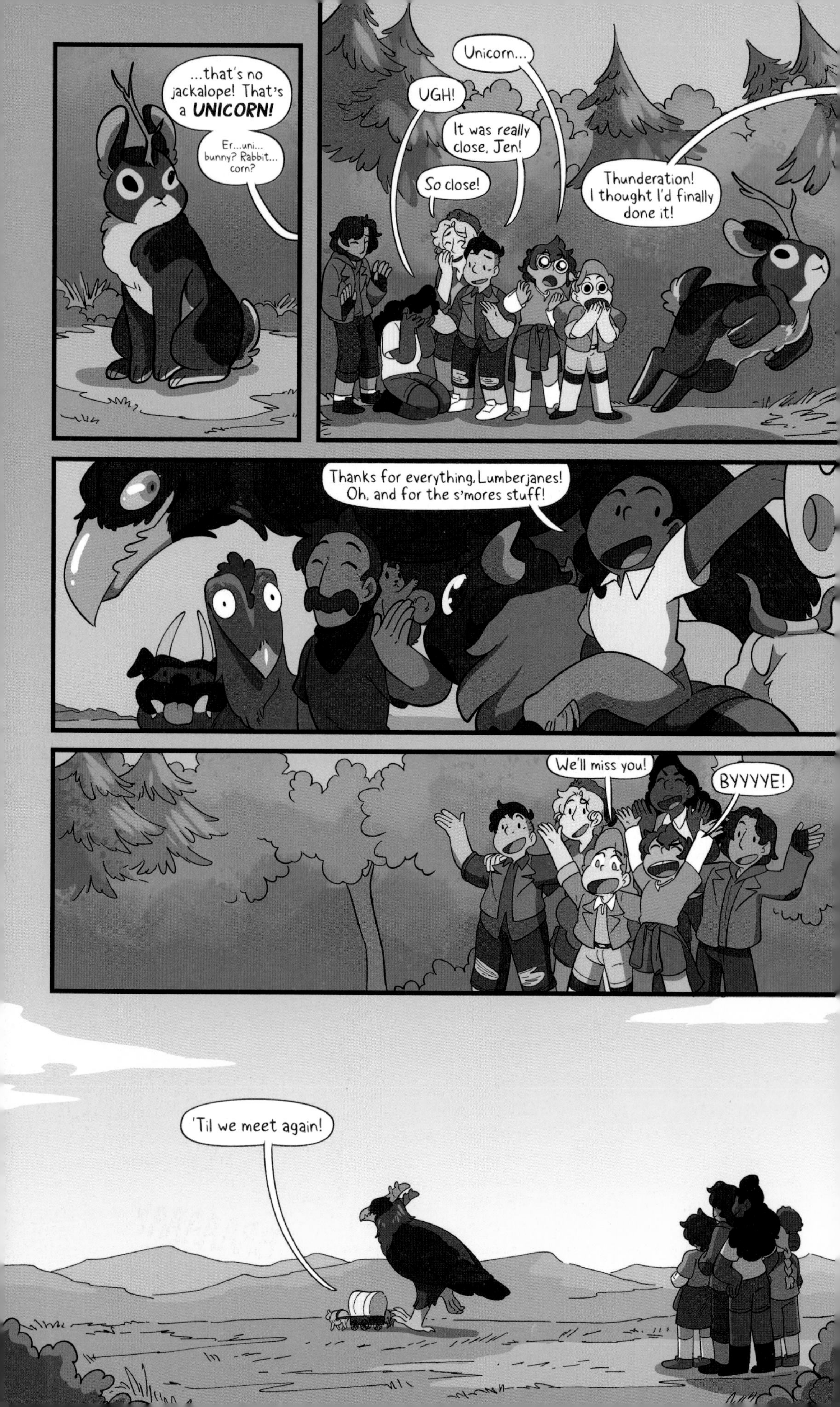
...that's no jackalope! That's a **UNICORN!**
Er...uni... bunny? Rabbit... corn?
Unicorn...
UGH!
It was really close, Jen!
So close!
Thunderation! I thought I'd finally done it!
Thanks for everything, Lumberjanes! Oh, and for the s'mores stuff!
We'll miss you!
BYYYYE!
'Til we meet again!

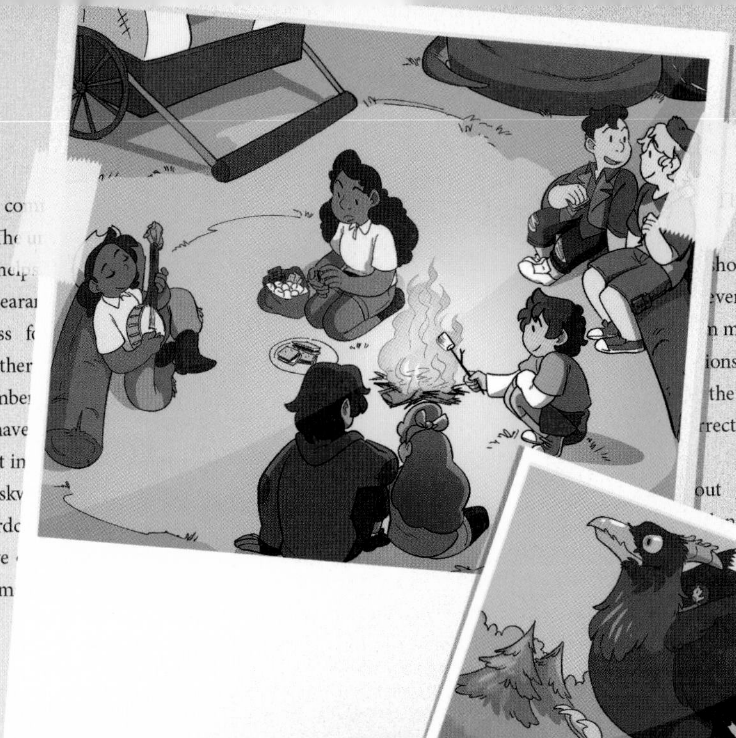

will co

The u

It help

appeara

dress f

Further

Lumbe

to have

part in

Thiskv

Hardc

have

them

IE UNIFORM

should be worn at camp

events when Lumberjanes

n may also be worn at other

ions. It should be worn as a

the uniform dress with

rrect shoes, and stocking or

out grows her uniform or

ter Lumberjane.

a she has

her

her

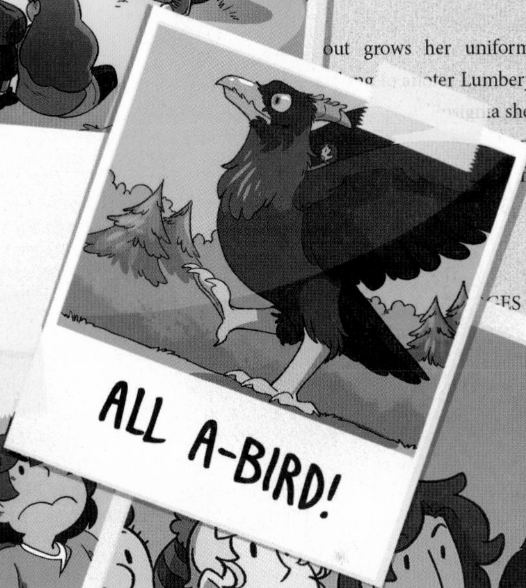
ALL A-BIRD!

The

yellow, short sl

emb

the w

choose

slacks,

made o

out-of-dc

green bere

the colla

Shoes ma

heels, rou ings or

socks shou with the shoes or wit

the uniform. Ne bracelets, or other jewelry do

belong with a Lumberjane uniform.

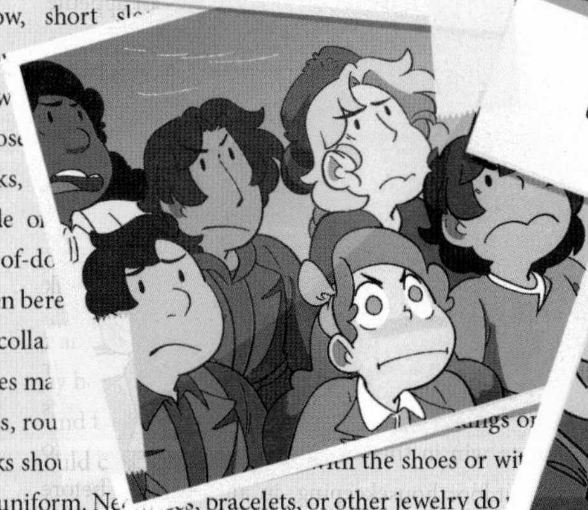

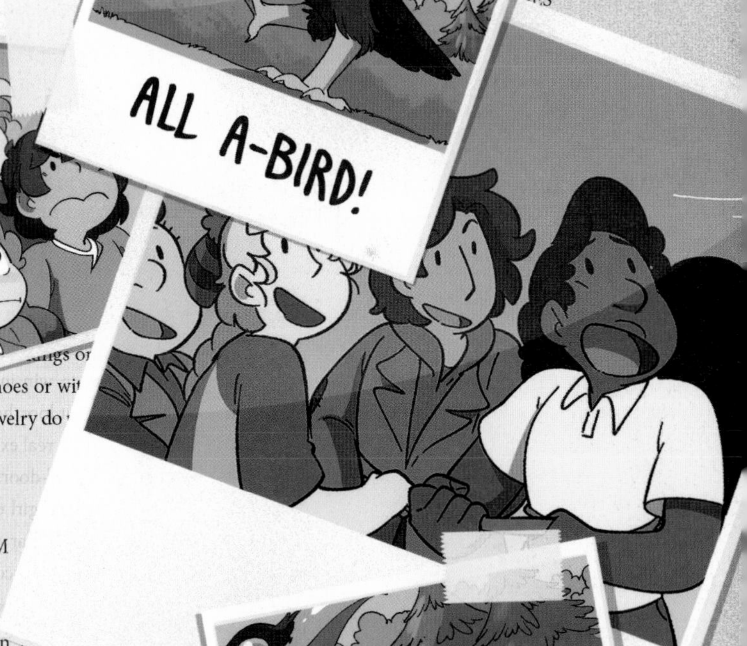

HOW TO WEAR THE UNIFORM

To look well in a uniform demands first of uniform be kept in good condition—clean pressed. See that the skirt is the right length for your own height and build, that the belt is adjusted to your waist, that your shoes and stockings are in keeping with the uniform, that you watch your posture and carry yourself with dignity and grace. If the beret is removed indoors, be sure that your hair is neat and kept in place with an insonspicuous clip or ribbon. When you wear a Lumberjane uniform you are identified as a member of this organization and you should be doubly careful to conduct yourself in a way that will show everyone that courtesy and thoughtfullness are part of being a Lumberjane. People are likely to judge a whole nation by the selfishness of a few individuals, to criticize a whole family because of the misconduct of one member, and to feel unkindly toward and organization because of the

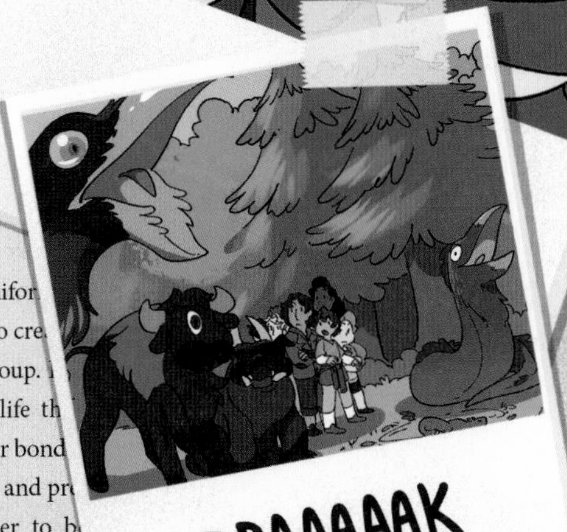
BRAAAAK

The unifor

helps to cre

in a group.

active life th

another bond

future, and pr

in order to b

Lumberjane pr

Penniquiqul Thi ore Lady

Types, but m es will wish to have one. They

can either bu , or make it themselves from

materials available at the trading post.

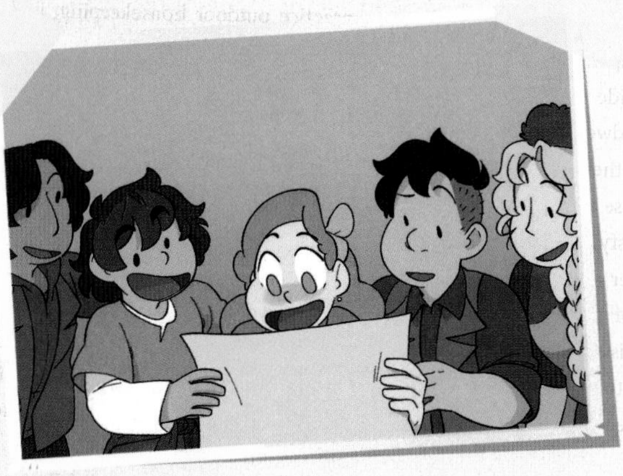

LUMBERJANES FIELD MANUAL

CHAPTER FORTY-EIGHT

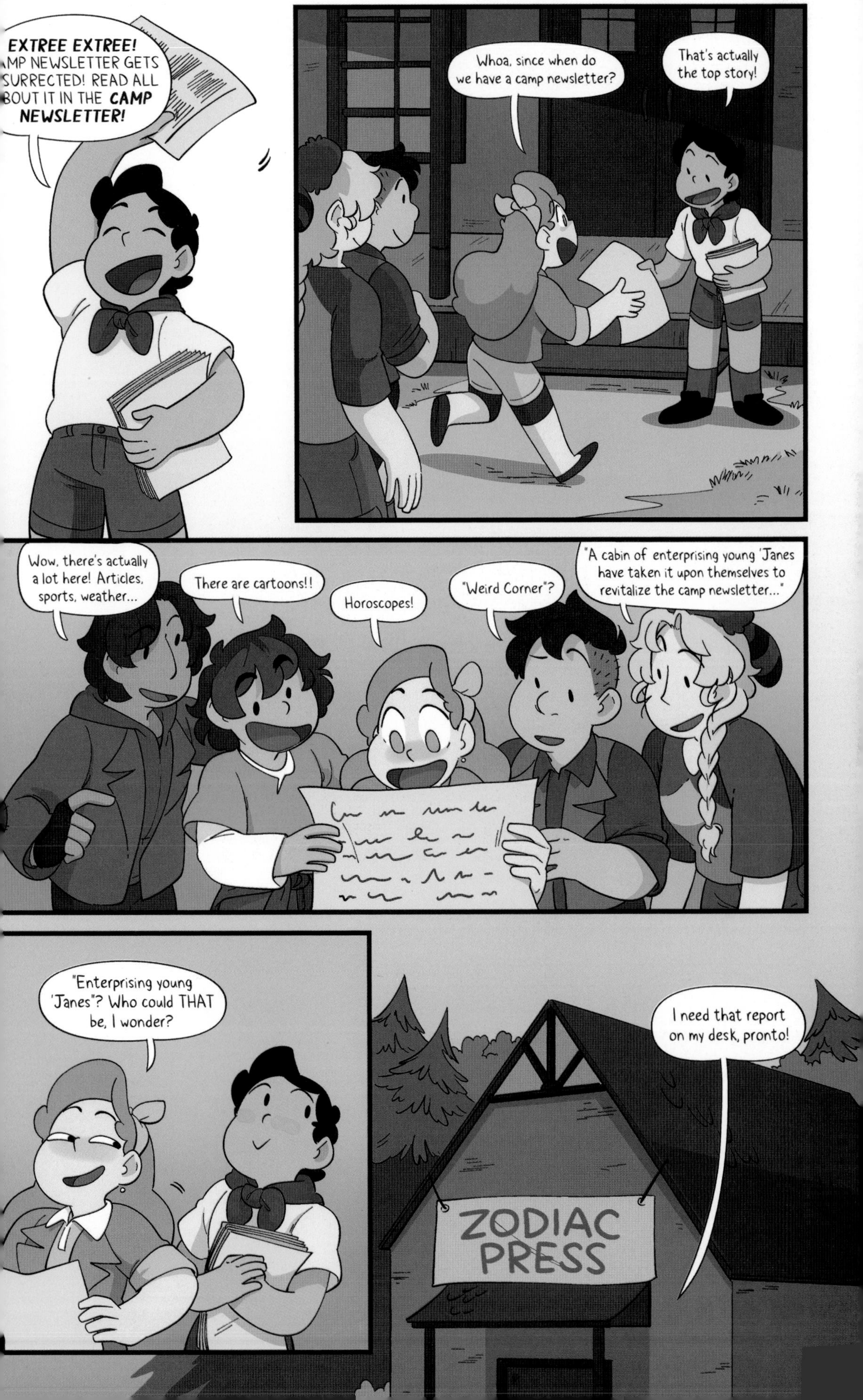
EXTREE EXTREE!
AMP NEWSLETTER GETS
SURRECTED! READ ALL
BOUT IT IN THE CAMP NEWSLETTER!
Whoa, since when do we have a camp newsletter?
That's actually the top story!
Wow, there's actually a lot here! Articles, sports, weather...
There are cartoons!!
Horoscopes!
"Weird Corner"?
"A cabin of enterprising young 'Janes have taken it upon themselves to revitalize the camp newsletter..."
"Enterprising young 'Janes"? Who could THAT be, I wonder?
I need that report on my desk, pronto!
ZODIAC PRESS

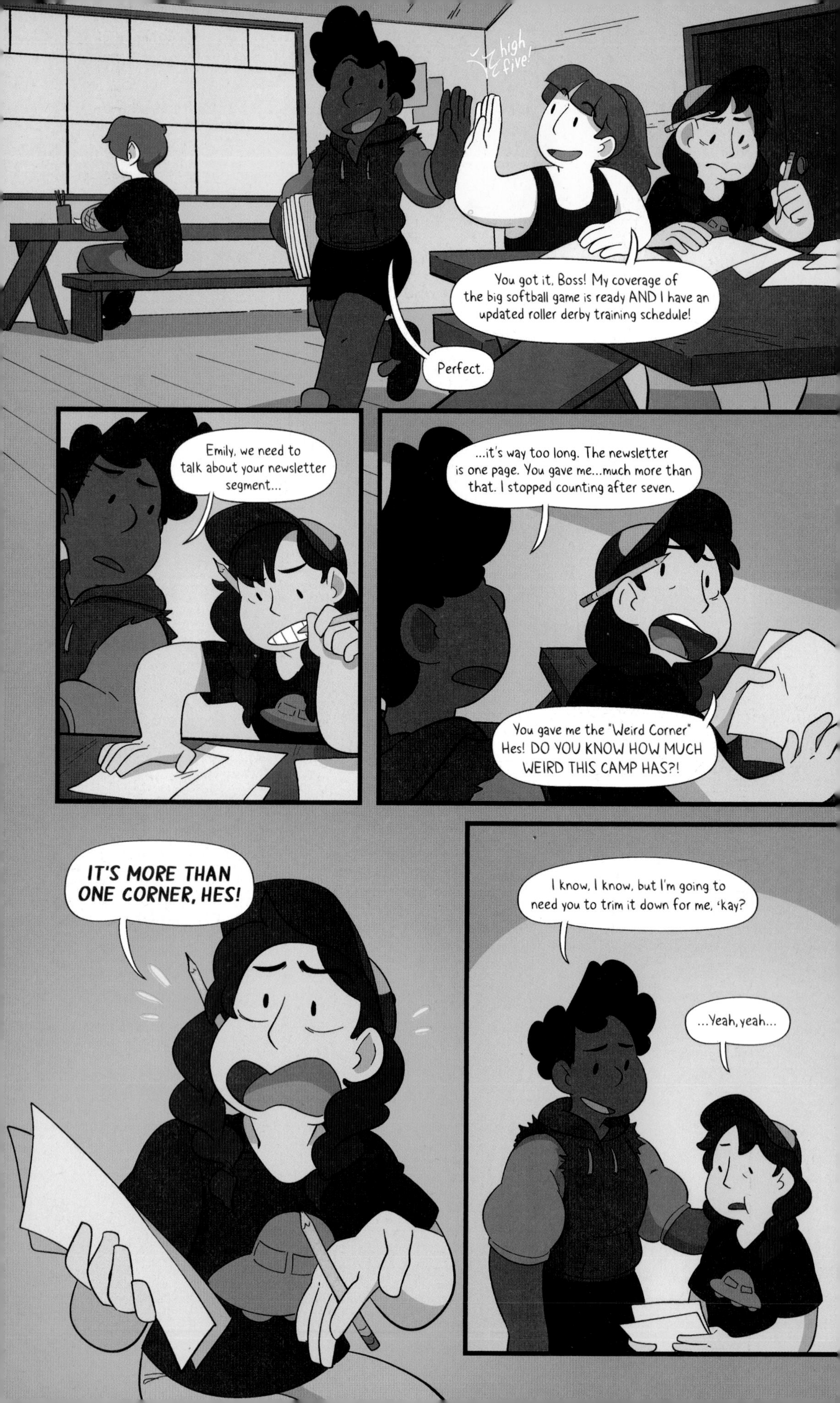
high five!
You got it, Boss! My coverage of the big softball game is ready AND I have an updated roller derby training schedule!
Perfect.
Emily, we need to talk about your newsletter segment...
...it's way too long. The newsletter is one page. You gave me...much more than that. I stopped counting after seven.
You gave me the "Weird Corner" Hes! DO YOU KNOW HOW MUCH WEIRD THIS CAMP HAS?!
IT'S MORE THAN ONE CORNER, HES!
I know, I know, but I'm going to need you to trim it down for me, 'kay?
...Yeah, yeah...

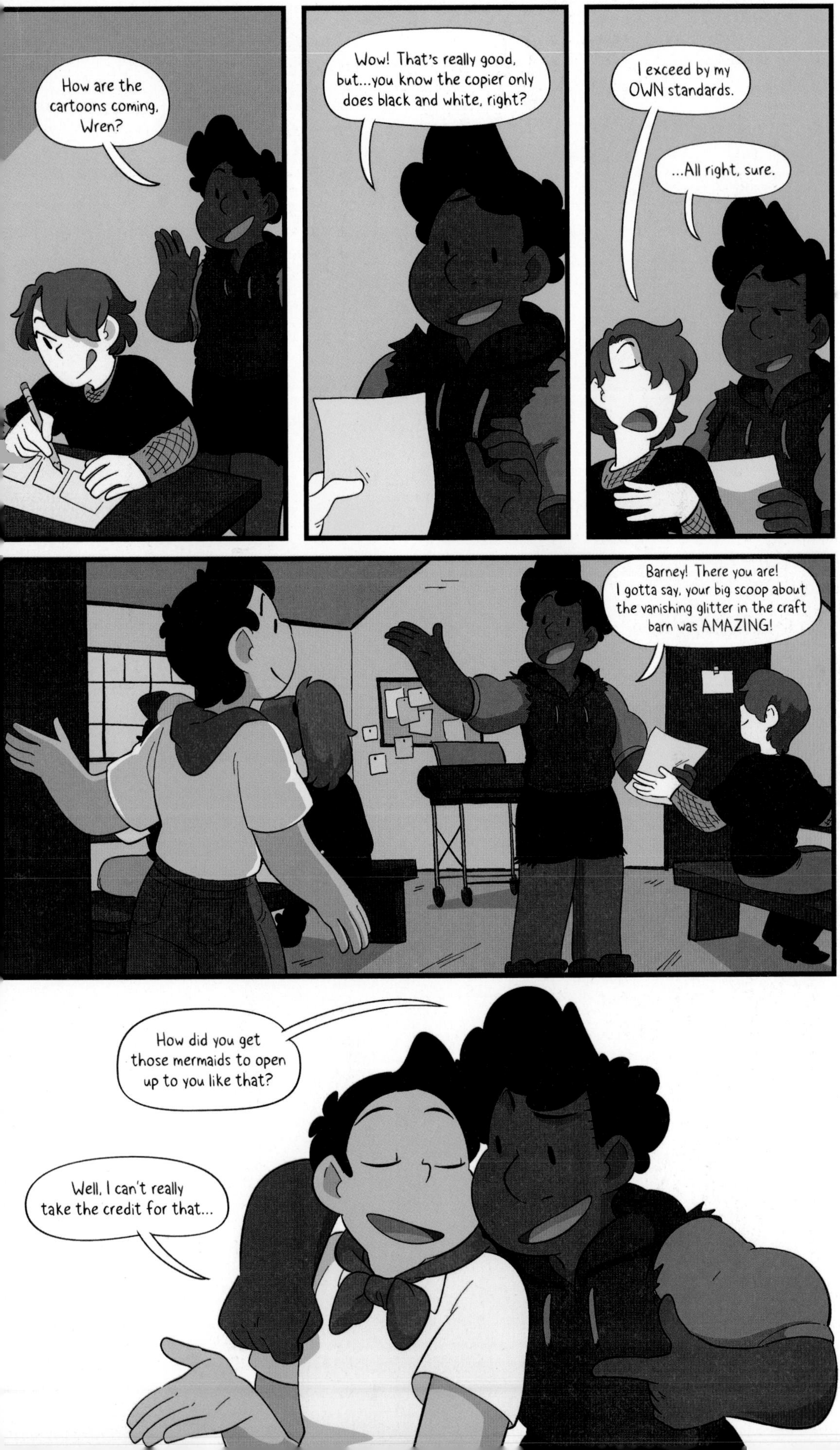
How are the cartoons coming, Wren?
Wow! That's really good, but...you know the copier only does black and white, right?
I exceed by my OWN standards.
...All right, sure.
Barney! There you are! I gotta say, your big scoop about the vanishing glitter in the craft barn was AMAZING!
How did you get those mermaids to open up to you like that?
Well, I can't really take the credit for that...

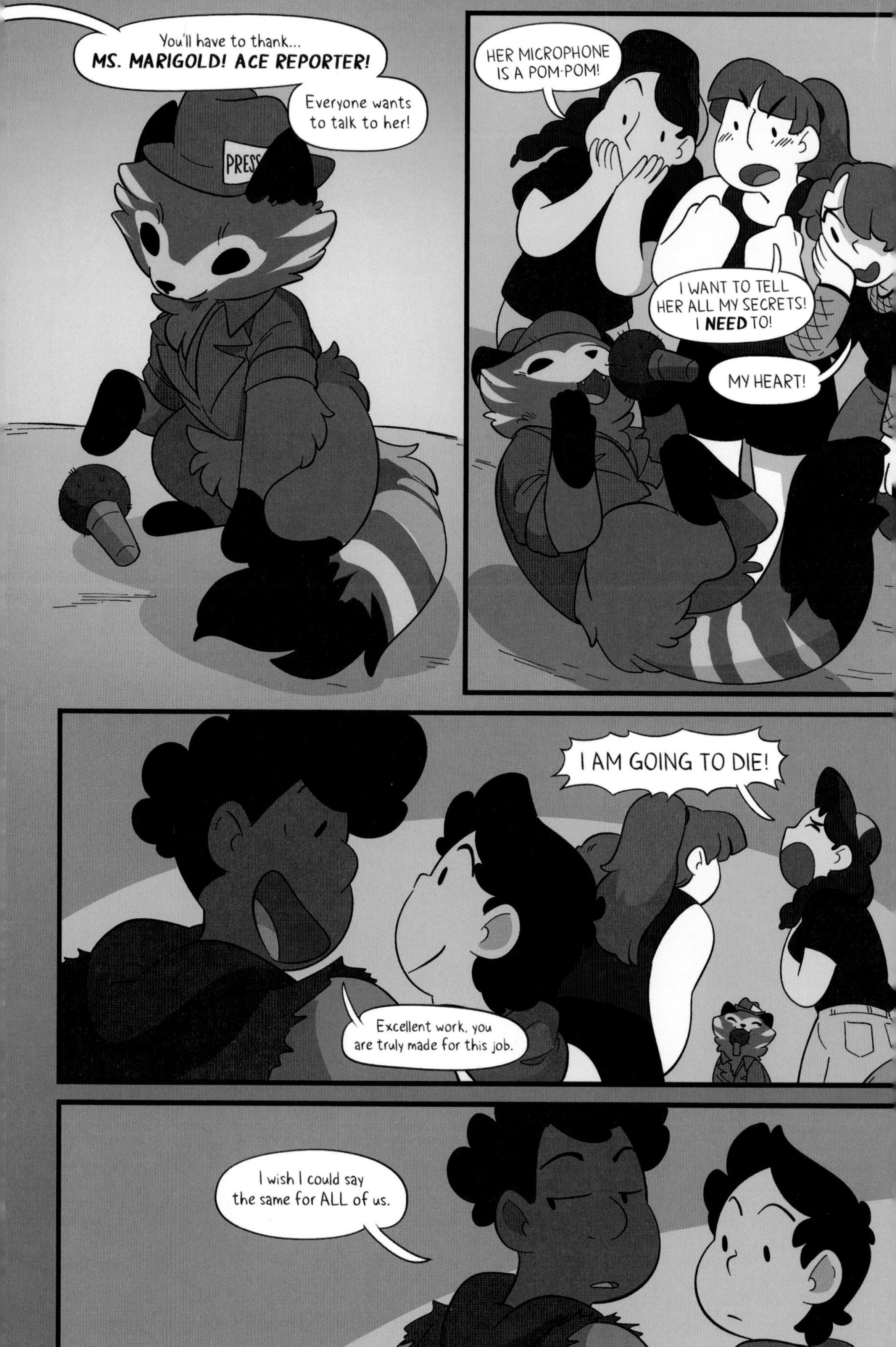
You'll have to thank...
MS. MARIGOLD! ACE REPORTER!
Everyone wants to talk to her!
HER MICROPHONE IS A POM-POM!
I WANT TO TELL HER ALL MY SECRETS! I **NEED** TO!
MY HEART!
PRESS
I AM GOING TO DIE!
Excellent work, you are truly made for this job.
I wish I could say the same for ALL of us.

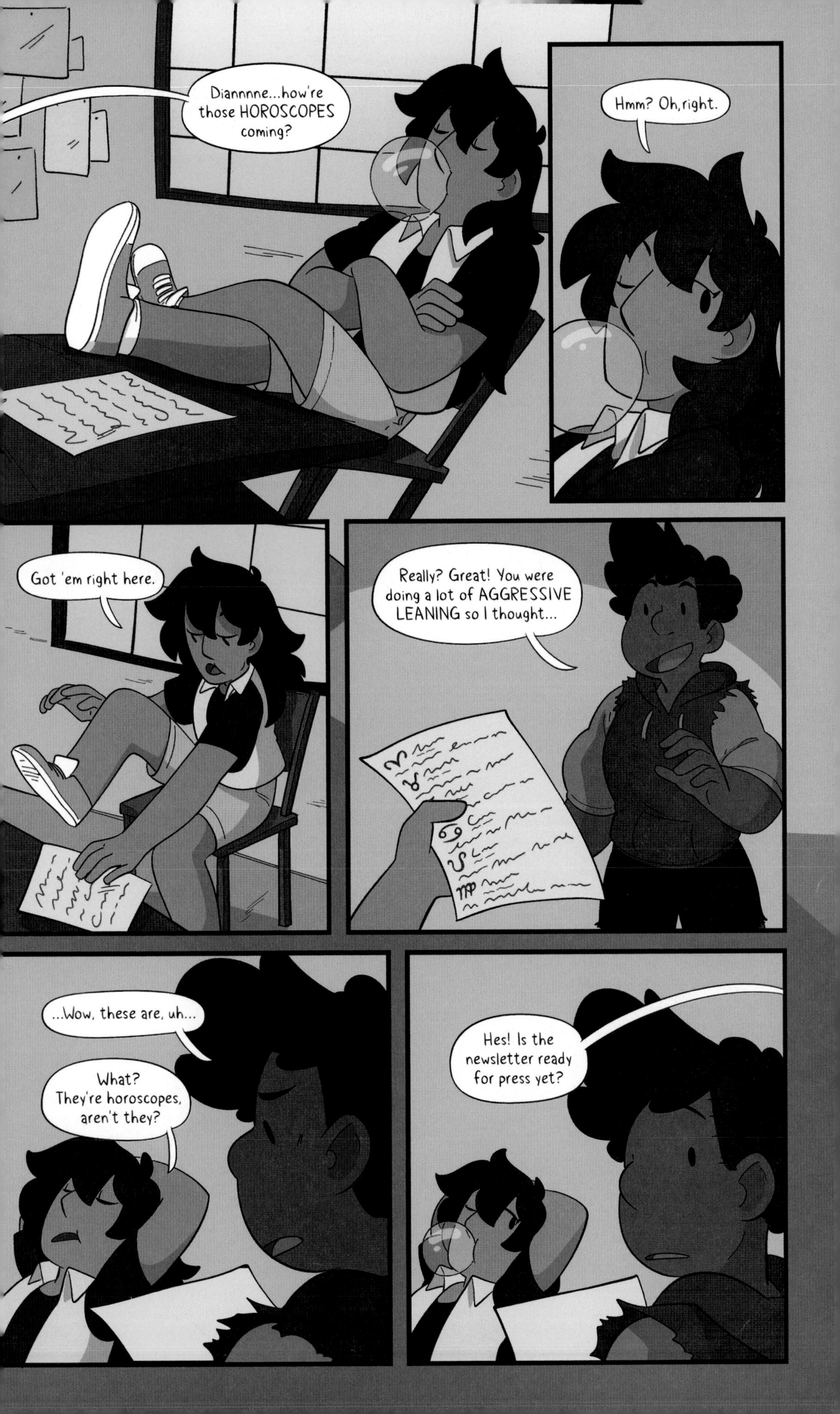
Diannnne...how're those HOROSCOPES coming?
Hmm? Oh, right.
Got 'em right here.
Really? Great! You were doing a lot of AGGRESSIVE LEANING so I thought...
...Wow, these are, uh...
What? They're horoscopes, aren't they?
Hes! Is the newsletter ready for press yet?

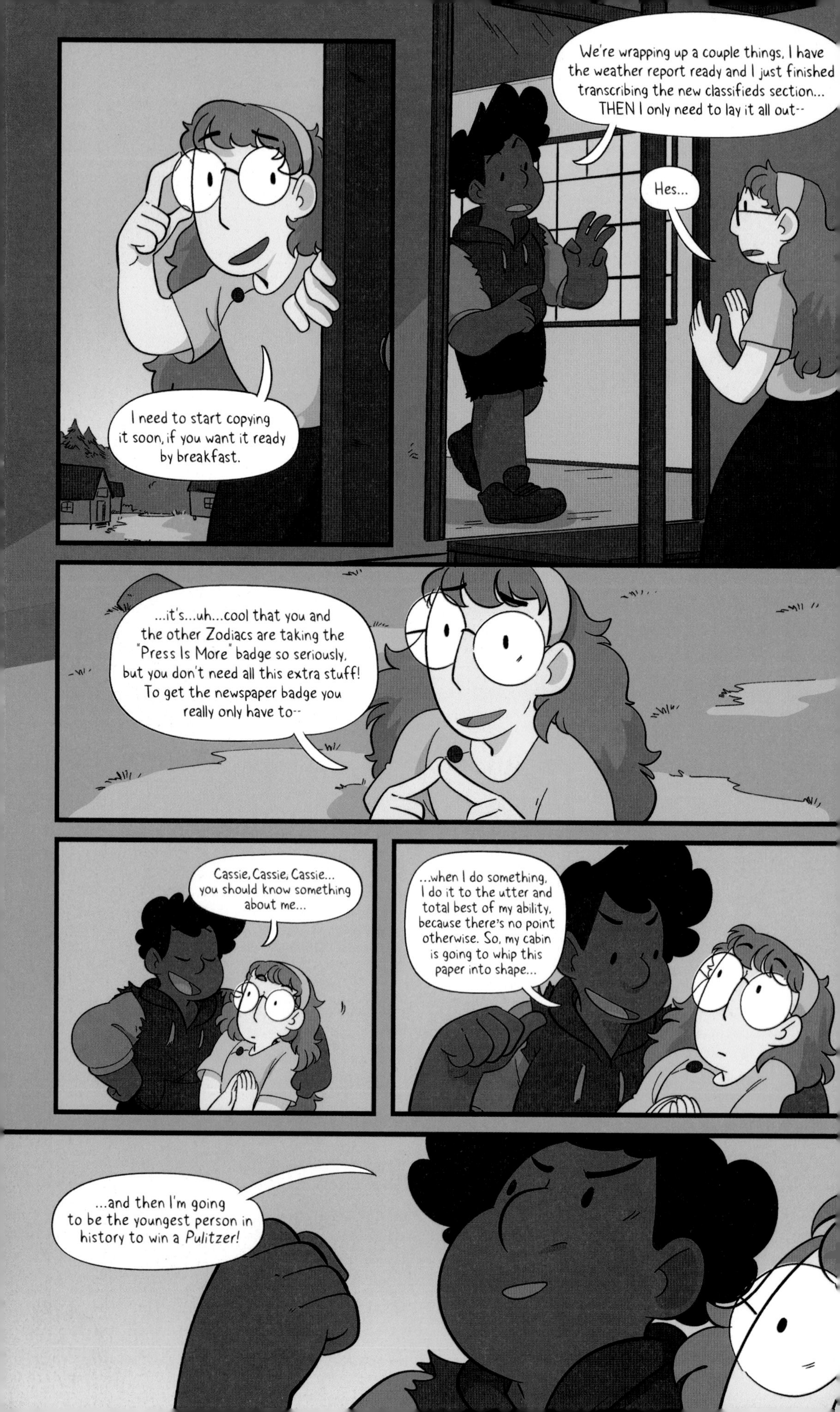
We're wrapping up a couple things, I have the weather report ready and I just finished transcribing the new classifieds section... THEN I only need to lay it all out--
Hes...
I need to start copying it soon, if you want it ready by breakfast.
...it's...uh...cool that you and the other Zodiacs are taking the "Press Is More" badge so seriously, but you don't need all this extra stuff! To get the newspaper badge you really only have to--
Cassie, Cassie, Cassie... you should know something about me...
...when I do something, I do it to the utter and total best of my ability, because there's no point otherwise. So, my cabin is going to whip this paper into shape...
...and then I'm going to be the youngest person in history to win a *Pulitzer*!

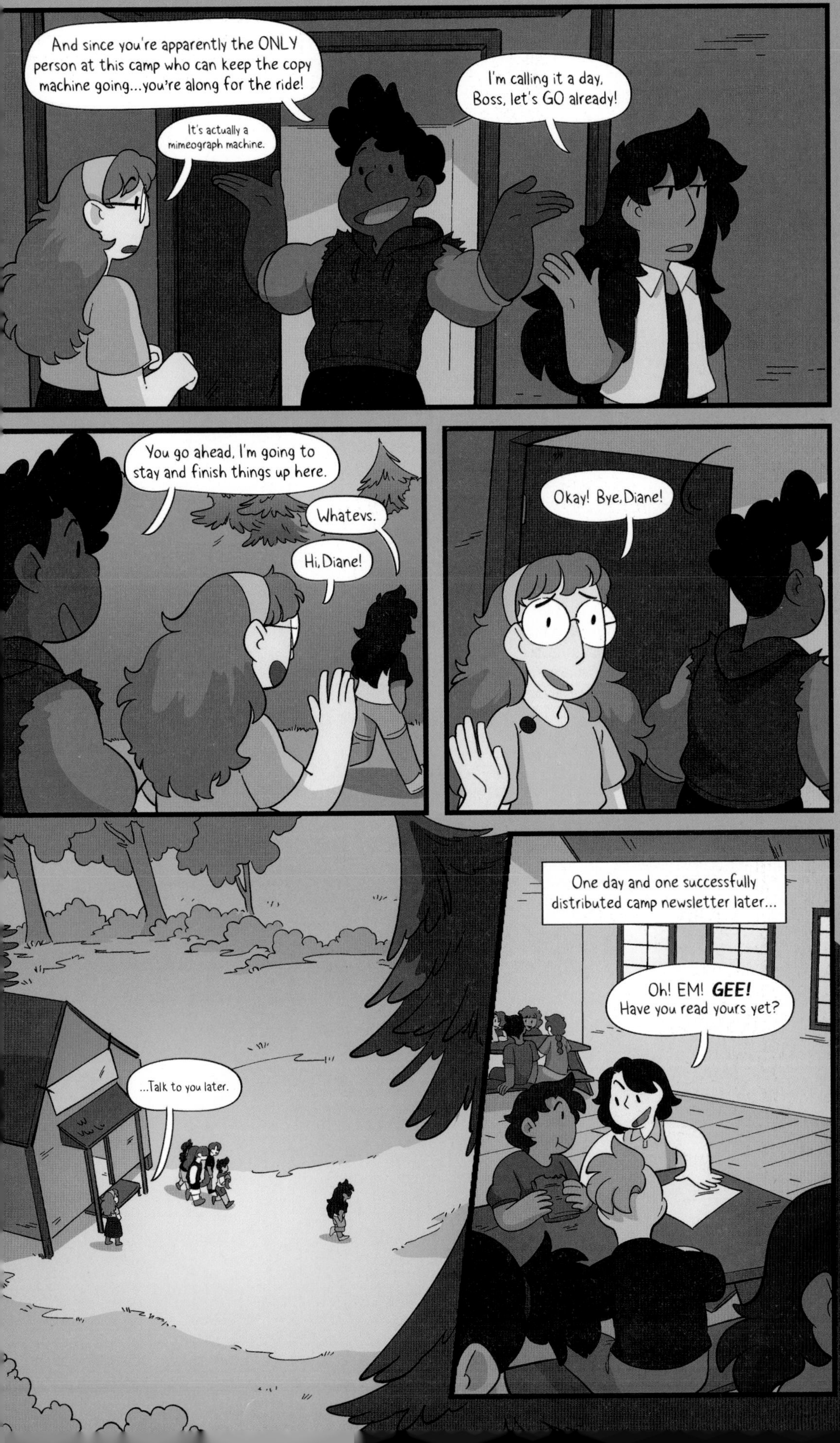
And since you're apparently the ONLY person at this camp who can keep the copy machine going...you're along for the ride!
It's actually a mimeograph machine.
I'm calling it a day, Boss, let's GO already!
You go ahead, I'm going to stay and finish things up here.
Whatevs.
Hi, Diane!
Okay! Bye, Diane!
...Talk to you later.
One day and one successfully distributed camp newsletter later...
Oh! EM! GEE! Have you read yours yet?

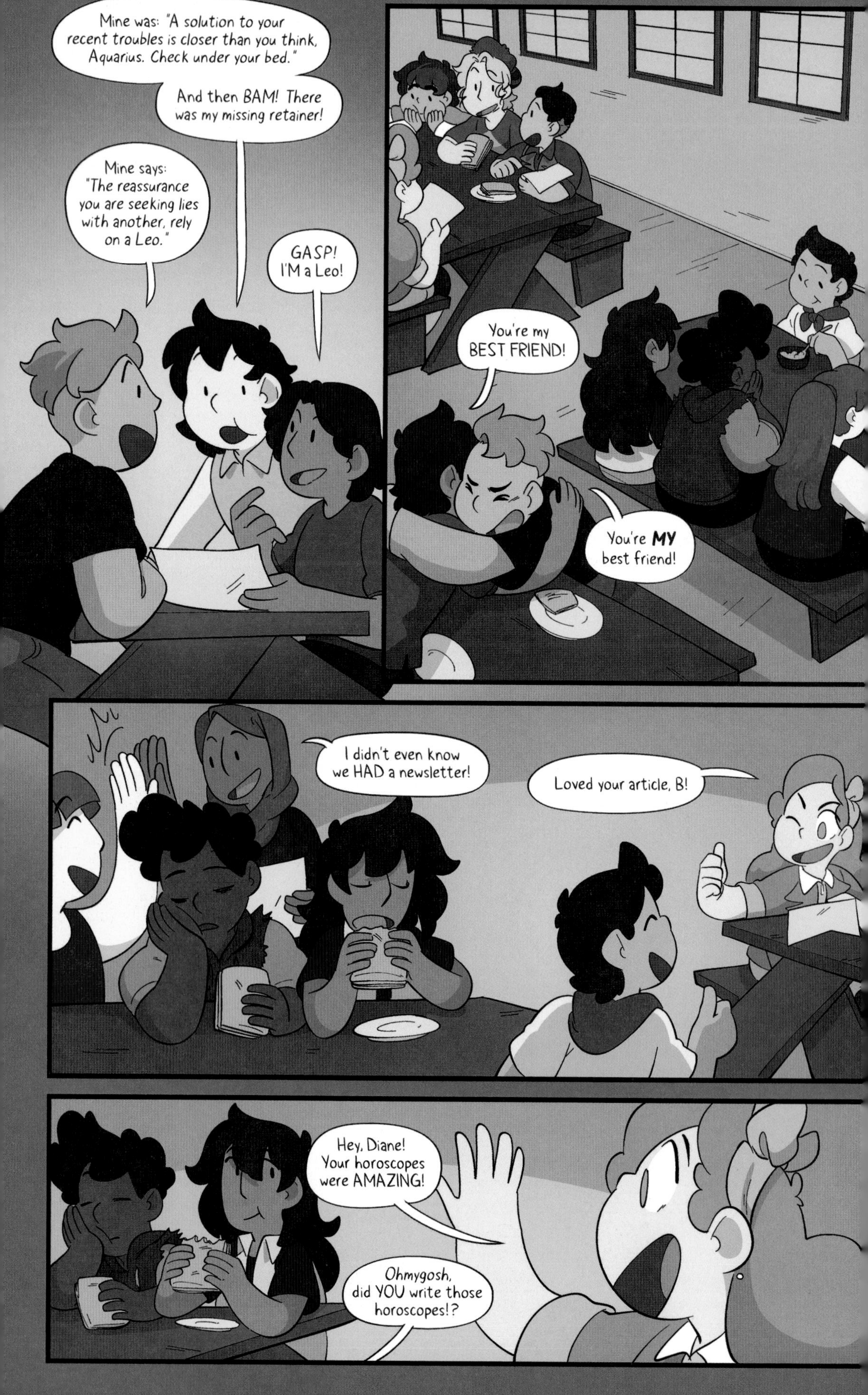

Mine was: "A solution to your recent troubles is closer than you think, Aquarius. Check under your bed."
And then BAM! There was my missing retainer!
Mine says: "The reassurance you are seeking lies with another, rely on a Leo."
GASP! I'M a Leo!
You're my BEST FRIEND!
You're **MY** best friend!
I didn't even know we HAD a newsletter!
Loved your article, B!
Hey, Diane! Your horoscopes were AMAZING!
Ohmygosh, did YOU write those horoscopes!?

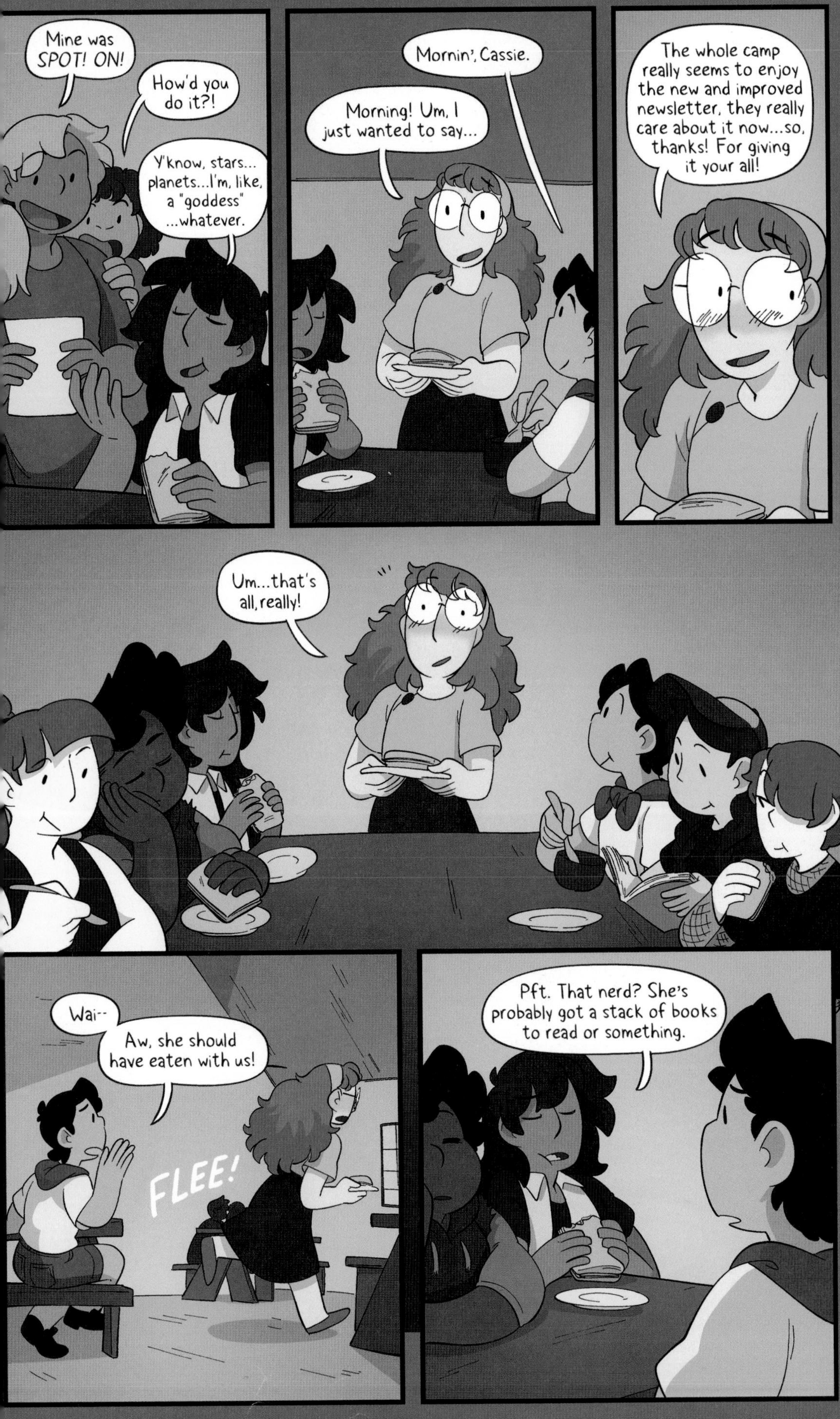
Mine was SPOT! ON!
How'd you do it?!
Y'know, stars... planets...I'm, like, a "goddess" ...whatever.
Mornin', Cassie.
Morning! Um, I just wanted to say...
The whole camp really seems to enjoy the new and improved newsletter, they really care about it now...so, thanks! For giving it your all!
Um...that's all, really!
Wai--
Aw, she should have eaten with us!
FLEE!
Pft. That nerd? She's probably got a stack of books to read or something.

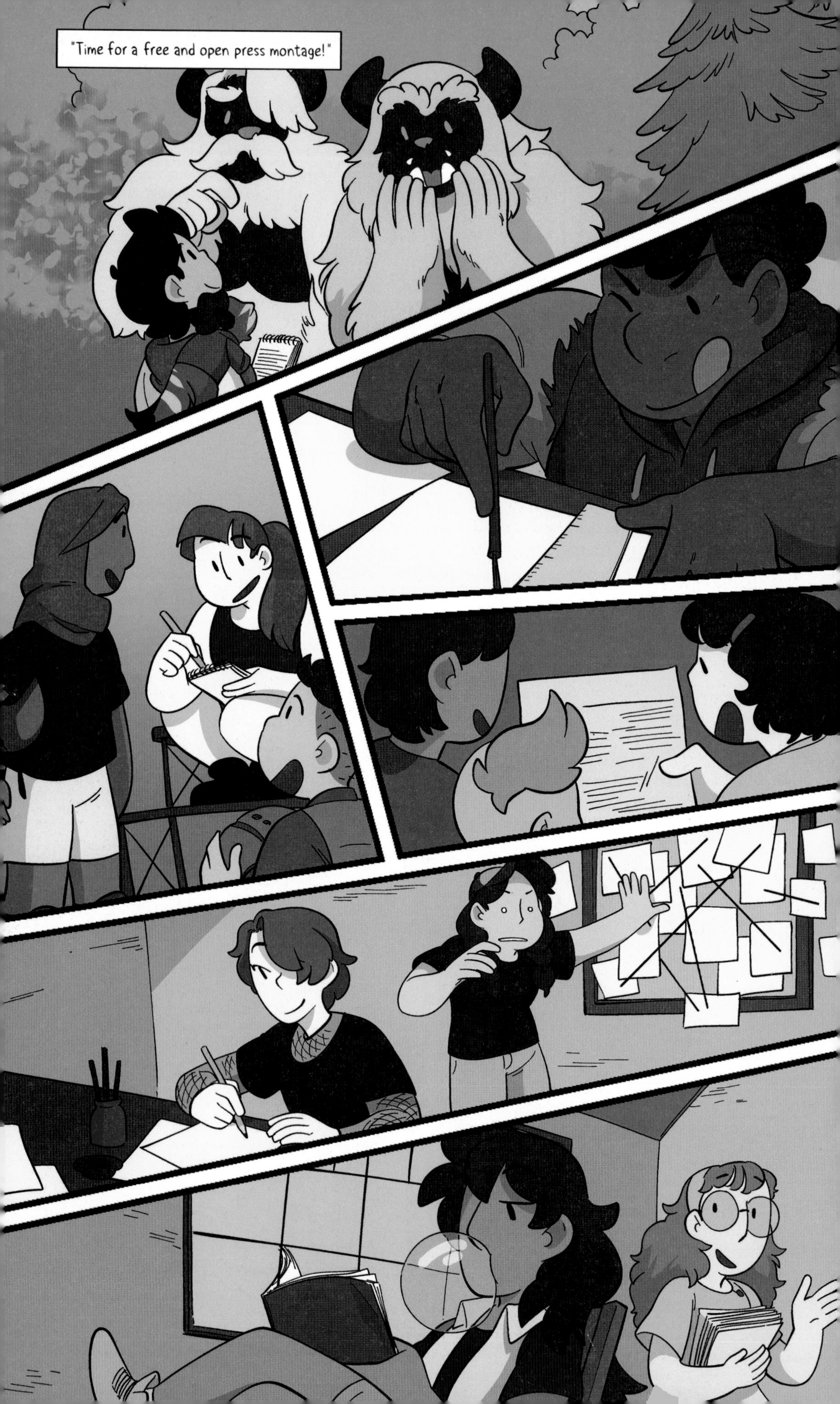
"Time for a free and open press montage!"

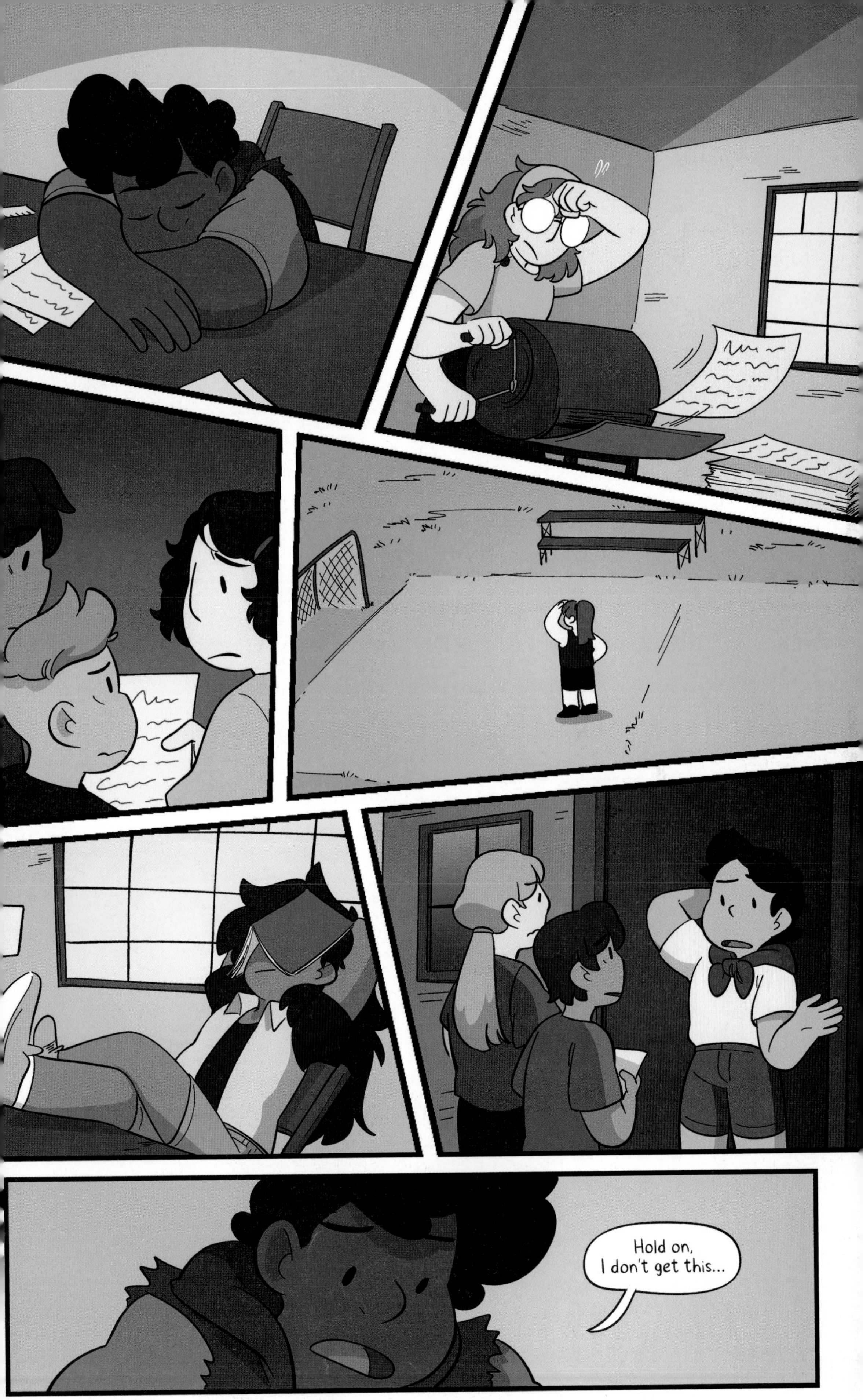
Hold on, I don't get this...

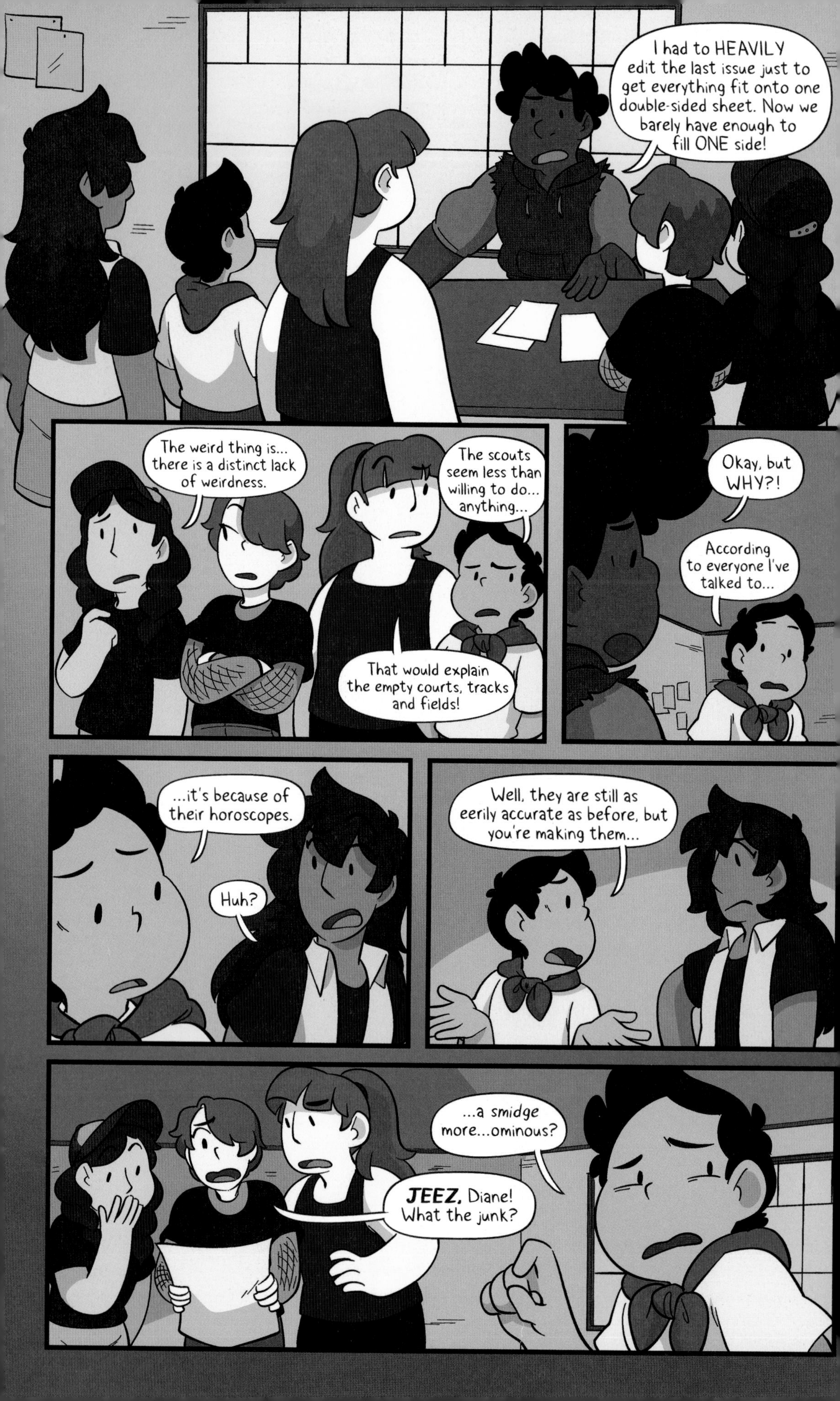
I had to HEAVILY edit the last issue just to get everything fit onto one double-sided sheet. Now we barely have enough to fill ONE side!
The weird thing is... there is a distinct lack of weirdness.
The scouts seem less than willing to do... anything...
That would explain the empty courts, tracks and fields!
Okay, but WHY?!
According to everyone I've talked to...
...it's because of their horoscopes.
Huh?
Well, they are still as eerily accurate as before, but you're making them...
...a smidge more...ominous?
JEEZ, Diane! What the junk?

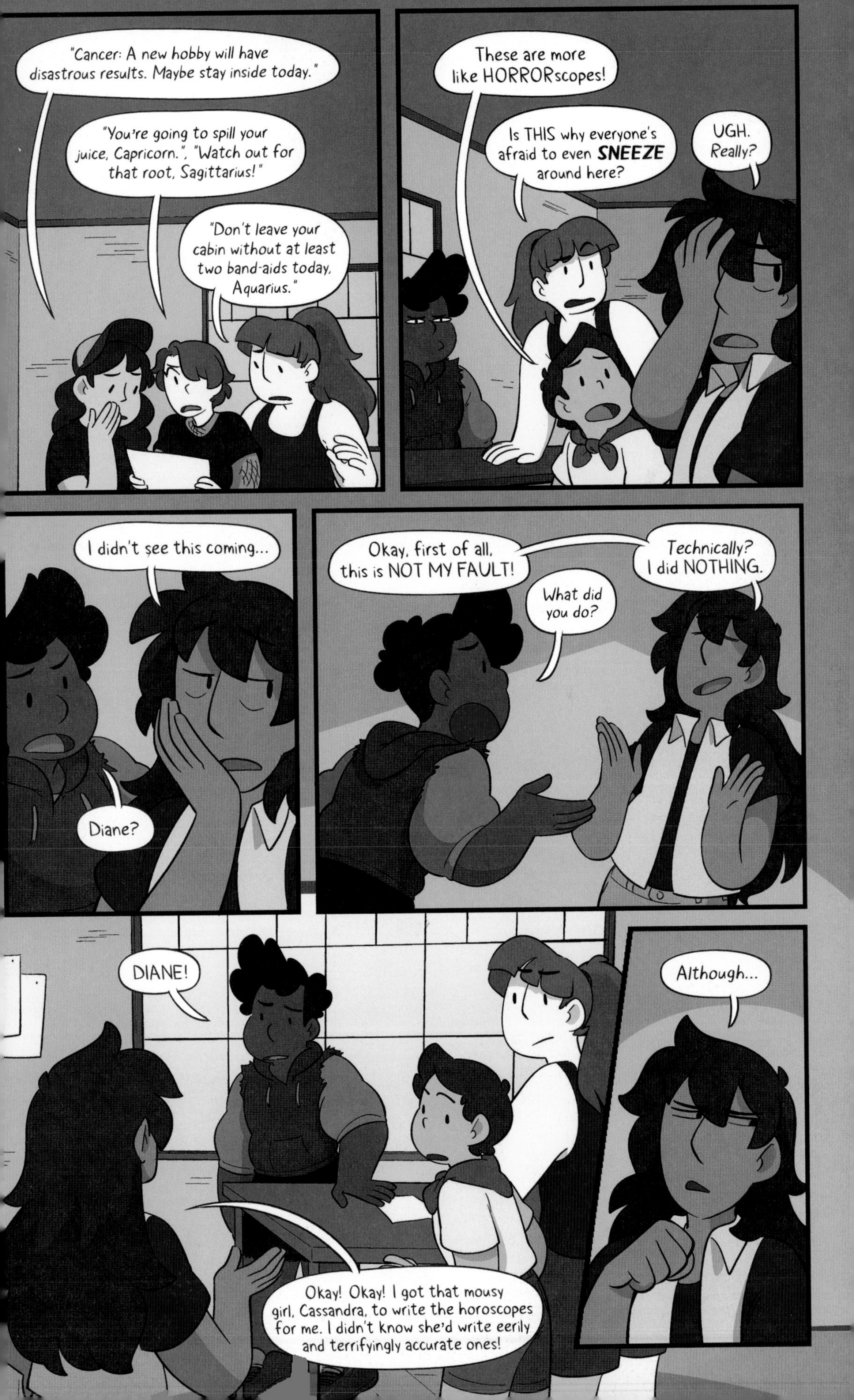
"Cancer: A new hobby will have disastrous results. Maybe stay inside today."
"You're going to spill your juice, Capricorn.", "Watch out for that root, Sagittarius!"
"Don't leave your cabin without at least two band-aids today, Aquarius."
These are more like HORRORscopes!
Is THIS why everyone's afraid to even **SNEEZE** around here?
UGH. Really?
I didn't see this coming...
Diane?
Okay, first of all, this is NOT MY FAULT!
Technically? I did NOTHING.
What did you do?
DIANE!
Okay! Okay! I got that mousy girl, Cassandra, to write the horoscopes for me. I didn't know she'd write eerily and terrifyingly accurate ones!
Although...

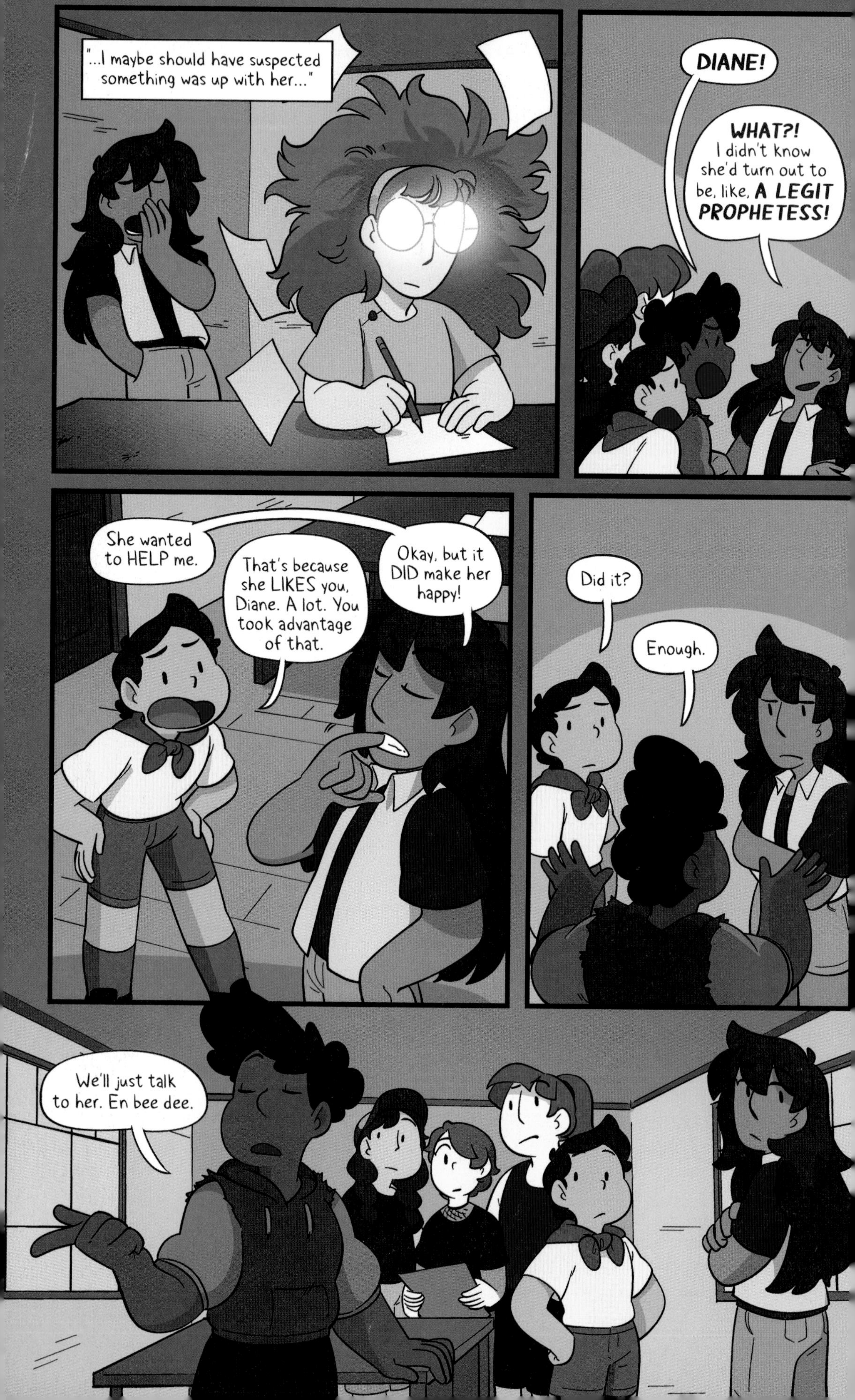
"...I maybe should have suspected something was up with her..."
DIANE!
WHAT?! I didn't know she'd turn out to be, like, A LEGIT PROPHETESS!
She wanted to HELP me.
That's because she LIKES you, Diane. A lot. You took advantage of that.
Okay, but it DID make her happy!
Did it?
Enough.
We'll just talk to her. En bee dee.

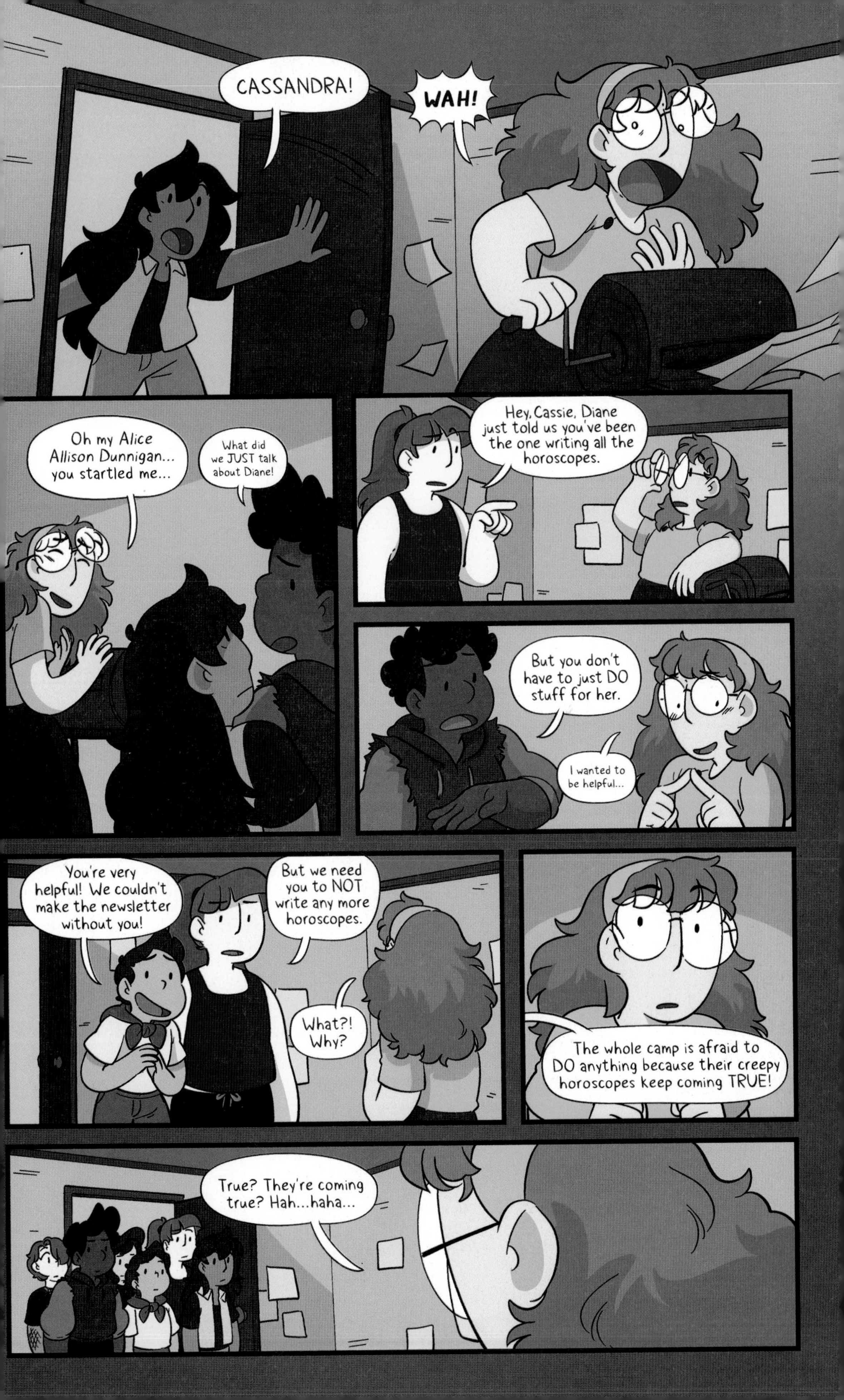
CASSANDRA!
WAH!
Oh my Alice Allison Dunnigan... you startled me...
What did we JUST talk about Diane!
Hey, Cassie, Diane just told us you've been the one writing all the horoscopes.
But you don't have to just DO stuff for her.
I wanted to be helpful...
You're very helpful! We couldn't make the newsletter without you!
But we need you to NOT write any more horoscopes.
What?! Why?
The whole camp is afraid to DO anything because their creepy horoscopes keep coming TRUE!
True? They're coming true? Hah...haha...

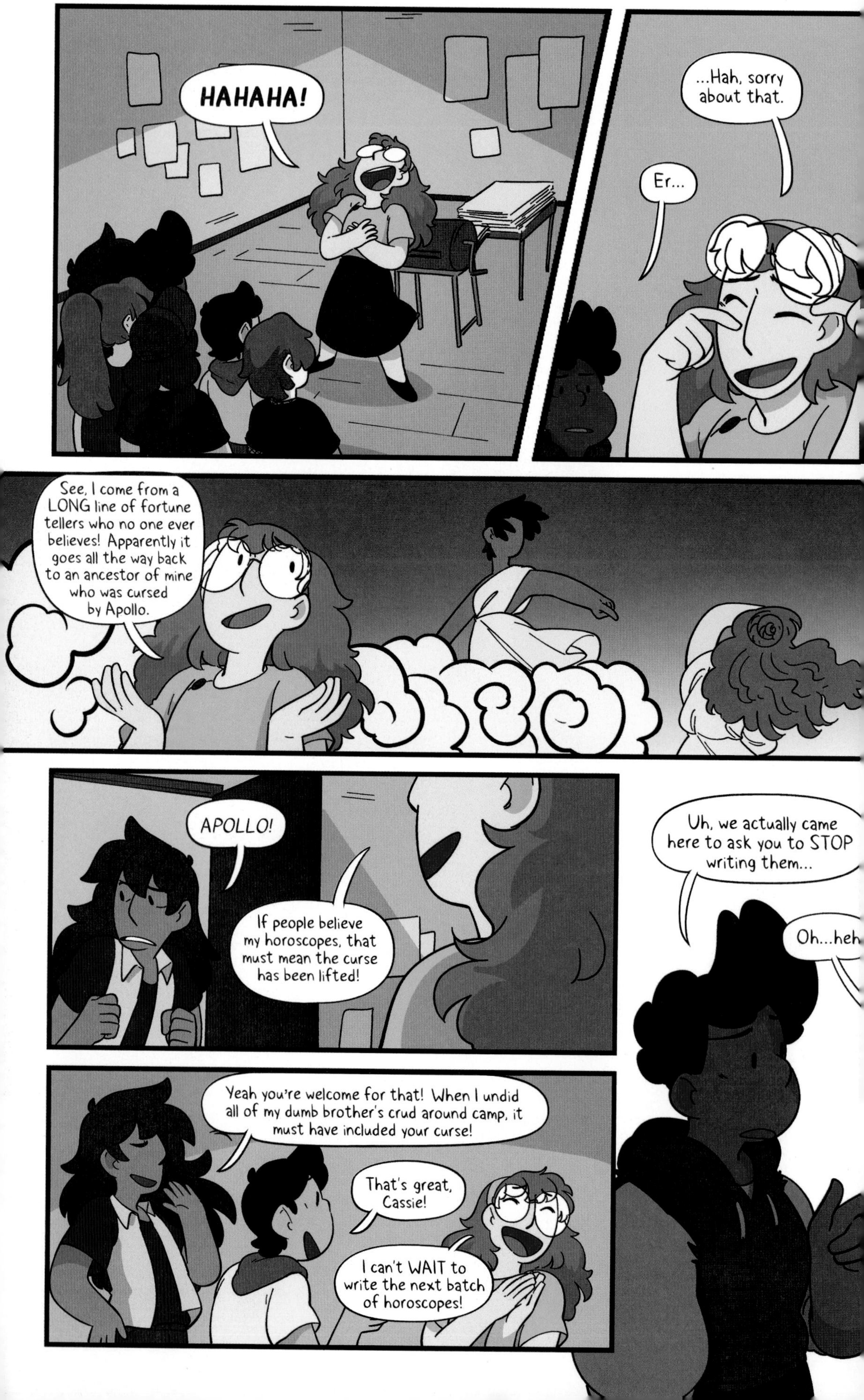
HAHAHA!
...Hah, sorry about that.
Er...
See, I come from a LONG line of fortune tellers who no one ever believes! Apparently it goes all the way back to an ancestor of mine who was cursed by Apollo.
APOLLO!
If people believe my horoscopes, that must mean the curse has been lifted!
Yeah you're welcome for that! When I undid all of my dumb brother's crud around camp, it must have included your curse!
That's great, Cassie!
I can't WAIT to write the next batch of horoscopes!
Uh, we actually came here to ask you to STOP writing them...
Oh...heh

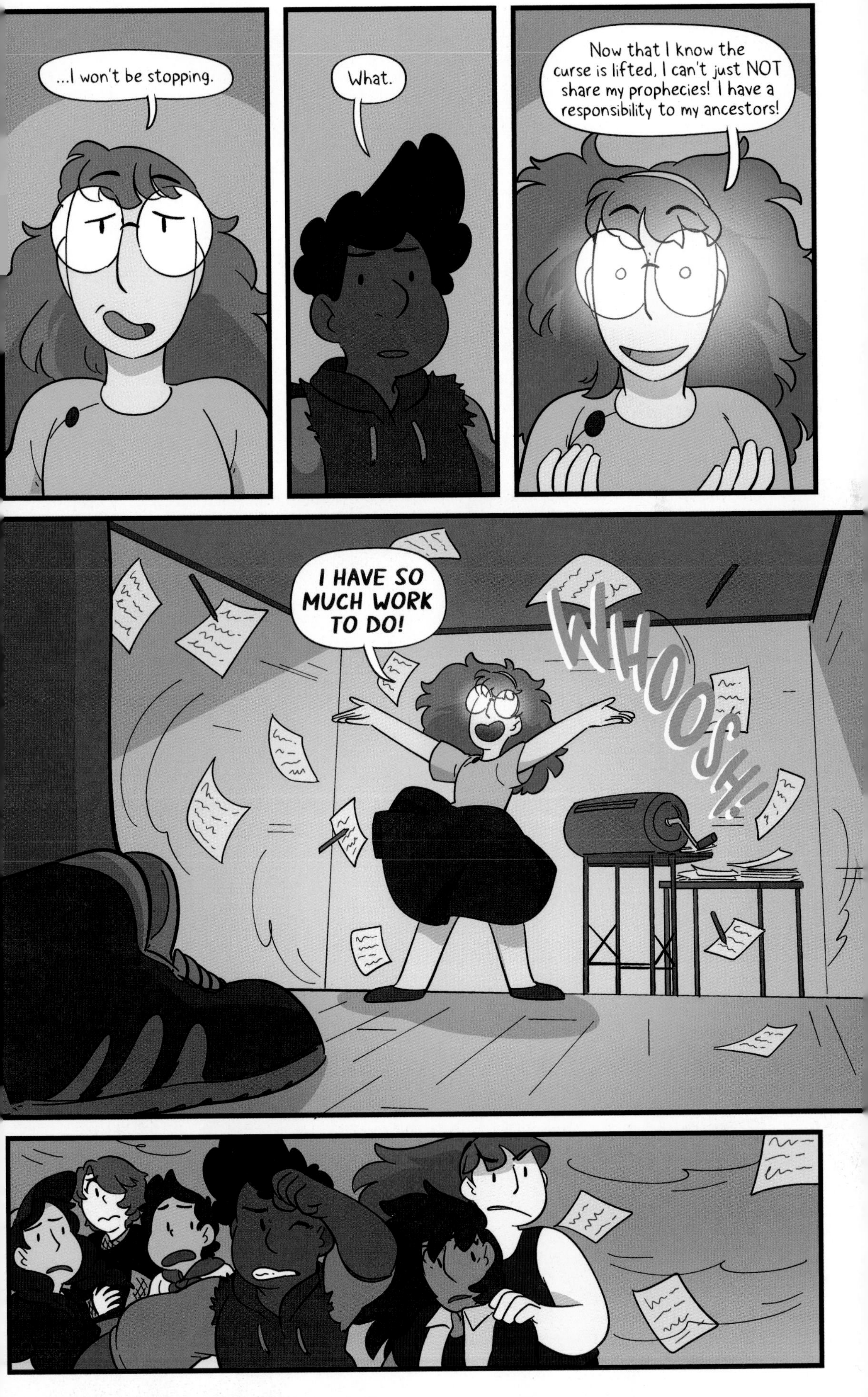
...I won't be stopping.
What.
Now that I know the curse is lifted, I can't just NOT share my prophecies! I have a responsibility to my ancestors!
I HAVE SO MUCH WORK TO DO!
WHOOSH!!

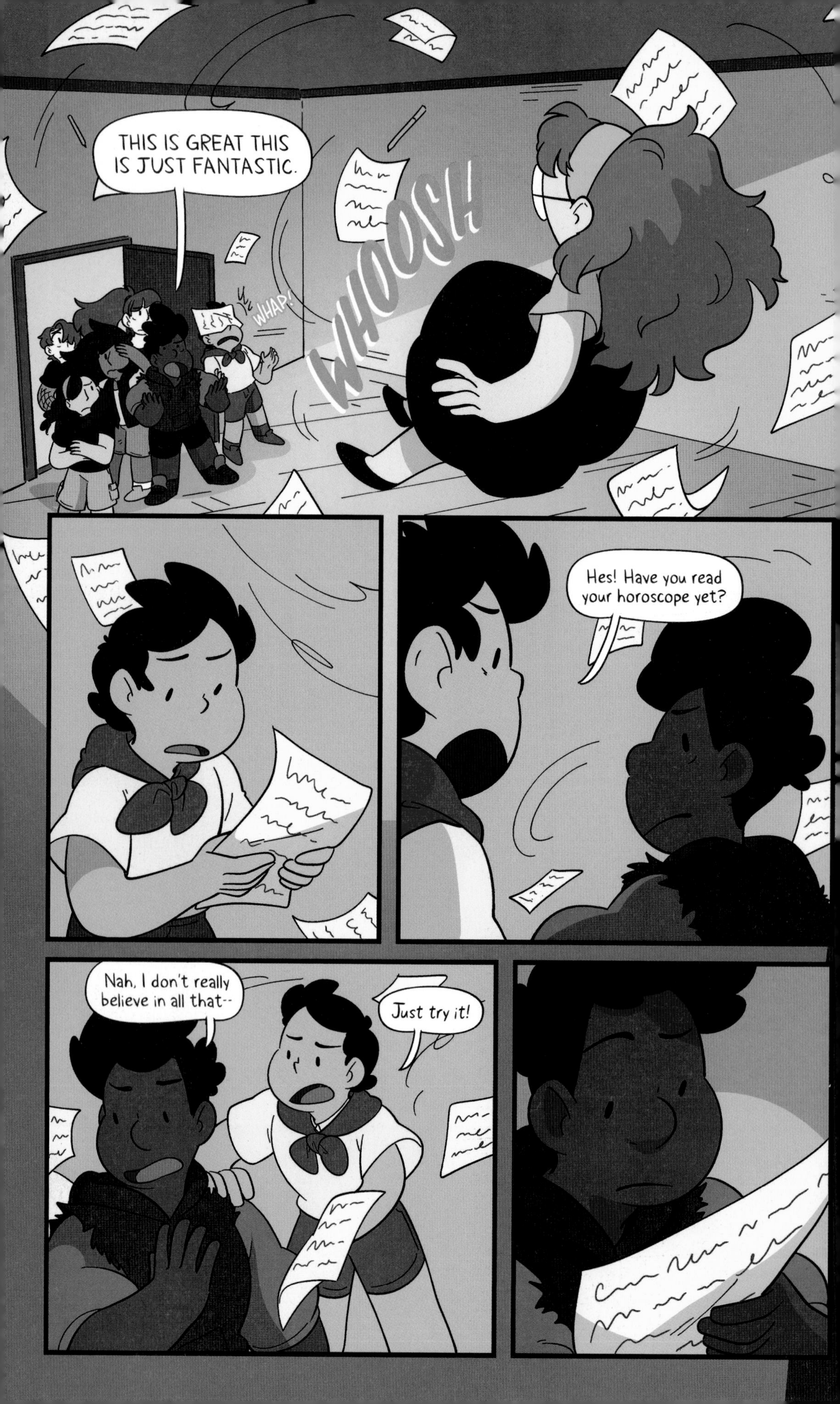
THIS IS GREAT THIS IS JUST FANTASTIC.
WHAP!
WHOOSH!
Hes! Have you read your horoscope yet?
Nah, I don't really believe in all that--
Just try it!

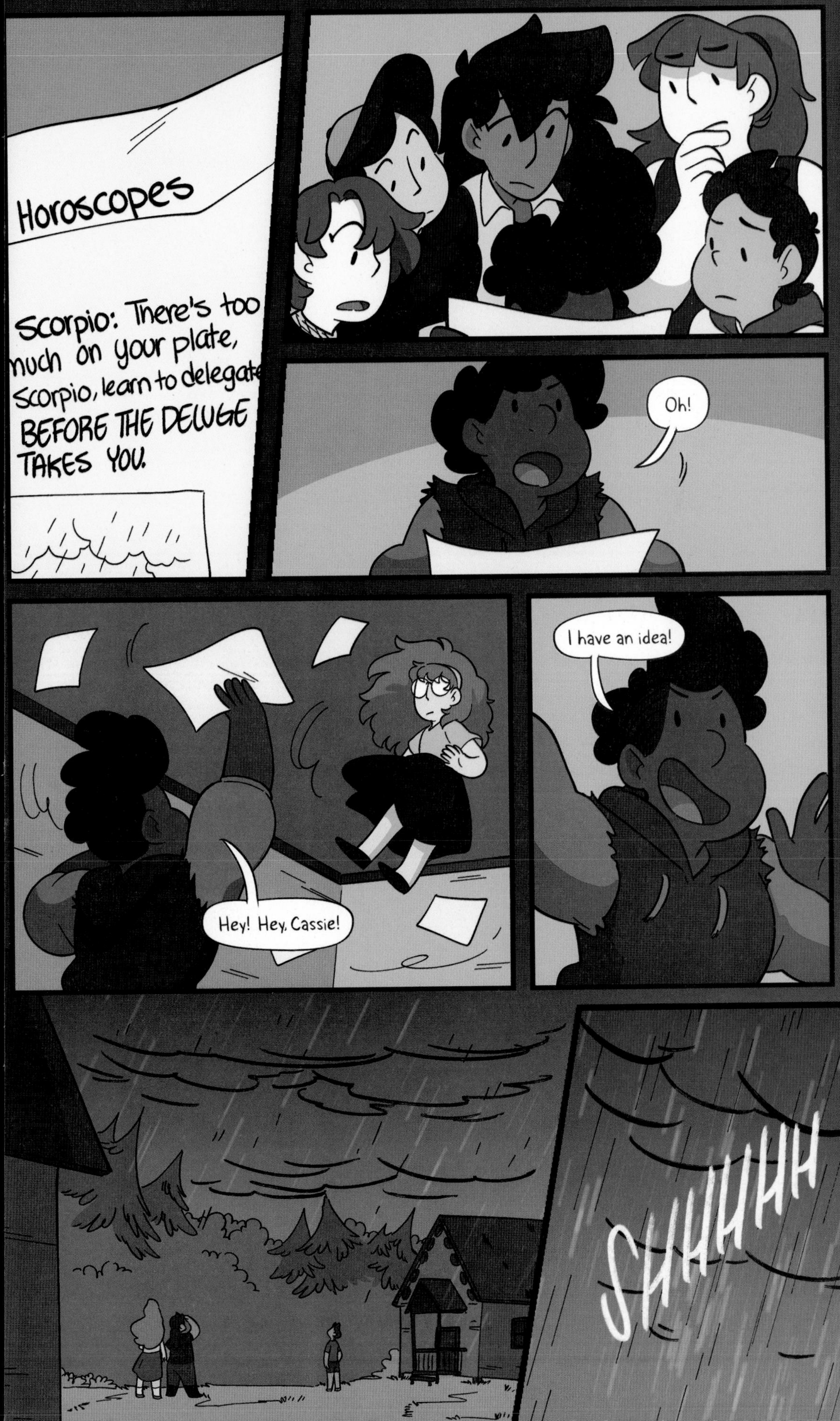
Horoscopes
Scorpio: There's too much on your plate, Scorpio, learn to delegate BEFORE THE DELUGE TAKES YOU.
Oh!
Hey! Hey, Cassie!
I have an idea!
SHHHHH

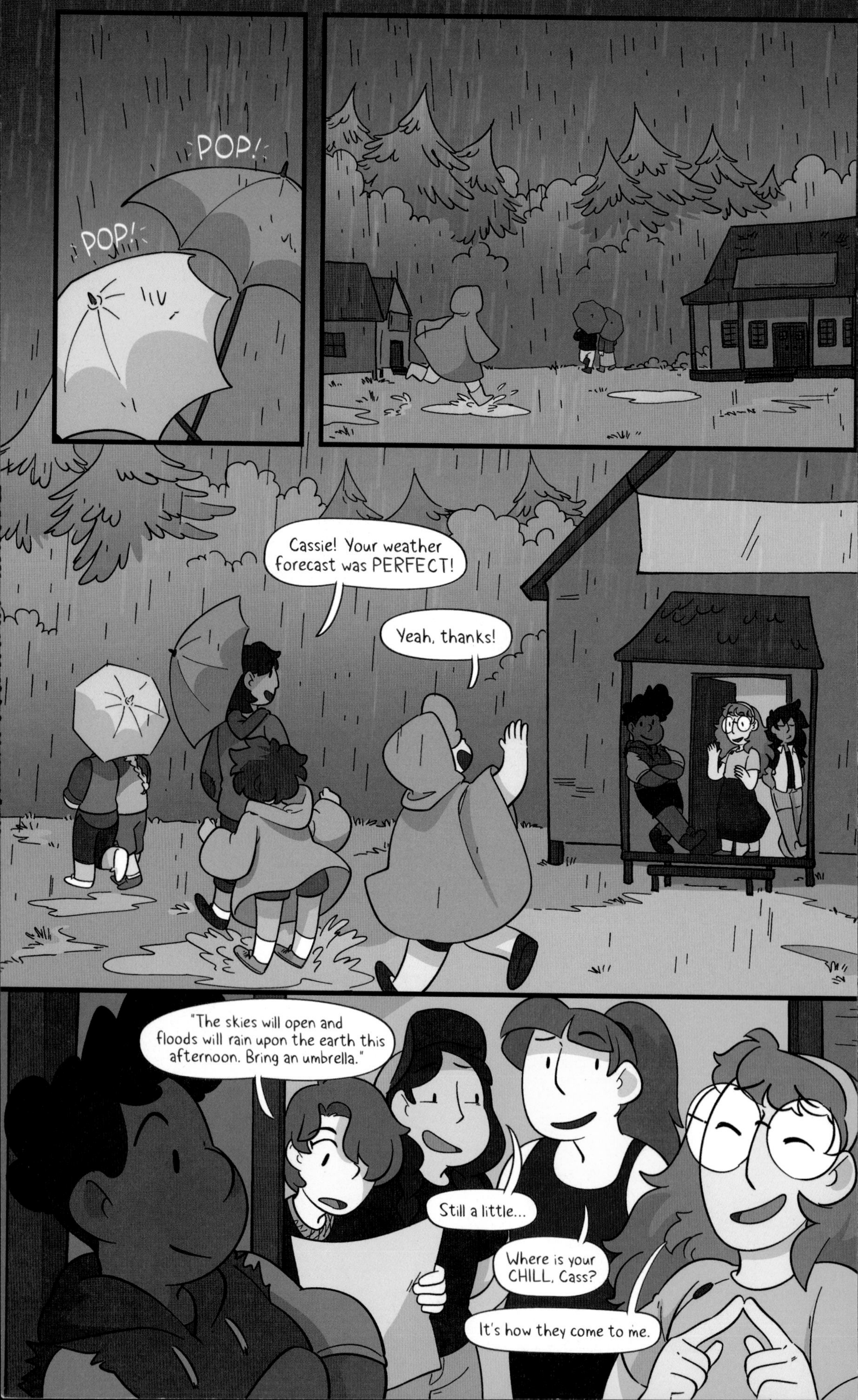
POP!
POP!
Cassie! Your weather forecast was PERFECT!
Yeah, thanks!
"The skies will open and floods will rain upon the earth this afternoon. Bring an umbrella."
Still a little...
Where is your CHILL, Cass?
It's how they come to me.

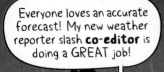

Everyone loves an accurate forecast! My new weather reporter slash **co-editor** is doing a GREAT job!

AH!

SPLASH!

'KENZIE!

HAHAHA!

Hey, so...

...So, like, you could have hated me or whatever 'cause my brother cursed your family and everything, so I guess it's cool you didn't blame me, or whatever... that's surprisingly cool of you...

Th-thanks Diane!

Hey! I wrote one last horoscope! It's yours! If you wanna read it...

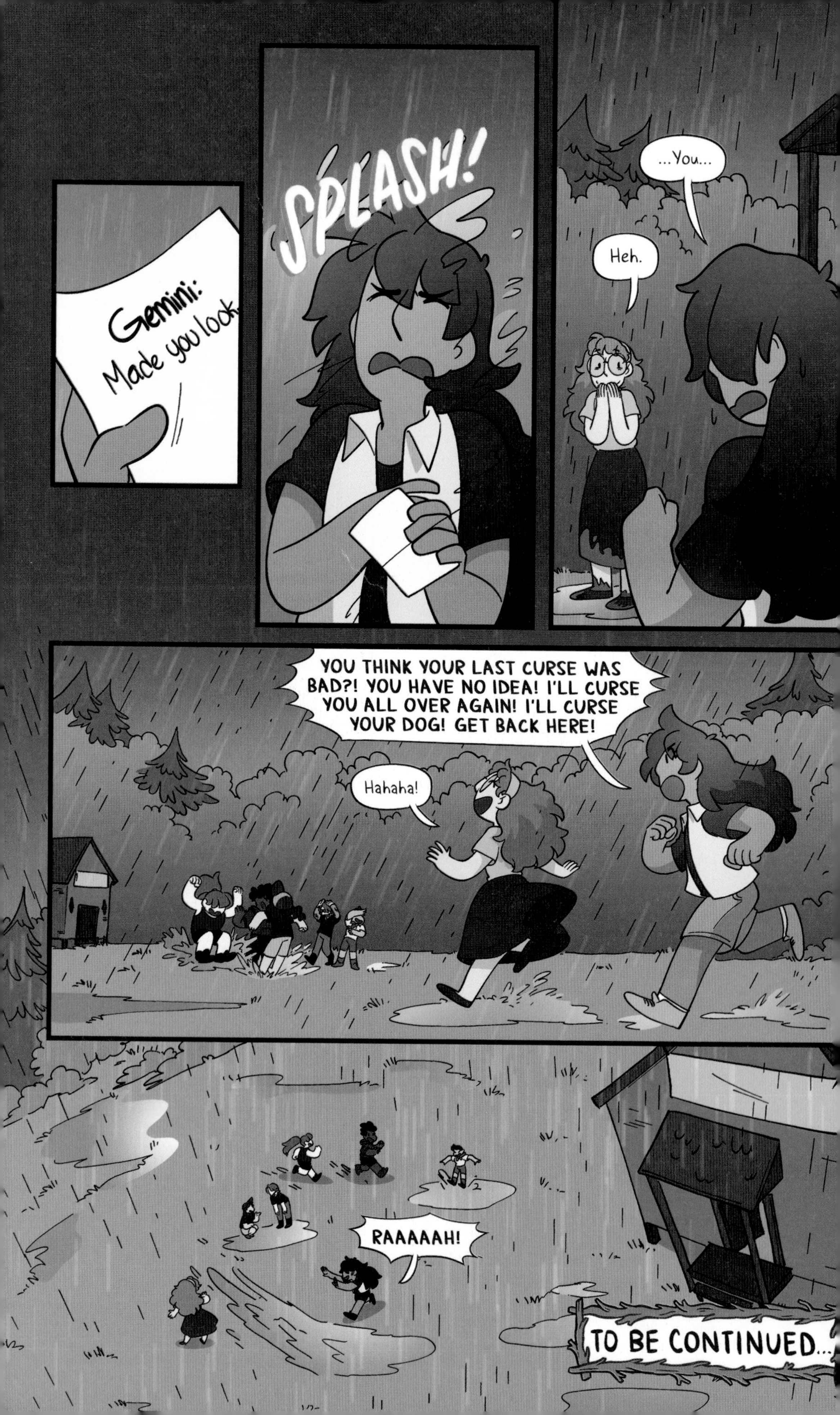
Gemini:
Made you look
SPLASH!
...You...
Heh.
YOU THINK YOUR LAST CURSE WAS BAD?! YOU HAVE NO IDEA! I'LL CURSE YOU ALL OVER AGAIN! I'LL CURSE YOUR DOG! GET BACK HERE!
Hahaha!
RAAAAAH!
TO BE CONTINUED...

will co...

The u...
It hel...
appearan...
dress f...
Further...
Lumber...
to have...
part in...
Thiskv...
Hardc...
have ...
them...

OH NO

...hould be worn at camp
...vents when Lumberjanes
...n may also be worn at other
...ions. It should be worn as a
...the uniform dress with
...rect shoes, and stocking or
...out grows her uniform or
...ng to another Lumberjane.
...signia she has
...n her
...f her

The...
yellow, short sl...
emb...
the w...
choose...
slacks, ...
made o...
out-of-do...
green bere...
the colla...
Shoes ma...
heels, roun...d t...ings or
socks shou...ld ...th the shoes or wit...
the uniform. Ne...es, bracelets, or other jewelry do...
belong with a Lumberjane uniform.

MARIGOLD, ACE REPORTER!

...elexplorer ...
...doors is just outside your door, whether
...d of a country dweller. Get acquainted
...over how to use all the ways of getting

HOW TO WEAR THE UNIFORM

To look well in a uniform demands first of ...
uniform be kept in good condition—clean ...
pressed. See that the skirt is the right length for your own
height and build, that the belt is adjusted to your waist,
that your shoes and stockings are in keeping with the
uniform, that you watch your posture and carry yourself
with dignity and grace. If the beret is removed indoors,
be sure that your hair is neat and kept in place with an
insconspicuous clip or ribbon. When you wear a
Lumberjane uniform you are identified as a member of
this organization and you should be doubly careful to
conduct yourself in a way that will show everyone that
courtesy and thoughtfullness are part of being a
Lumberjane. People are likely to judge a whole nation by
the selfishness of a few individuals, to criticize a whole
family because of the misconduct of one member, and to
feel unkindly toward and organization because of the

The unifor...
helps to cre...
in a group. ...
active life th...
another bond ...
future, and pr...
in order to b...
Lumberjane pr... 
Penniquiqul Thi...re Lady
Types, but m...es will wish to have one. They
can either bu...he uniform, or make it themselves from
materials available at the trading post.

INTERVIEW WITH A YETI

COVER GALLERY

Lumberjanes "Out-of-Doors" Program Field

ZOO IT YOURSELF

"You can always trust a wet nose and toe beans."

Whether they're tiny tadpoles, or elephants the size of your house, the animals we share our homes and world with are all important in their own, unique ways, and the desire to care for animals is one that many young scouts share. As children, we are so used to being cared for and looked after, that having an opportunity to nurture something else, be it a goldfish or a puppy, is often our first chance at true autonomy. So whether you have one pet or a menagerie, or even if you're simply pet-sitting, we hope that you will enjoy earning your Zoo It Yourself badge.

A major goal of modern zoos is conservation, public education, and ensuring that the animals in their care live the happiest, healthiest lives possible. And while you might not have a chance to look after or interact with lemurs, giraffes, or other wild creatures, keeping those values in mind when you are spending time with pets makes an excellent first step!

Consider the unique needs and personalities of different types of animals, and work with your troop or counselors to learn what they require and how best to read their moods and preferences. A good place to start is meeting the pets your fellow Lumberjanes have at home, or volunteering at an animal shelter! You will quickly come to find out that each pet prefers different food, toys, and bonding activities, and that the best thing to do is to give to each according to their needs. What makes a dog happy may not suit a cat, a horse, or even a different dog!

Think about what a zoo run by you would look like. Draw a map to plan the sizes of enclosures and the layout, or put together a menu that reflects each animal's dietary needs and place in the food chain. Try your hand at writing descriptions of habits and habitats, to think about how you would like to teach the public about the incredible animals in your care!

And remember, no matter how interested we are in them, not every creature is meant to be kept, whether in a home or in a zoo. Just as we try to respect our pets' wishes when it comes to playtime and petting, we should also strive to respect that some creatures are simply not meant to be kept away from the wild, and instead do our best to create a world that will be hospitable to them.

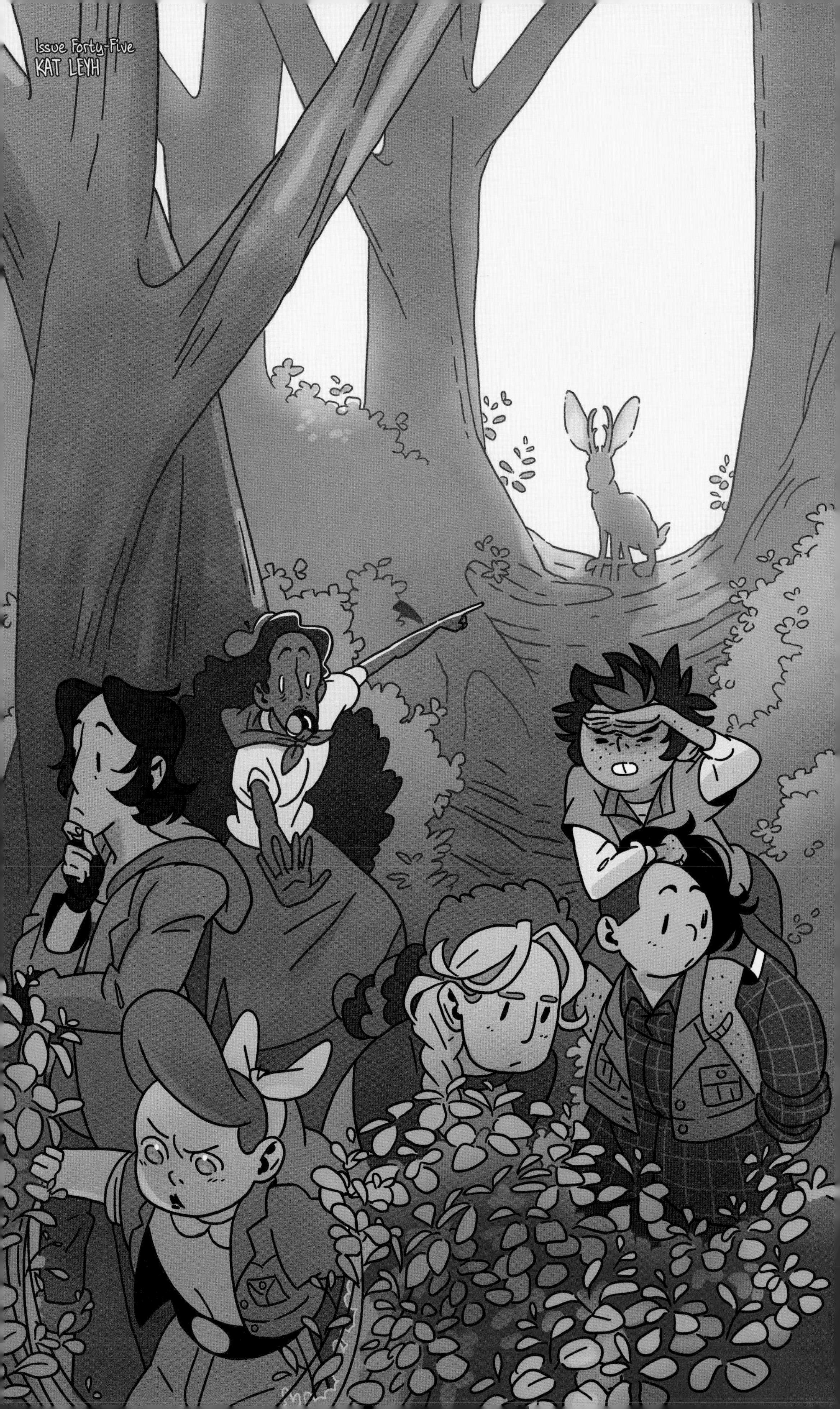
Issue Forty-Five
KAT LEYH

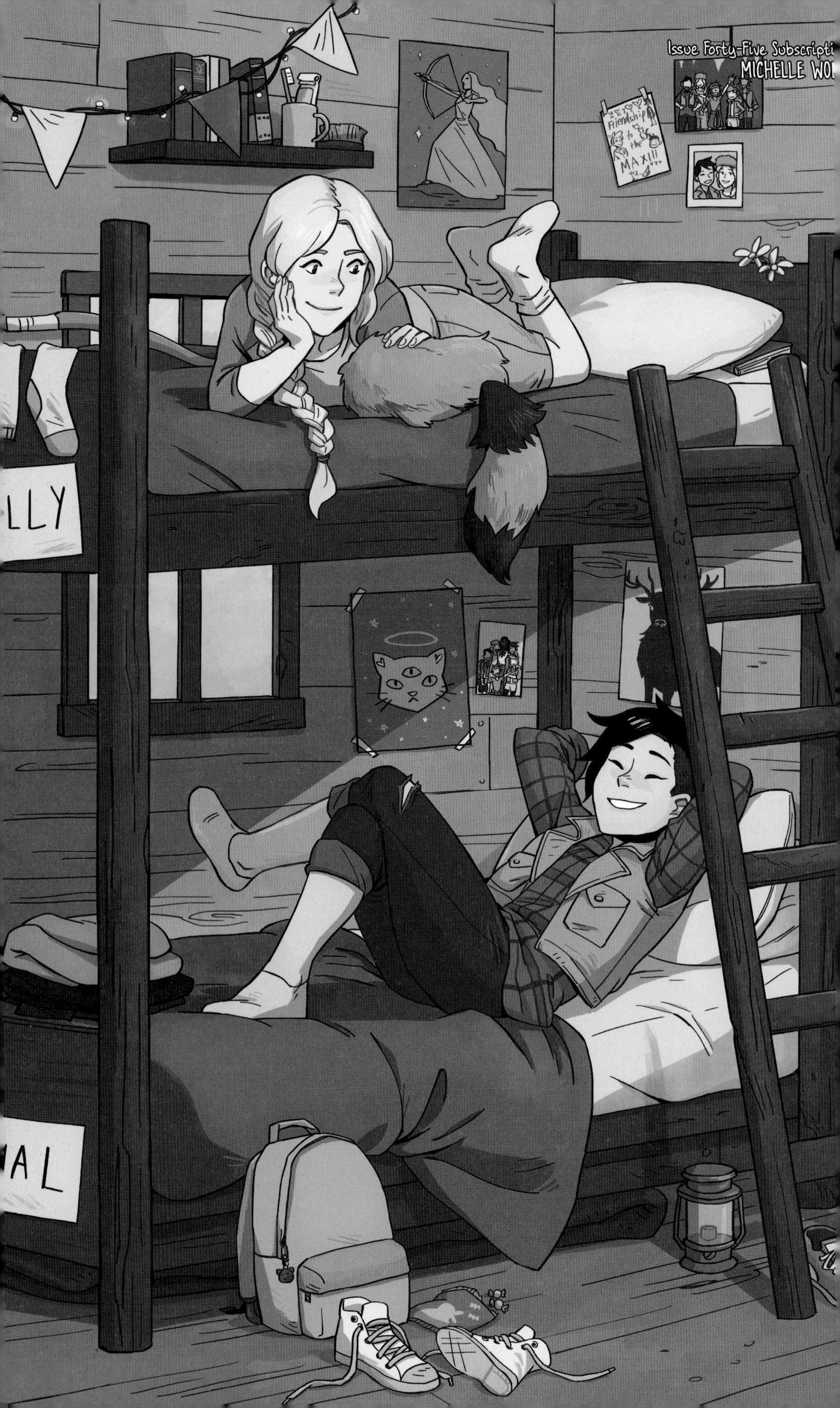
Issue Forty-Five Subscripti
MICHELLE WO
Friendship to the MAX!!!
LLY
AL

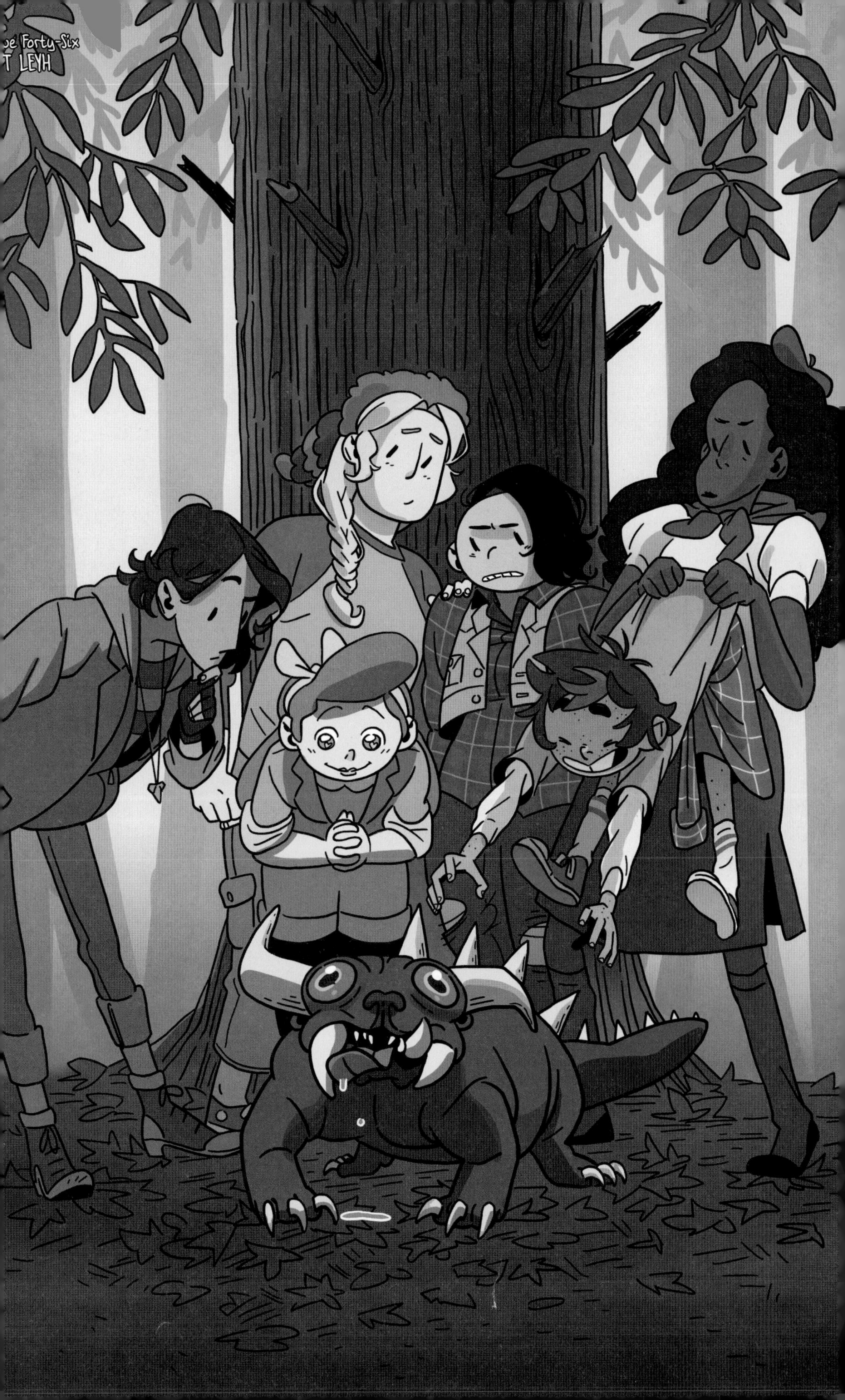

Issue Forty-Six
T LEYH

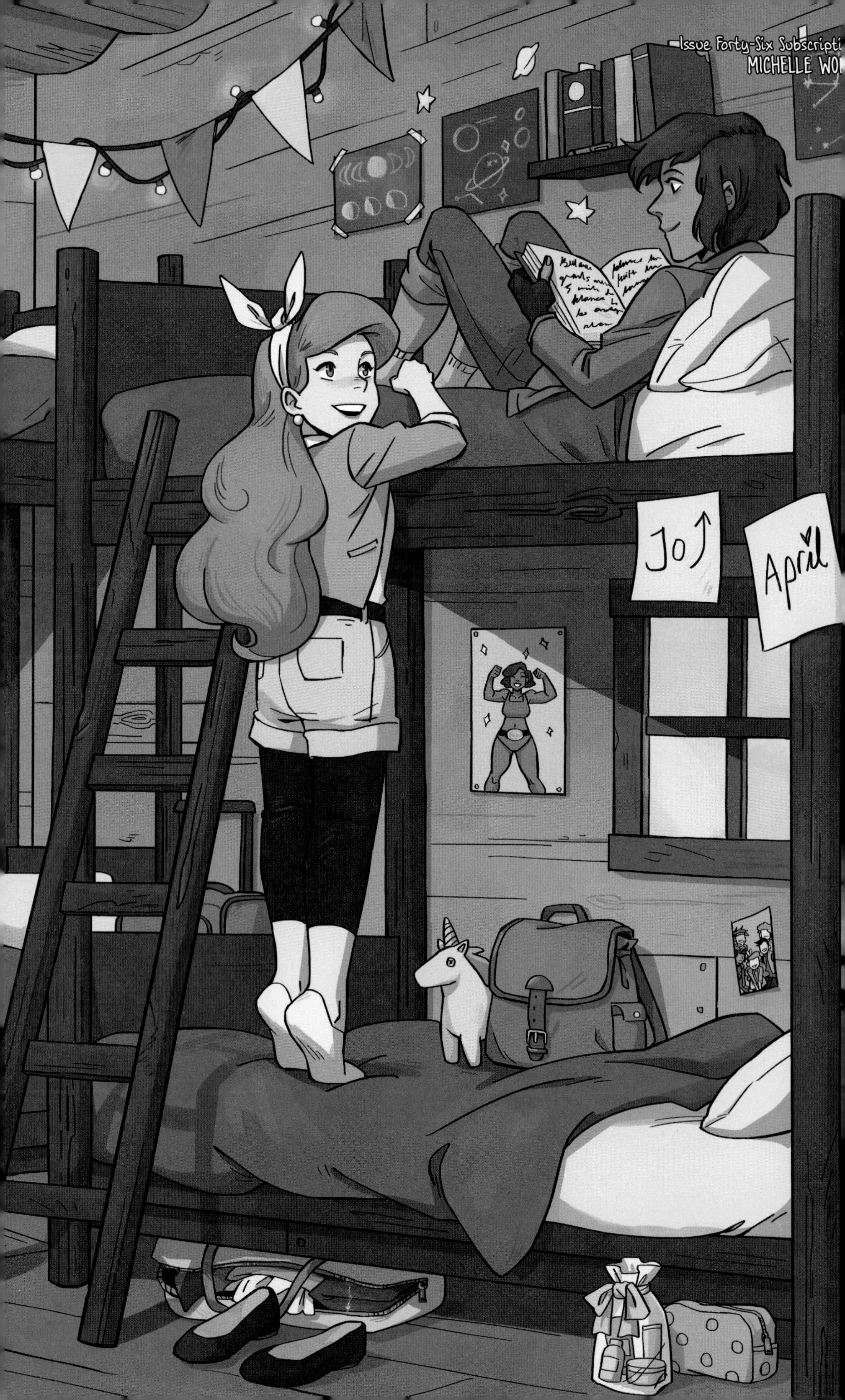
Issue Forty-Six Subscripti
MICHELLE WO
Jo ↑
April

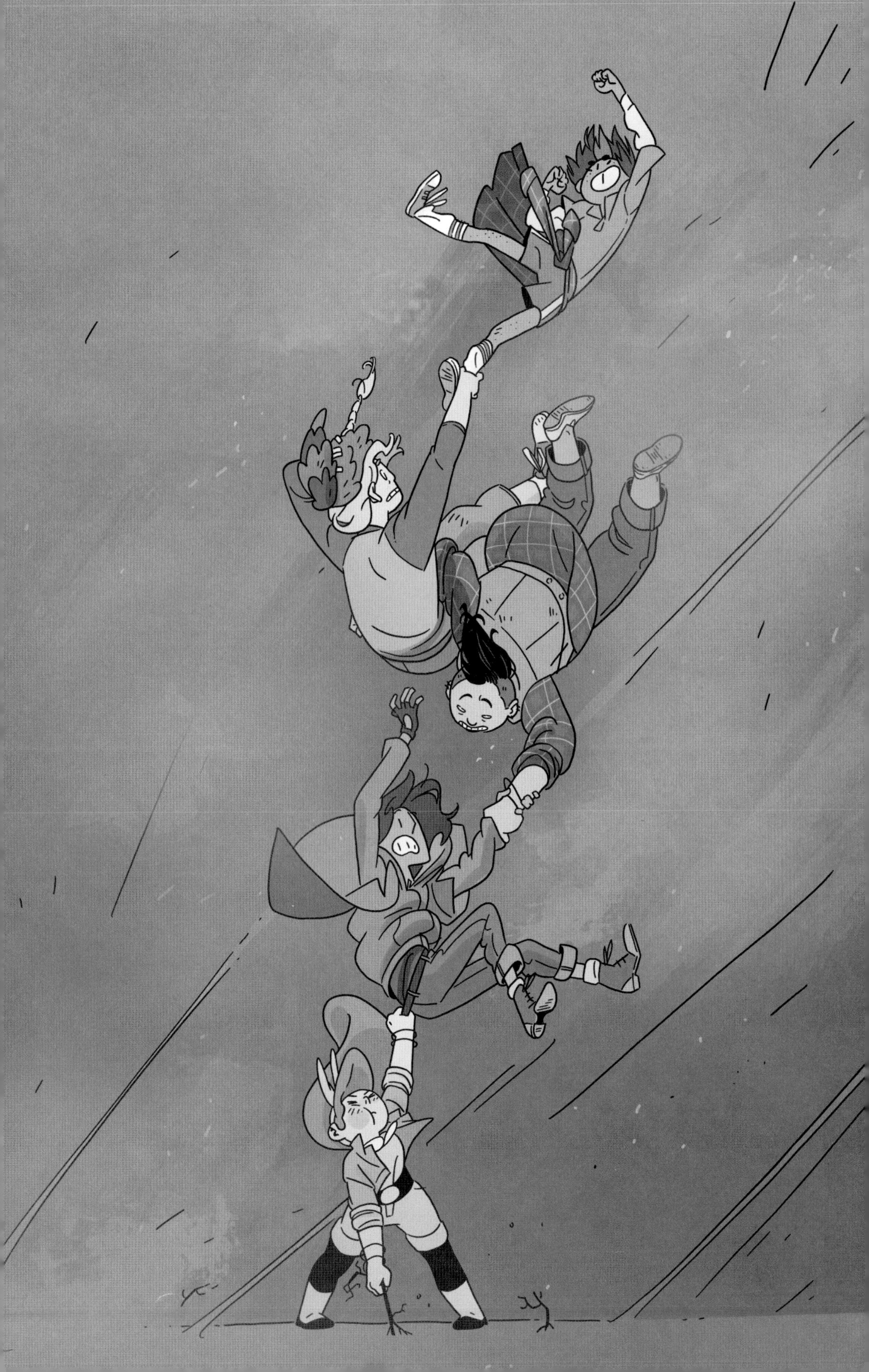

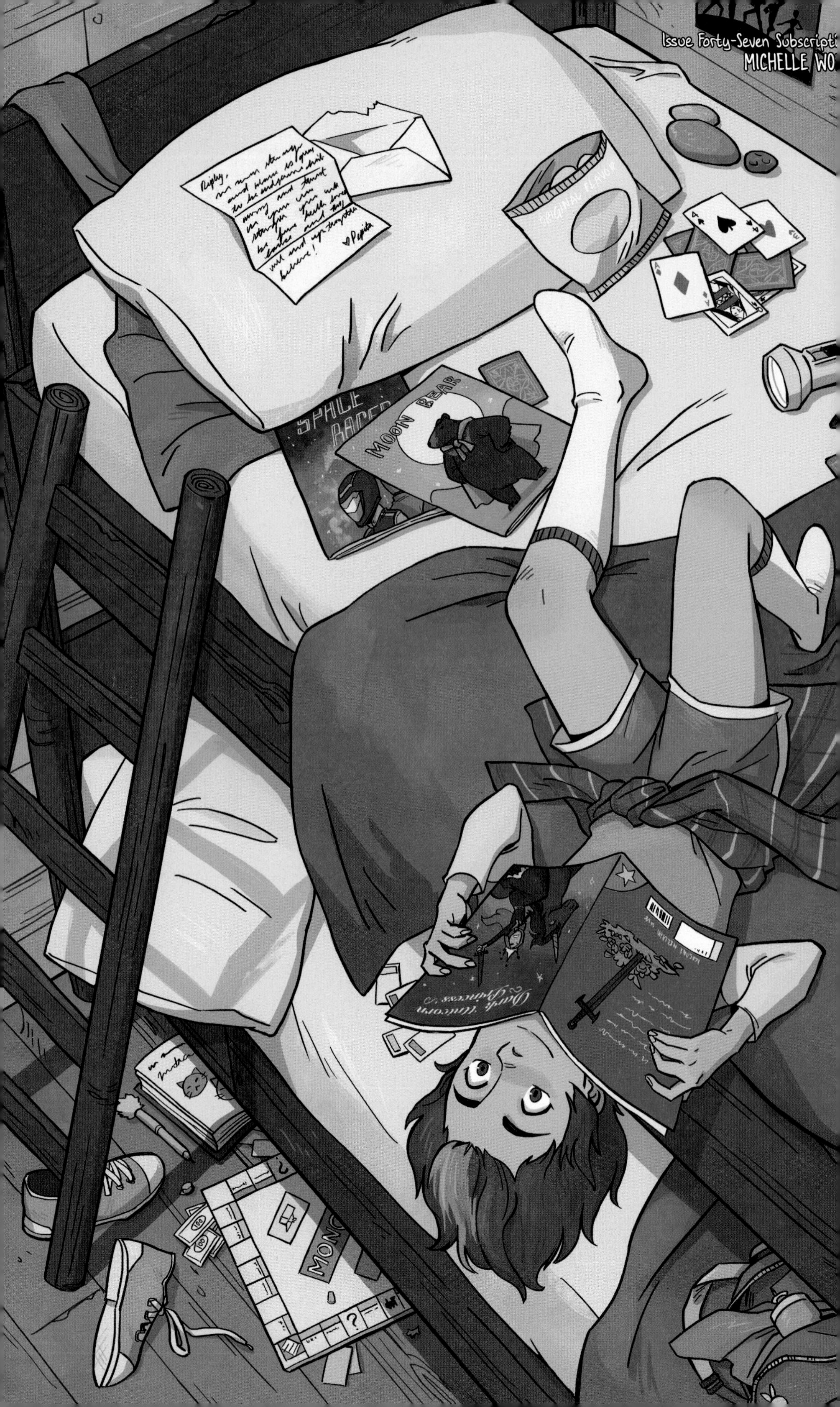

Issue Forty-Seven Subscripti
MICHELLE WO
ORIGINAL FLAVOR
SPACE RACER
MOON BEAR
Ripley,
♡Pepita

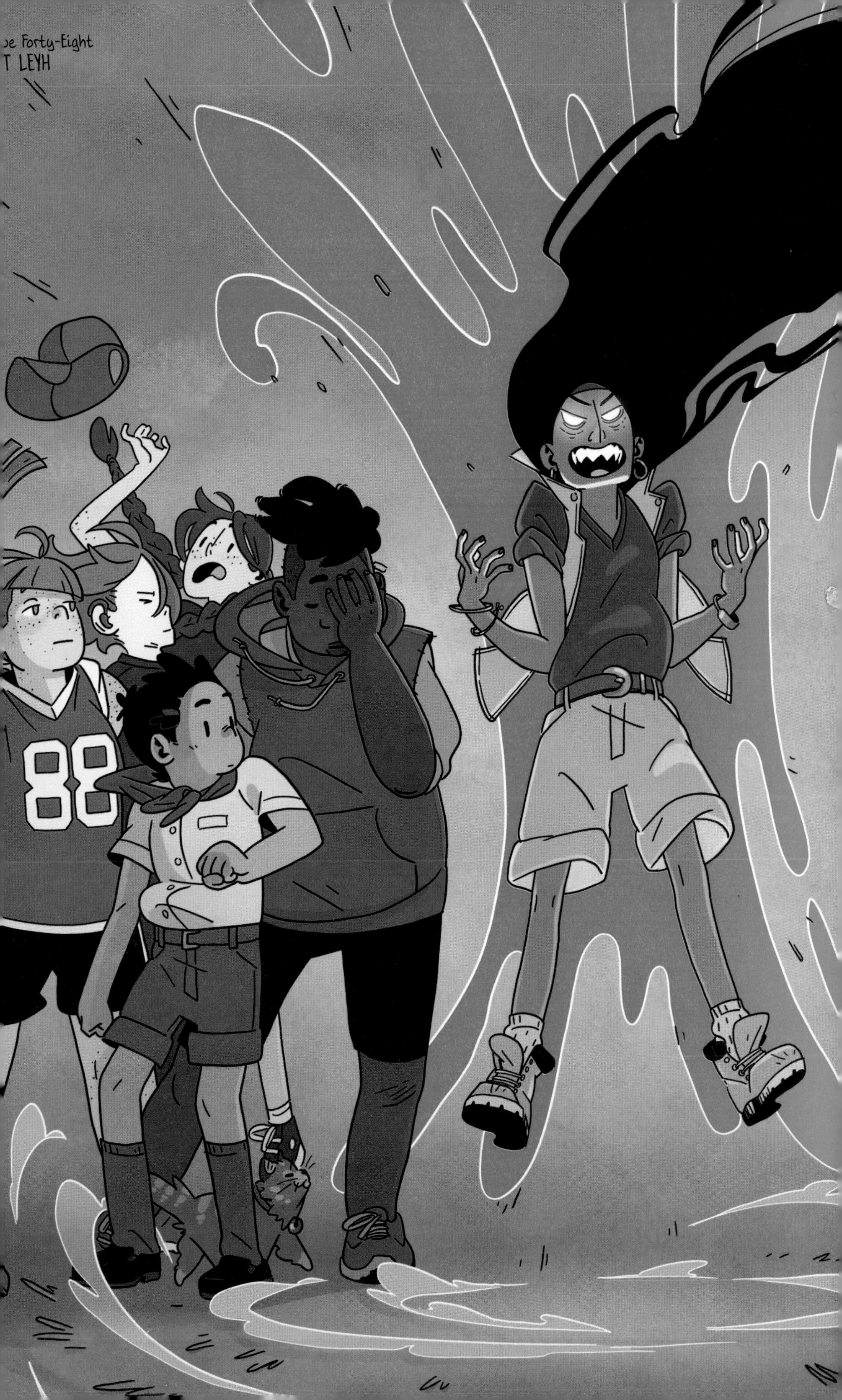

e Forty-Eight
T LEYH
88

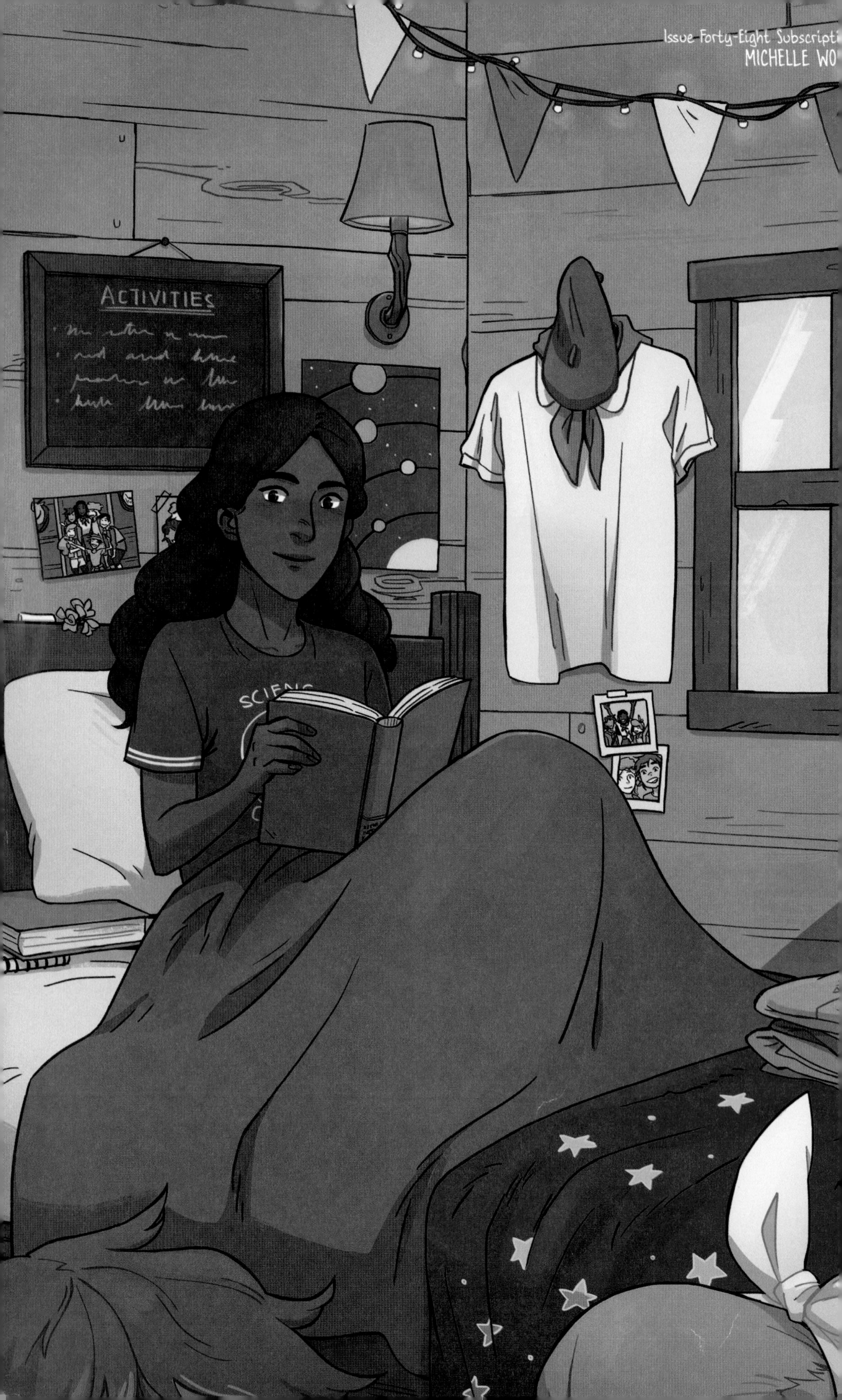
Issue Forty-Eight Subscripti
MICHELLE WO
ACTIVITIES

LJ

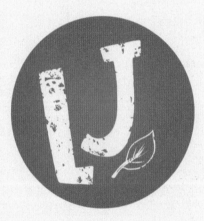

DISCOVER
ALL THE HITS

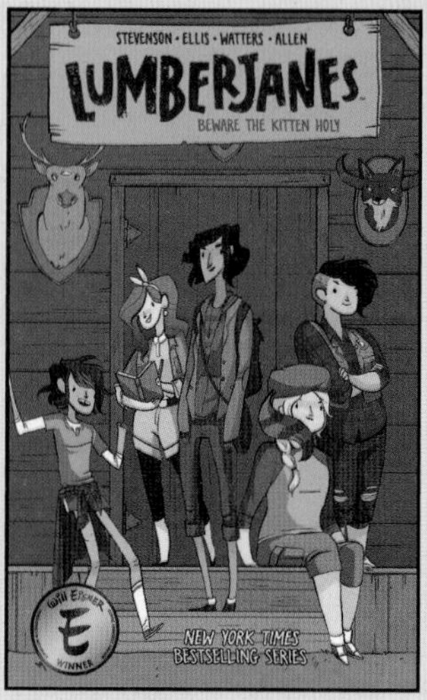
STEVENSON • ELLIS • WATTERS • ALLEN
LUMBERJANES
BEWARE THE KITTEN HOLY
NEW YORK TIMES BESTSELLING SERIES

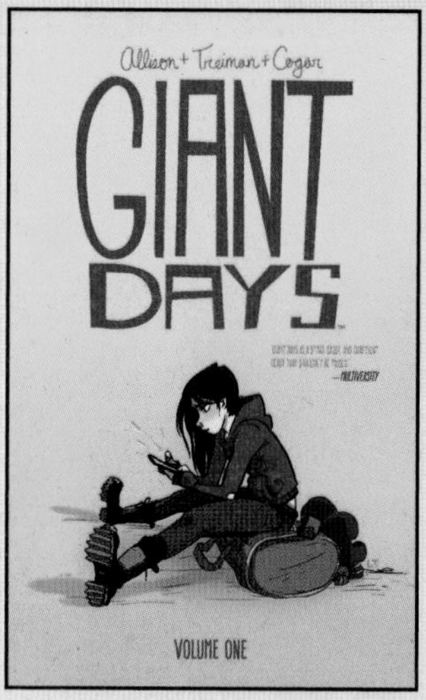
Allison + Treiman + Cogar
GIANT DAYS
VOLUME ONE

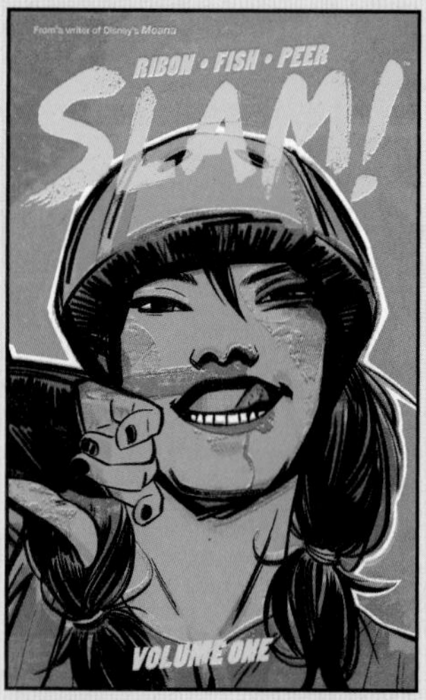
RIBON • FISH • PEER
SLAM!
VOLUME ONE

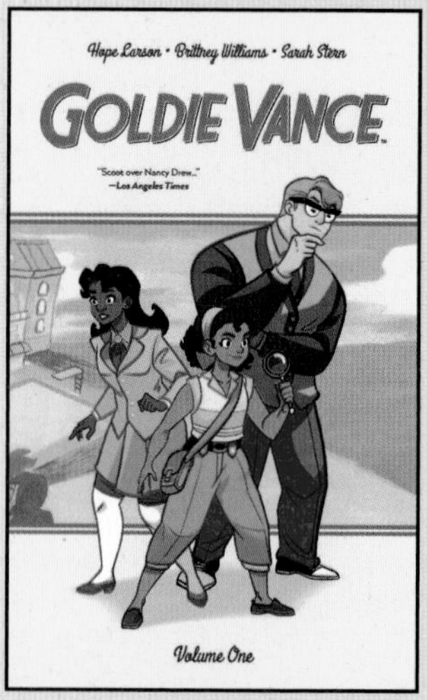
Hope Larson • Brittney Williams • Sarah Stern
GOLDIE VANCE
"Scoot over Nancy Drew..." —Los Angeles Times
Volume One

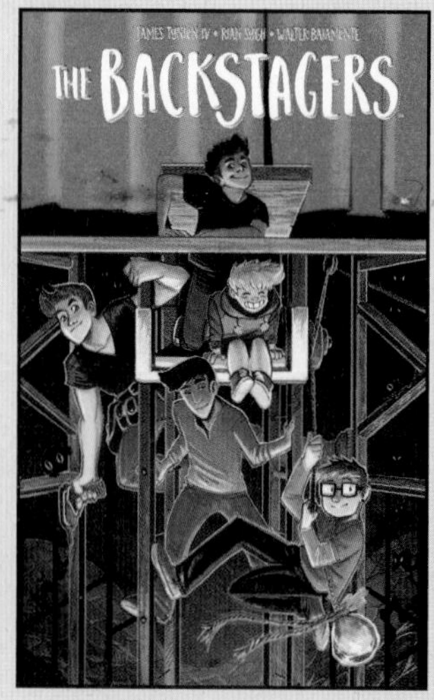
THE BACKSTAGERS

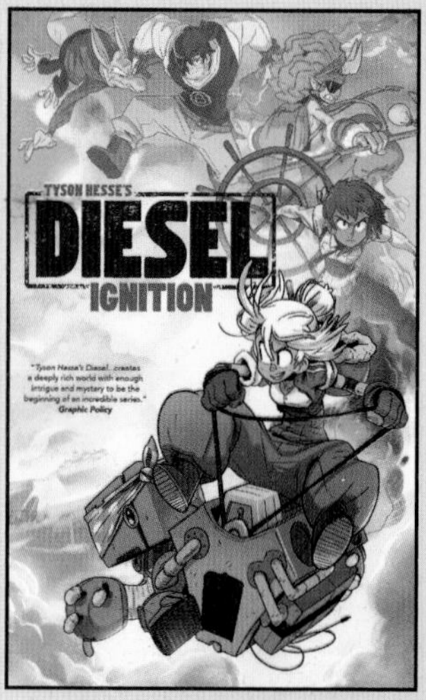
TYSON HESSE'S
DIESEL
IGNITION

Lumberjanes
Noelle Stevenson, Shannon Watters, Grace Ellis, Brooklyn Allen, and Others
Volume 1: Beware the Kitten Holy
ISBN: 978-1-60886-687-8 | $14.99 US
Volume 2: Friendship to the Max
ISBN: 978-1-60886-737-0 | $14.99 US
Volume 3: A Terrible Plan
ISBN: 978-1-60886-803-2 | $14.99 US
Volume 4: Out of Time
ISBN: 978-1-60886-860-5 | $14.99 US
Volume 5: Band Together
ISBN: 978-1-60886-919-0 | $14.99 US

Giant Days
John Allison, Lissa Treiman, Max Sarin
Volume 1
ISBN: 978-1-60886-789-9 | $9.99 US
Volume 2
ISBN: 978-1-60886-804-9 | $14.99 US
Volume 3
ISBN: 978-1-60886-851-3 | $14.99 US

Jonesy
Sam Humphries, Caitlin Rose Boyle
Volume 1
ISBN: 978-1-60886-883-4 | $9.99 US
Volume 2
ISBN: 978-1-60886-999-2 | $14.99 US

Slam!
Pamela Ribon, Veronica Fish, Brittany Peer
Volume 1
ISBN: 978-1-68415-004-5 | $14.99 US

Goldie Vance
Hope Larson, Brittney Williams
Volume 1
ISBN: 978-1-60886-898-8 | $9.99 US
Volume 2
ISBN: 978-1-60886-974-9 | $14.99 US

The Backstagers
James Tynion IV, Rian Sygh
Volume 1
ISBN: 978-1-60886-993-0 | $14.99 US

Tyson Hesse's Diesel: Ignition
Tyson Hesse
ISBN: 978-1-60886-907-7 | $14.99 US

Coady & The Creepies
Liz Prince, Amanda Kirk, Hannah Fisher
ISBN: 978-1-68415-029-8 | $14.99 US